SEA GLASS HEARTS

BAYTOWN BOYS

MARYANN JORDAN

This book is a work of fiction. Names, characters, places, and incidents either are products of the author's imagination or are used fictitiously. Any resemblance to actual persons, living or dead, events, or locales is entirely coincidental.

Cover: Graphics by Stacy

ISBN ebook: 978-1-947214-86-6

ISBN print: 978-1-947214-87-3

❀ Created with Vellum

1

It was a dark and stormy night. The famous, or rather, infamous, first words from Edward Bulward-Lytton's 1830 novel ran through his mind. Sheriff Liam Sullivan's high school English teacher had used it as an example of a melodramatic style of fiction writing. And yet, as the windshield wipers on his Acawmacke Sheriff's SUV flew back and forth, slinging water to the side as fast as they could and still not making visibility any better, he thought the phrase to be the perfect example of truth.

If he remembered correctly, the rest of the line was just as descriptive of his situation. *It was a dark and stormy night; the rain fell in torrents—except at occasional intervals, when it was checked by a violent gust of wind...*

As though on cue, his SUV was rocked sideways by just such a violent gust of wind. Keeping both hands on the steering wheel, he drove slowly south on the main road that bisected the Eastern Shore of Virginia, heading toward his home from the station. The Eastern

Shore was unusual in that it was not connected by land to the rest of Virginia. It was a peninsula that was land-locked by Maryland to the north, only consisted of two counties, and connected by a seventeen-mile bridge-tunnel over the Chesapeake Bay to Virginia Beach. While they could count on the Virginia State Police, the North Heron and Acawmacke Counties' law enforcement relied heavily on their shared cooperation.

Tapping his radio before gripping the wheel again, he called in to the dispatcher. "Highway Thirteen clear from Mile Marker Nineteen to Mile Marker Six."

"10-4. All others reporting same."

"Any updates?"

"They're saying the storm turned fast, but you know that. Still claiming Cat 5."

He stifled the curse threatening to erupt at the thought of the damage a Category 5 hurricane could do to the Eastern Shore—roofs gone, buildings demolished, power and phone lines down, homes lost. And all to one of the poorest areas of Virginia. *But please, God, no loss of life.*

"You headin' home for the night to ride out the storm, Sheriff Sullivan?"

"Yes. Should be there in about ten minutes if I can keep the vehicle from blowing off the road."

"Be safe."

"10-17." Signing off, he was glad that from all reports the roads were clear as the residents had heeded the emergency warnings and fled to the inside of their homes, and the visitors had found lodging with the few hotels in the area or left the day before to go back to their homes.

Another gust of wind slammed into the side of his vehicle, and he jerked on the steering wheel to hold it onto the road as he slowed, tapping the brake lightly. At this rate, he wouldn't make it home in ten minutes, and that was saying a lot considering he wasn't far away.

A strange flash of light through the water hitting the windshield caught his eye, and he squinted, leaning forward to discern what he was looking at. Visibility was limited to the second after the wiper had swiped, instantly dimmed by the pounding water. Slowing even more, the sight of a trailer on the side of the road became barely discernible, and a small SUV was attached to the front. It was parked on the side of the road with the emergency flashers on. He noted the Ohio license tags. Rental vehicle. *Christ Almighty, who the hell is driving tonight, pulling that load in the middle of a Cat 5 hurricane?* He backed up slightly and pulled to the side. "Possible 10-46, Mile Marker Seven."

Calling the tags into dispatch, he waited the moment it took to run them. They were indeed to a rental. Swallowing the growl that erupted, he ignored his hat, knowing the wind would send it sailing. Instead of throwing open the door in irritation, he opened it with caution, holding it tightly so the raging wind didn't pull it off the hinges. Climbing down, assaulted immediately by the pelting rain, he turned his back toward its force and shut the door carefully. With his high-beam flashlight raised, he stalked past the trailer toward the SUV, taking care to remain upright.

Shining his light inside, he called out, "Acawmacke Sheriff's Department. Is there an emergency?" He bent slightly to peer inside, the illumination of the light shining onto the driver twisted in the seat as she shifted her ass over to the passenger side. A pair of wide, sky-blue eyes stared back at him. His gaze dropped to the rest of her as the sound of screeching hit his ears. *Fucking hell!* His hand shot out to the door, throwing it open.

2

TWO DAYS EARLIER

Liam Sullivan sat in his office, attempting to work on the monthly report while keeping an eye on the computer screen that had been on one of the national weather stations for the past day. Hurricane Henry had finally moved off their radar, having hit the Gulf states and leaving flooding and destruction along a path from Alabama, through Georgia, and into the Carolinas. The Eastern Shore of Virginia had received no more than a heavy spring rain.

But now, on Henry's heels, was Hurricane Ivy. This storm was just as large, having skimmed the east coast of Florida, moving partially out to the Atlantic only to veer back toward the Outer Banks of North Carolina. He hated for that area to take another direct hit but inwardly rejoiced that while the coast of Virginia would get the aftereffects, it wouldn't slam into them with quite such voracity.

"Sheriff?"

He looked up at one of the newer deputies, Ron

Taylor, standing in his doorway, his uniform neatly pressed, his hair regulation cut, and—God bless him—his baby face red with embarrassment. *What now?*

"Yes?" He tried to keep the irritation from his voice but heard it leak through. Clearing his throat, he repeated in a calmer tone. "Yes, Ron? What do you need?"

"Um… Margaret's gone to lunch and there are a couple of women with pies for you up at reception. I tried to put them off, but… they kind of insisted…"

Liam thought if Ron's ears turned any redder, he'd look like he had two ripe tomatoes stuck to the side of his head. He scrubbed his hand over his face and shook his head. Margaret Hoover was the long-time receptionist for the Acawmacke Sheriff's Department, hired out of high school more years ago than anyone could remember. She joked that she was at the department from the time the county was established in 1663. The way she ran things, she might have been right.

She'd worked for numerous sheriffs, watched over the construction of their new facility, and knew the ins and outs of the whole county as well as the neighboring county of North Heron. She was indispensable to their staff and to him as Sheriff.

And when she was on duty, she kept the casserole and pie committee well away from him.

Liam sighed heavily, turning his gaze up to the hound dog expression on Ron's face. "Deputy Taylor. You want to stay with this department and prove to your superiors that you can handle the job, and yet, you stand before me admitting you can't handle a couple of overzealous, matchmaking women?"

Ron's face scrunched as though in pain. "Sheriff, those women won't take no for an answer. They insist it's their God-given right to make sure the Sheriff is properly and rightly taken care of."

Standing, he stalked toward the door so quickly Ron had to scoot back, almost tripping over his feet in his haste to get out of the way. He made his way down the hall, ignoring the grinning faces coming from the open office doors of his Chief of Deputies, Lieutenant of Investigations, Lieutenant of Patrol, Lieutenant of Corrections, and lastly, Captain.

Stepping into the reception area, now behind a wall of safety glass which he hated and simultaneously appreciated, he halted, seeing the faces of four women glaring at each other. *Well, three glaring and one with a greenish, nervous appearance.*

A vision of his grandmother standing in her kitchen when he and his brothers, with dirt on their shoes, ran through after she'd scrubbed the floor. She'd throw her hands into the air and cry, "Lord, give me strength." *Grandma... I get it now. I really do.*

Moving to the glass barricade after deciding to not go around to the visitor side, he nodded at the oldest woman first, making sure to follow the southern decorum. "Mrs. Traynor."

"Why, Sheriff Sullivan, I know the rain is coming, so I wanted to make sure you had something to eat. This is my niece, Charlene, and we made you this chicken noodle casserole. Well, mostly she made it but used my family recipe. She's visitin', and I thought you should have a chance to meet her in case you see her out and about."

He nodded to the pale young woman being pushed forward by her aunt, looking about as uncomfortable as he felt. "Welcome to the county, Miss Charlene."

Mrs. Mack plopped her heavy pie dish onto the counter, elbowing Charlene to the side. "Sheriff, while Lucinda offers you her old-fashioned recipe, I brought an apple pie 'cause I know how much you like it. And to invite you to church on Sunday. If you can't make the service, stop by for the potluck lunch afterward. My daughter has moved back into the area, and she'll be there. You remember Priscilla? I'm sure you do."

Before he had a chance to speak, the next woman stepped forward, her tall frame dwarfing the others out of the way. "Sheriff." The sultry voice came from a woman closer to Charlene's age but with a worldly huskiness that was the result of practice, along with the lowering of her head as she glanced up at him through her thick, false lashes.

"Rachel," he acknowledged. He and Rachel went way back—in years but not in anything else. Attending North Heron High School at the same time, she'd been known as a flirt and a tease, flaunting her daddy's money. She'd cast her net toward the jocks. That included some of his friends, but back then, he'd been too busy to date, much less even try to hook up under the bleachers. She'd gone off to college, married early, and divorced. At last count, she'd gotten rid of husband number two when he was caught with his assistant, and she'd been discovered having long *sessions* with her personal trainer. Not that he cared, but Margaret kept him up on all gossip whether he wanted to know it or not.

And now, looking for husband number three, she'd turned her sights to him, or rather, any halfway decent-looking man with a steady job. Forcing a polite-but-not-encouraging smile onto his face, he glanced down at the obviously store-bought pie in her hand.

She tucked a strand of salon-perfected blonde hair behind her ear before tapping a long, red fingernail on top of the wrapped dessert. "I thought I'd bring something for you. I'm sure my *pie* is much better than any you've been offered."

Refusing to rise to her adolescent bait regardless of the snicker coming from behind him and the double "harrumphs" from Mrs. Traynor and Mrs. Mack, he swallowed his sigh.

"The Sheriff's Department thanks you for your culinary offerings, and they'll be taken back to the break room for everyone to enjoy. In the future, you may leave them here with the duty officer." With a practiced smile and nod, he turned and walked toward his office, his shoes tapping smartly along the tile. On his way, he shot Ron a glare with a lifted brow, indicating that he did not expect to be disturbed again. Turning the corner, he flipped off a few of his Lieutenants as they continued to grin as he passed by their open office doors.

Slumping into his chair, the familiar creak of the leather as well as the scent of lemon oil the cleaning crew used on the wooden furniture settled over him, easing his irritation. He dropped his chin to his chest, breathed in deeply, then lifted his head as he twirled in his chair and looked out the window.

The view wasn't much, but he'd take any window that gave him a chance to look outside. Located on the back corner of the L-shaped building, he was able to have a partial view of the historic courthouse, which drew visitors since it was no longer used. The much larger modern courthouse was located on the other side of the Sheriff's Department building.

He remembered his high school history class taking a field trip to several of the historic sites on the Eastern Shore. They'd entered the courthouse after being admonished to stay very quiet. While his friends with their adolescent eagerness to get back outside hurried through, he'd been drawn to the photographs that lined the wall of the many sheriffs and deputies that had served throughout the years. Uniforms with perfect creases. Hats worn low on their forehead. Gun belts banded about their waists. For a poor boy growing up in a poor area, he couldn't imagine a better job.

He'd aspired to become a deputy, never believing that he would eventually be sworn in as Sheriff. But the view out his window was a daily reminder. It was strange that some of his closest friends in high school had returned to the area, several of them also in law enforcement. Mitch Evans, the Police Chief of Baytown. Grant Wilder, an officer for the Baytown Police. Colt Hudson, his counterpart as Sheriff of North Heron County. And Wyatt Newman as Chief of Manteague.

Turning his head to the side, he could see trees in the background, another part of his view that he loved. Looking upward, he spied the clouds forming, darker in the distance, and prayed the hurricane would stay out to sea.

Releasing a cleansing breath, he pushed all thoughts of the casserole committee out of his mind, turned his chair back around to his desk, and continued to complete his end-of-month report. It wasn't a task he relished, but he could hardly ask his staff to stay on top of their paperwork if he wasn't willing to do the same.

By the end of the day, he'd said his goodbyes, making sure to speak to each deputy he met on the way out of the building. Camaraderie and loyalty were built on mutual respect, something he emphasized to the members of the department. Climbing into his SUV, he pulled out onto the road and turned toward the south.

When he came back from the Army and was hired as a deputy, he'd moved into the family home as a way to help his mom as well as save money. When he finally decided to buy his own house, he could have chosen anywhere in the county, from the northern tip near Chincoteague to the middle near the county seat, or further south. While he looked at many houses, the combination of wanting to stay close to his family while loving the familiarity of the southern end of the county caused him to choose a house only five miles away from the Acawmacke-North Heron line.

As though she knew he was thinking of her, his phone rang, and he glanced down to see it was his mother. "Hey, Mom. How are you?"

"Just the question I was going to ask you, Liam. I'm sure you've kept your eye on the weather today."

"Yeah. Don't mind telling you that I'm glad it's turning south. Hopefully, we'll just get rain."

"I remember a storm when you were just a baby that came tearing through. I thought the roof was going to blow off the house, and your daddy kept telling me it wasn't. It was only later that he told me he was afraid of the same thing but didn't want me to worry. Course, I told him that I was smart enough to know wind that strong could blow the roof off the house!"

Liam imagined his father trying to pat his mother on the arm while assuring her everything was fine. His mom was in the mood to chat, and he was happy to let her do so, her voice filling the cab of his SUV as he drove.

"You need to call your sister sometime soon. Sue's got a bee in her bonnet about Harold not coming to her baby shower. He says it's for women, and your sister insists that baby showers are *coeducational* now, and it's his husbandly duty to be there."

Choking back a snort, Liam said, "Co-ed, Mom. It's just co-ed. Men and women together."

"That's what I said. *Co*-educational!"

"Look, Harold's a good husband and a good father. Maybe he just doesn't want to sit around and play party games."

"Sue's got men coming. Your brothers-in-law are coming. Several of the women are bringing their husbands and both your brothers should be there. And don't you even think about not coming, Liam Sullivan!"

He remembered opening the pink and blue envelope a few weeks ago but, like Harold, figured it was mostly for women, so he hadn't even put the date on the calendar. He hoped he still had the invitation. "Sure, Mom. I'm pretty sure I got it on the calendar at home, but send me a text with the date and time again just so I'll have it on my phone."

"Uh-huh. I'll do that."

Her voice indicated that she didn't believe for one moment that he'd put anything on his calendar. As always, she put aside any irritation she had toward her children and continued to tell him the latest exploits of his three sisters, two brothers, nieces, nephews, and neighbors. She was happy that her family had all settled nearby, their gatherings large, loud, and loving.

Turning into his driveway, he said, "Okay, Mom, I'm home. I know the storm is supposed to just be rain, but have you got everything you need?"

"Oh, yes. I'm taken care of and blessed. But I wish you weren't alone, son."

"I've got a whole county to take care of. Not many people would want to share me with that."

"Humph," she groused again. "Just because one didn't work out doesn't mean there isn't someone special out there."

"I hear you, Mom, but I've really got to go. Talk to you later."

"Bye, sweetheart."

Disconnecting, he continued down his drive, the sight of his house filling him with pride and peace. The two-story, custom-built house was new, and he'd bought it for a good price. It had been almost finished for a couple who suddenly had a change in plans and needed someone to buy it quickly. He was thrilled with the three-bedroom home with a large owner's suite, an office downstairs, and open floor plan that allowed his living room to extend into the dining room and the large kitchen connected. He knew his family wondered why he bought the house if he didn't have a spouse and children on the way, but for him, it represented a chance to relax at the end of the day in a space that was all his.

Pulling into his garage, he lowered the door behind him. Moving into his neat laundry room, he took off his uniform after securing his weapon and tossed the clothes into the hamper. He grabbed a pair of clean sweatpants and a T-shirt that he kept on a shelf and pulled them on. With socked feet, he padded into the pristine kitchen, throwing open the massive refrigerator door and seeing what he could have for dinner. He still had leftovers from his mom's roast beef and veggies she'd sent to him earlier in the week. Heating them, he took his plate and beer out to the deck that overlooked the line of trees in his backyard, the sunset visible over the bay through their limbs.

After eating, he leaned back in his chair, watching as the sunset disappeared behind the dark clouds still forming. His mom's mention of his dad brought back more memories. Liam was the oldest of six kids and his memories the sharpest. His dad worked at one of the farms in the area, starting as a field worker when he was a teenager, then moving into supervision, and finally into the produce factory by the time Liam was ten years old. His mom was a housewife but sold her canned fruits and vegetables at the farmer's markets during the growing seasons.

As the oldest, Liam was used to herding his younger siblings around and helping with chores, but most of his memories were of having fun. He studied hard and played ball in middle school and ninth grade.

Until the fall day he and his siblings got off the school bus when he was thirteen years old.

Met at the door by their minister, he heard the sound of sobs coming from his mom. Leaving the younger ones on the front porch with a few of their neighbors, he went in alone to find out what was happening.

His mother wrapped him in her arms, managing to tell him through her broken sobs that their father had died of a heart attack. As he staggered up to his room, his heart ripped from his chest, he knew he was now the man of the house.

The vibration of his phone jolted him from the rabbit hole musings he had slipped down. Pulling it out of his pocket, he saw that it was Mitch. "Hey, man, what's up?"

"Any chance you'd have a problem switching the LEL meeting tomorrow to Baytown instead of Seaside?"

The two sheriffs and the four police chiefs in the two Virginia counties got together monthly for a Law Enforcement Leaders' meeting. With Mitch, Colt, Wyatt, and him being longtime friends and the other two having held their positions for several years, the six leaders were close, determined that by cooperation they stood a better chance of being effective in their duties to the citizens they protected.

"That's fine with me."

"Thanks. Dylan said that due to a past leak, the Seaside Police Station is having roofing work completed tomorrow. I volunteered the Baytown Station."

"Sounds good. I'll see you there. Give Tori my best. I need to get a baby gift to you two."

"Don't worry about it, man. Between her family and mine, we've got enough diapers, blankets, and onesies to last."

Disconnecting, Liam chuckled. He had no idea what a onesie was but hoped his sister had enough of them as well. He knew he would have to go to his sister's baby shower and their chaotic household would be overwhelming, but he could stand it for a couple of hours.

Walking back into his house, the neatness filled him with a sense of calm. As he passed the extra bedrooms across from the master, he knew that one day he'd like to marry and have children, but so far, there had only been one woman who'd tempted him to take the plunge. His job had been the impediment she couldn't get past. She wanted a different life for them, and he wasn't about to give up his lifelong dream for someone who wanted more money and status. *When I find someone who fits into my life, then I'll be ready.*

3

Parking in the small Baytown Police Station's parking lot, Liam alighted from his vehicle, his eye toward the sky. The clouds were darker and beginning to roll. When he'd eaten breakfast, he'd listened to the weather station again, hearing divergent hurricane path predictions.

Once inside, he smiled at the receptionist, one who rivaled his Margaret in the length of service. She was on the phone or he had no doubt she would offer her opinion on where the hurricane would land.

Inside the station's workroom, he greeted Mitch on his way to the coffee pot, glad to see it full and strong. "Good morning."

Mitch already had a cup and sat at the round table. "Morning. I guess you've seen the reports."

Colt Hudson walked in, his face hard. It was a look he used to have before his wife Carrie and her son came into his life. Nowadays, it was a smile that usually graced Colt's face. "Fuckin' storm. I wish it was more predictable. My county's Board of Supervisors won't make a call about opening emergency centers until the governor calls for the funds to operate them. The governor won't make that call until the predictions are in, definitely saying that it's coming." He stopped at the coffee pot and glanced at Liam, nodding toward his cup. "Is it strong?"

"Hell, yeah."

"Good." Colt poured his cup and sat at the table across from Mitch.

Liam sat next to him. "We're all in the same boat, Colt. My Board of Supervisors hasn't made a decision yet either. Hell, they're probably waiting on your county's board's decision."

Hannah and Dylan walked into the room. The police chiefs for the little towns of Easton and Seaside were also a couple, soon to be married. Hannah sat down and Dylan filled two cups with coffee. Placing one in front of her, he turned to Colt. "Any word on—"

"No."

The room was silent for a few seconds before the others began laughing. "Damn, Colt. Besides Hurricane Ivy and the county's Board of Supervisors, what's got your boxers in a twist?" Liam asked.

"Sorry," he said, scrubbing his hand over his face. "Carson is only sleeping about two hours at a time. Carrie's exhausted, and I'm not much better."

Liam nodded as the others expressed sympathy, but looking at Colt, he was glad his house was quiet. The idea of a raging storm outside with a raging baby on the inside made him sorry for his friend.

Wyatt hustled in, apologizing as he grabbed his coffee. The Police Chief for Manteague, a fishing town on the ocean side of Liam's county, appeared as flustered as the rest of them. Liam knew it wasn't just the storm; they'd all worked through hurricanes that brushed by the Virginia coast before. But with the unpredictable Ivy, they had little time to prepare when the county's monies and resources were tied up in politics.

"What's the most up-to-date?" Hannah asked.

Mitch tapped on his tablet before turning it around, letting the others see the screen. "One of the American forecast models shows the hurricane turning out to sea, not doing anything more to the East coast than some drenching rain. Another model shows it going out to sea then turning back, coming in toward New England, but that track doesn't seem to have a lot of popularity. What I can tell, the most accurate model is the European one, which doesn't bode well for us."

Liam leaned closer, looked at the map Mitch was indicating, and observed the European model's track that predicted Hurricane Ivy skimming past North Carolina before turning inward at a direct hit to Virginia. *Right on top of us. Fuck!*

"Why the hell are they so different?" Dylan grumbled.

Hannah rolled her eyes as she looked down at her tablet. "Why else? Funding." Glancing up, she shrugged. "The American scientific endeavors are funded, or defunded, at the whims of the politicians in charge at the time. The European research centers and scientists seem to have a steadier flow of funds to do their job. When you look at the history to see which model has been the most accurate, it's the European."

A collective groan came from the table, and Liam reached to squeeze the back of his neck, hoping to ease the tension. "We need to plan for the worst. If it's really going to happen, then the governor can declare a state of emergency, and the State Police can handle the evacuation routes. Our supervisors can work with the emergency shelters." He looked over at Colt. "Are you bringing more people into the station or keeping them spread out over your county?"

"I'm going to keep them spread out. I'd rather have more of my deputies at home with their families scattered all over the county, ready to be called to whatever area might need them the quickest. That makes more sense than having an excess amount of them just sitting at the station."

Liam nodded. "I agree. That's what I'm going to do."

"Have you got enough staff for the Regional Jail?" Wyatt asked Colt. Each of the smaller towns' police stations had a few cells, but they wouldn't keep anyone during a major storm. If needed, they would have them transferred to the large Regional Jail.

"Yeah, we've got it covered," Colt replied.

"Any word on the Chesapeake Bay Bridge-Tunnel?" Liam asked.

"They will start restricting travel once the winds hit forty mph. So, all those campers will have to travel north toward Maryland if they don't go ahead and leave. Cars can continue to cross even at sixty-five mph winds. Once it gets above that, they'll shut it down."

"We'd better hope the governor goes with the European model and starts getting things ready soon," Liam said to the nods of agreement from the others. "But until then, I'm going back to the office and telling my people that's what we're preparing for."

As the meeting concluded, they each offered grim-faced goodbyes before heading out. Normally, after their LEL meetings, they had lunch at one of the local establishments. But today, with the unpredictable Ivy staring them down, they were each ready to hustle back to their stations.

The rest of the day was a blur of planning, meetings, and activity. The winds increased, and by mid-afternoon, it appeared as though the Euro model was correct. Every office, including reception, had the TV on the weather stations as they sent their high-profile field meteorologists to Virginia Beach. They stood on the sand, the wind gusts beginning to whip their thin jackets, while daredevils played in the surf waves in the background.

Liam sighed, knowing the Virginia Beach law enforcement would have to take time to chase off the idiots who didn't heed warnings. *Christ, I hope Mitch doesn't have to deal with that.* Baytown had the only public beach in the area, and he hoped their small staff didn't have to endanger themselves trying to save people who weren't smart enough to stay out of the storm.

By the end of the day, the storm had stalled, but in

doing so over the water, the meteorologists talked of how Ivy was growing and predicted that by the time she headed to the coast, she would still be a Category 5.

Pulling into his garage that evening, he was glad he had time to secure his house. The original owners had opted for hurricane shutters on most of the windows, for which he was now grateful. It took almost an hour to go to each window and lower the metal grate that slid down on the outside and secure it in place. It was an expense he wouldn't have sprung for but was glad the couple who'd had the house built had decided on the upgrade.

Turning on the television in the living room, he moved to the kitchen and fixed a simple but hot dinner. If the storm knocked the electricity out, his generator would kick on, keeping his meals from just being sandwiches. Eating at the dining room table, keeping an eye on the television, he watched as the predictions for the storm's path kept it hitting the coast of Virginia directly, but the timing had slowed. Instead of the force of the storm hitting early tomorrow morning, they were now predicting a late evening landing.

Closing his eyes, Liam sighed heavily. He would have preferred the worst of the storm to be during the daytime, not in the black of night. Rinsing his dishes, he placed them into the dishwasher, wiped the counters, and tossed the dishtowel into the hamper in the laundry room before hanging a clean towel over the stove handle.

Flipping off the lights, he double-checked the doors and climbed the stairs. His nighttime routine was uninterrupted—a shower, clothes for the next day laid out, shoes shined, then climbing into bed to read.

But tonight, sleep was hard to find. The wind had picked up outside, and while the windows were covered and secure, he could still hear the whistling around the back corner of his house. He'd called his mom, checked in with his siblings, and made sure everyone was prepared. They were all adults, all taking care of their families and each other, but he couldn't stop the feeling of needing to be responsible.

He rolled over, thinking of what his youngest brother, Corby, had said. *"Jesus, Liam, you've got a whole county to take care of. We're good, and we've got Mom. Stop worrying about us."* It might be true, but easier said than done.

He'd called his oldest sister, Ellen, to check on her family and ask if she felt safe in her home. *"Brother dear, while my kids love their Uncle Liam, they want to spend the storm in a house they can play in, not one that looks like a model home!"* He knew she was right also. Sighing, he punched his pillow. *There's nothing wrong with liking a neat space to call my own.* He loved his family and never regretted stepping up to the plate to help raise his boisterous siblings, but the chaotic house made him promise that when he could finally have a place of his own, it would be calm perfection.

Rolling to his back, he sighed heavily, the sound of his breath leaving his lungs mixed with the wind against his empty house.

The station was a hive of activity the next morning. Hurricane Ivy had finally quit pissing around over the open water and had turned decidedly toward the Eastern Shore. As the day progressed, the winds increased, and the Chesapeake Bay Bridge-Tunnel administrators made their calls accordingly. They closed to trucks and campers by noon, and it was predicted that soon only cars would be able to pass.

He met with his Captain and Lieutenants, ensuring all departments were covered and staffed. "For those deputies at home, make sure they have their emergency contact in place and radios on. We'll be better able to get to any area of need quicker if they travel from their homes instead of just this station. And if not needed, then they'll be able to pass the storm with their families."

Ross, his Captain, nodded. "They appreciate that, Liam." His sentiments were met with nods from his other top staff. At only thirty-four years old, Liam knew he was young to be the Sheriff, but it was a position he'd wanted and knew he could do a good job. For the first couple of years, he worked hard to prove himself, glad that now he seemed to be accepted as more than competent. He stuck to the rules, didn't put up with the previous Sheriff's good-old-boy mentality that fostered favoritism as well as racism, and made sure the staff was well-trained and taken care of.

Tom, the Lieutenant of Corrections, spoke next. "The jail's generators have been checked out, and everything is in working order. My staff is in place, including food and health, so we're good to ride out the storm."

By the end of their meeting, the winds had picked up and the rain had started. Skipping lunch, he made a trip over to the jail to check on the sixty-two inmates currently held. The previous day, the few that had medical conditions had been transported to the Regional Jail in North Heron. He chatted with the deputies that would be staying for the duration, thanking them for volunteering to ride the storm out on duty, and promised the county would reimburse them for their overtime.

Stepping out onto the sidewalk, he ducked as the wind threatened to whip his hat off his head. The sky was already dark, the evening sun long hidden behind the swirling clouds and slashing rain.

He jogged back into the Sheriff's office, his long coat barely able to keep most of him dry. Once inside, he made his last rounds, stopping to stare at the TV in the corner. The bridge-tunnel had closed to all traffic other than cars with no luggage on top and had warnings posted that they would be closing completely by dark. The hotels and B&Bs were filled. The county had set up emergency shelters at the local schools, and Liam made sure they were staffed with a few of his deputies for the night.

The latest predictions still had Ivy hitting the Shore as a Category 5 hurricane and then stalling once it hit land. The sustained winds and rain might last two days. He dropped his chin to his chest, his fists landing on his hips. *Well, hell.*

4

Now, driving home in the dark storm, the torrential rain kept his windshield wipers busy at full speed, and yet, their effectiveness was minimal as he leaned forward to try to see the highway. He called in to the dispatcher to give all-clear updates on the part of the highway he was traversing, glad to hear that his other deputies were reporting the same. *Thank God, people had heeded the warnings and were off the road.*

"Any updates?"

"They're saying the storm turned fast, but you know that. Still claiming Cat 5."

He stifled the curse.

Close to the turnoff for his home, he hoped to be in his driveway in about ten minutes. Another gust of wind slammed into the side of his vehicle, and he gripped the steering wheel tighter.

A strange flash of light through the windshield caught his eye, and he squinted, leaning forward to try to discern what he was looking at. Slowing even more, the sight of a trailer on the side of the road became barely visible through the rain, a small SUV attached to the front. Parked on the side of the road, the emergency flashers were on, and he noted the Ohio license tags. *Christ Almighty, who the hell is driving tonight, pulling that load in the middle of a Cat 5 hurricane? And going south? The fucking bridge is closed!*

He backed up slightly and pulled to the side. "Possible 10-46, Mile Marker Seven."

Calling the tags into dispatch, he discovered the vehicle and trailer were indeed rentals. Swallowing the growl that erupted, he ignored his hat, knowing the wind would send it sailing. Instead of throwing open the door in irritation, he opened it with caution, afraid of the raging wind catching it. Climbing out of his SUV, he squinted as the rain pelted his face. He turned his back toward its force and shut the door carefully. With his high-beam flashlight raised, he braced himself against the wind and stalked past the trailer toward the SUV.

Shining his light inside, he called out, "Acawmacke Sheriff's Department. Is there an emergency?" He bent slightly to peer inside, the illumination of the light shining onto the driver twisted in the seat, a pair of wide, sky-blue eyes staring back at him. His gaze dropped to the rest of her. *Fucking hell!* His hand shot out to the door, throwing it open.

The woman had shifted to the passenger side and was now facing the driver's door, her large, pregnant belly prominently displayed. *Shit!*

He bent forward and leaned into her space, his hands moving toward her ankles to assist her to a more comfortable position. "Ma'am, I'm with the Sheriff's Department. Are you in labor?"

Her brows lowered as she slapped at his hands. "Stop that! What are you doing?"

"Are you in labor? Ma'am, do you need an ambulance?"

As the sound of screeching from the back seat hit his ears, he jerked his head around, eyes wide at the sight of a small child in a car seat staring back at him, her mouth open in a scream. Blonde hair, the front pulled up in two pieces that stuck straight up with pink bows, reminded him of his nieces. She held a juice box in her hands, but most of the purple contents appeared to be all over her shirt.

"Ma'am, do you need an ambulance?" he repeated, his gaze moving back to her pregnant belly as she slapped his hands again.

"No, I need to get a cloth. And thanks to you, my daughter is terrified!"

Rain was blowing in behind him, soaking the interior. He shuffled forward and climbed into the driver's seat, shutting the door.

"What are you doing in my car?" The woman's voice jumped an octave by the end of her question.

His radio squawked. "Sheriff, do you need assistance?"

"Negative. Assisting stranded motorist."

"I'm not stranded!"

He twisted his head, shooting her a glare that would

have most people snapping their mouths shut, but she met his expression with one of her own that made him wonder who would win the glare battle. She broke first, only because her face contorted with a grimace, and her hands went to her stomach.

"Ma'am, do you need assistance?" he repeated for what seemed the tenth time, frustration mixed with concern.

She shook her head, her facial muscles relaxing, and moved her gaze to him before looking toward the back seat. She shifted with difficulty, managing to get to her knees, and leaned between the front seats, her body pressing against his arm and shoulder as she reached toward her child. "No, I'm not in labor. I've had a few pains but it's not labor."

He tried to shift out of her way, but with his left side plastered against the door handle of her small SUV, he had no more room to maneuver. "Well, then—"

"Rosie, honey, don't cry. The nice man is just checking on us. Mommy will get a new shirt as soon as we get to Baytown, and I can get you out of the car. Do you want a cracker instead of the rest of your juice?"

The cries turned to sniffles. "I… I… want y… you."

"Oh, baby, I can't let you out of your car seat right now, but as soon as this nice man leaves, we'll be on our way."

What the fuck? "Ma'am, this nice man isn't leaving."

She settled her weight back onto her calves, still kneeling backward in the seat as her head swung around to pin another glare onto him. "What? What do you mean you're not leaving?"

He stared, incredulity pouring from him as he wondered if her reality was starkly different from his... and he knew his was right. "Ma'am, it's dark outside."

She glanced toward the windshield. "Uh... yeah."

Huffing, determined to count slowly before he lost his cool and upset the now-quiet-but-still-sniffling child in the back. "And it's storming. We're in the beginning of a Category 5 hurricane."

"Do you always state the obvious?"

He blinked just as a drop of water fell from his hair and landed in his eye. "Ma'am, I'm the Sheriff of Acawmacke County, and the streets have been ordered to be cleared. You have not obeyed that order and are costing the county resources by taking our time."

Her bravado slipped, and she swallowed audibly. As he stared, he now observed her pale complexion and the bluish circles underneath her eyes. "I'm sorry, Sheriff. I'm not trying to be a problem, and I want out of the storm as much as you. We just need to get to Baytown."

"What's in Baytown?"

"The Sea Glass Inn. It's a bed-and-breakfast. Rosie and I have a room there. I knew a storm was coming but I was so close, and we don't have anywhere else to go."

"Ma'am, the inns are all full—"

"No, Tori's expecting me."

"Tori?"

Her honey-blonde hair moved as her head nodded. "Yes, Tori. Tori Evans. She owns the Inn and—"

"I know who Tori is. I also know her husband is the Police Chief there. Are you saying they are expecting you in the middle of this storm? They know you're traveling?"

"Well… yes, sort of. Tori knew I was on my way. It's taken longer to get there than I thought."

Just then, another blast of sustained wind hit the SUV and it rocked slightly. The little girl in the back whimpered, and the woman's eyes shot open wider.

"Baytown may only be about thirty minutes away in normal conditions, but in this storm, it would take you over an hour and a half. Plus, there's no way I can let you continue driving down the road with hurricane-force winds, even if you weren't pulling this trailer. We're going to have to find an alternative, ma'am," he declared, his mind searching for what that alternative plan could be. *There's not a hotel nearby, and they're all filled anyway. The closest emergency center is as far away in the other direction as Baytown.* It only took a second to flip through his relatives' homes in his mind. *Shit, none are closer than mine.*

The winds picked up and the rains pelted the windshield harder. Looking to the side as the woman leaned her arms over the back of the seat, wiping the little girl's face, he sighed. "Ma'am, we have no choice. I live a few minutes from here in a house that's secure and safe. I know it's not ideal, and you don't know me, but I have got to get you out of this storm immediately."

She settled her thighs on her calves again, knees still bent in the seat, and stared. The car rocked again, and she blinked. Sucking in a deep breath, she let it out, her head nodding in a jerking motion. "I can't believe I'm saying this, but you're right. I can't keep driving in this. I was trying to get Rosie and myself to safety, but the storm hit quicker than I thought."

He wanted to point out that the storm had actually stalled for a day but, glad that she wasn't arguing, decided to placate her. "After it stalled out over the ocean, it turned quickly. If you're not used to the way hurricanes can move, I'm sure it caught you off guard." He twisted and glanced to the very back, seeing suitcases. "I'm going to pull up beside you and transfer your suitcases over to my vehicle—"

"Can't I just follow you there?"

"Absolutely not! You're pulling a trailer which adds stress to your vehicle every time the wind hits it. You've been lucky so far, but the wind is increasing in velocity, and there's a good chance it could flip the trailer over, your vehicle following."

"Damn," she breathed, her shoulders slumping.

Not giving her another chance to come up with a different scenario that he would waste more time explaining, he said, "Ma'am, I'm telling you how this is going to go. I'm gonna pull up next to your vehicle and transfer the suitcases over. Then we're going to get your child's car seat into the back of my SUV and get her transferred safely as well—"

Her head nodded in jerks again. "Yes, thank you. Just tell me what I need to do for Rosie and we'll get her into your vehicle."

Glad that the severity of the situation had now struck her, he continued. "We'll leave your vehicle and trailer here." Her mouth opened, but he continued talking. "There's no debate. We have to leave it here. As soon as the storm gives us a bit of a break, we can come to get it."

Once again, she simply nodded, her bravado slipping as the severity of the situation finally hit. "I don't know you. I need to talk to Tori."

"We need to get going, but you're right. Let me give Mitch a call. I'll put it on speaker." She remained silent as he dialed, glad when the call was answered quickly. "Hey, Mitch, it's Liam. I've got—" He turned and looked toward her, his head cocked to the side.

"Amy Carruthers."

"Amy Carruthers. Yeah, she and her daughter were on their way to Baytown but the storm halted their progress. No, it's okay, they're fine. I've got them and we're not far from my house. Yeah… my house. It's the closest safe place I can get them to. No, it's all good. Is Tori there? Amy wants to talk to her." Mitch called for Tori, who must have been listening to the conversation, and hit the speaker button.

"Oh, my God, Amy! Are you okay?" Tori asked, her voice raised.

"Yes, yes, we're fine. I wasn't stranded… well, at least not exactly. Rosie had spilled her juice box, was screaming, and I just needed to pull to the side to deal with the mess and a very upset pre-schooler."

"How lucky you are that Liam found you!"

"Well, that's partially why I'm calling. He wanted me to find out the scoop on him since we're going to his house."

"Oh, you're in the best hands. Liam is the Sheriff. Mitch grew up with him, and I've known him for several years. He's the best person who could have come across you in a storm, and you can absolutely trust him."

Liam grinned at Tori's resounding reference. He glanced to the side, seeing Amy's chest heave as she let out a sigh of relief. "Thanks, Tori."

"Listen, you stay with Liam and stay safe. We'll get together when the storm passes. I can't wait to see you again and meet Rosie."

With goodbyes said, he looked at her, waiting. She nodded. "Okay, it seems as though you're the man to trust right now."

With no more objections, he opened the door and squinted against the sting as the force of the rain hit him in the face. Making it to his vehicle, he climbed inside and started the engine, pulling to the side of her SUV. Calling dispatch, he reported. "Sheriff Sullivan. The 10-46 stranded vehicle was not mechanical. Pregnant woman and small child. Out of state, traveling to Baytown. I've got them and taking them… to safety."

Disconnecting, he shook his head. *I must be crazy!* Even as he climbed from his vehicle again, already drenched to the skin, he could not come up with an alternative plan that would ensure the safety of the woman and child. At least for the night they would be warm, dry, and fed. As soon as the winds slowed, he'd drive them to Baytown, getting a deputy to follow in her vehicle so he could be sure they arrived safe and sound.

The woman had unlocked the back of her vehicle

from inside, and he lifted the hatch. Grabbing the two largest suitcases, he transferred them to the back of his SUV. Ducking his head, trying to keep the rain from hitting him straight in his face, he transferred the other smaller bags, one obviously filled with toys. Slamming the back of both SUVs, he walked around to her side.

"Do you think it's best if I just hold her in my arms?"

Shaking his head, he replied, "No, ma'am, I'm sorry. It's against the law in Virginia to transport a child that's not in a car seat." He looked into the back, seeing the little girl staring back at him, a curious look in her big blue eyes, so similar to her mother. "How old is she?"

"She's almost four but little for her age. She's very quiet and won't talk much until she gets used to someone."

"I'll have you take her out of the seat, and I should be able to transfer it to my backseat quickly with both our doors open. I've even got an extra jacket that I can throw over it so it won't get wet. It'll take a couple of minutes to make the transfer and get it secured properly in my vehicle."

"That's fine."

He glanced back to her and she smiled. It struck him that that was the first time he'd seen her smile since they'd met. It also didn't miss his attention that her smile made an already beautiful woman appear even more exquisite. He wanted to ask why she was on the road by herself. Why wasn't her husband with her? Why was she making such a move late in her pregnancy? And why was she heading to a bed-and-breakfast with a trailer full of possessions? There was no time for questions now, but as soon as he got her settled, he wanted answers.

He waited while she unbuckled the child—*Rosie*—and brought her to the front seat where the little girl nestled on her mom's lap, laying over the baby bump, her face pressed against her mom's chest, watching him carefully. Opening the back door, and with an extra coat over the top of the car seat, he managed to get it unbuckled and transferred into his vehicle with only a modicum of difficulty. Once it was secure, he closed her back door and then turned to the front passenger seat.

"Okay, ma'am, it's time. I don't want to upset Rosie, but the ground is slick, and I can't be sure that you won't fall trying to carry her yourself. So, I'm gonna take her from you, get her buckled in, and then I'm going to come back for you. I know she'll cry, but she'll be safe."

She held his gaze for just a few seconds, then turned and smiled widely at her daughter. "Sweetie, you're going to have to be a really brave girl for Mommy. This nice man is going to carry you and put you in his big car, and then he can help Mommy get in, too. We're going to go for a fun ride."

Rosie's arms tightened about her mom. "Mommy, I don't wanna go."

"Baby, you've got to be a big girl and let the nice man take us to his house to play. He's taking your toys, too." Amy gently unwound her daughter's arms and leaned back, allowing Liam to pull her against his chest, but she screamed.

"Bubbie!"

"What?" He jerked, looking around in confusion.

"Oh, I'm sorry." Amy leaned over the seat again and grabbed a very worn stuffed rabbit. "Here's her Bubbie. She won't go anywhere without him."

Liam reached out and took the stuffed animal from her and handed it to Rosie. She clutched it tightly, growing still and quiet. Breathing a sigh of relief, he wrapped the extra jacket over Rosie's head before he carried her, careful to keep the pelting rain from slashing against the little child. She was whimpering by the time he got to his vehicle, but he managed to get her buckled into her car seat. Just as the tears begin to fall in earnest and a wail left her lips, he hustled back into the raging storm to get Amy.

She had slung her purse strap crossways over her body and swung her legs out of the car. With his hands holding her firmly, he assisted her to a standing position, wrapping her body in his large jacket, pressing her close to his chest. The wind knocked her even closer to him, and they walked slowly to his vehicle. He wanted to hurry but didn't want her feet to slip out from under her.

Making it to his passenger door, he opened it. She stepped away from his chest, and he moved his hands downward, but her expanded waistline didn't allow him to have a firm grip. Sliding his hands upward, he grasped her under her armpits and lifted her into his SUV. He grabbed the seat belt and settled it across her body, snapping it into place. As he looked up, their faces just inches apart, both blinked the water from their eyes. Jerking back, he stepped away and closed her door securely.

He hurried back to her vehicle to make sure it was locked and secure. His lungs heaved, the gale-force winds having knocked the breath out of him. Now, completely drenched, he bent forward to stagger back to the driver's side of his SUV and climbed inside. His door slammed shut easily, and he wiped his hand over his face, careful to not sling water toward his passenger. Glancing to the side, he noted she was only slightly less drenched than he and probably wouldn't have felt any more water coming her way.

Her gaze had been on the back seat keeping an eye on her daughter when she turned and focused on him. "Thank you for rescuing us and offering us shelter for the next few hours."

He nodded then jerked slightly, realizing an important step he'd completely forgotten. Reaching into his pocket, he pulled out a leather case and flipped it open. "I'm sorry. I know I was in uniform and driving a Sheriff's vehicle, but I never showed you my full badge and identification. That was incredibly remiss of me."

She leaned forward, seeing his photograph as well as his title. *Sheriff, Acawmacke County.* "I think the hurricane has everyone a bit discombobulated. After all, you thought I was in labor." Sticking her hand forward, a smile curving her lips. "Well, Sheriff of Acawmacke County, if you're going to take us to your house, we really should be formally introduced as friends. I'm Amy Carruthers, and this is my daughter, Rosie. We're pleased to meet you."

She cocked her head to the side, her hand still held out toward him, and he grinned. Sliding his palm against hers, he wrapped his fingers around her small hand. "Amy, it's nice to meet you and Rosie. Just call me Liam. Now, let's get you home."

5

Amy twisted her neck around so that she could keep an eye on Rosie sitting in the back seat. It dawned on her after she was buckled into the front seat that she should have insisted on sitting in the back with her daughter, but the hurricane seemed to have short-circuited her already-pregnant brain, and she simply hadn't thought of it in time. Rosie was no longer crying, was safe and dry, and was curiously looking around.

Her chest heaved with a great sigh, and she let it out heavily. *Could this day have gone any worse?*

Glancing at the handsome Sheriff behind the wheel, she knew her day *could* have gone a lot worse. An accident. Stalling on the side of the road. The trailer flipping in the wind. An unscrupulous character stopping to help. *Oh, hell yeah, this day could have gone a lot worse!*

She watched Liam's concentration focus out the windshield where she hoped he could see further than she could. She'd never been in a hurricane before and couldn't believe how quickly the weather had changed. Totally unaware of an impending storm when she'd left Ohio, she and Rosie had spent their time listening to children's books and music, not having the radio on. This morning when she checked out of their hotel was the first time she'd learned of the threatening weather. The receptionist mentioned that the storm had stalled out over the ocean, and she was sure she had time to get to Baytown. While driving, she listened to the radio and heard the forecasters talk about the storm turning and heading directly toward them, but she was sure they'd be able to make it.

Closing her eyes, a shiver ran through her at the thought of the dangerous situation she'd placed herself, Rosie, and her unborn child in. *What an idiot I was. I should've stopped at a hotel hours ago.* But even as they traveled, the radio was also reporting about all the filled hotels and how there were no vacancies available, fueling her desire to get to Baytown, to her friend's bed-and-breakfast.

She felt the blast of heat and opened her eyes. Liam glanced toward her. "I saw you shiver and thought you might be cold."

"Thank you. Actually, I think I'm just mind-numb over the events of today."

"We're almost to my house."

She looked out the window, the headlights barely piercing the black of the night, mostly illuminating the slanting sheets of rain. A house loomed ahead, the garage door gliding up. He pulled inside, and suddenly, the silence of the rain no longer hitting the vehicle sounded strange, as though her ears had grown accustomed to the constant noise.

Before she had a chance to say more, he alighted from his side. She unbuckled and twisted around, her smile wide as she caught Rosie's eyes. Her daughter was staring around, holding onto her bunny. "Are we gonna live here?"

"Just for the night, Rosie. Just until the rain stops. Now, let's get you out of your seat."

Her door opened, and Liam's hand held onto her arm, assisting her down. "Your shoes are soaked, so they'll be slick. Let me get her for you."

She stared up into his face, his wet, dark hair and five o'clock shadow giving him a devil-may-care appearance, and yet, his touch was so gentle. She nodded, not trusting her voice.

He opened the back door, and she heard him soften his voice. "Hey, there, Rosie. I'm going to get you out of your seat, and then you and your mommy can get inside where it's dry, okay?"

"Okay," came the whispered reply as Rosie clutched her bunny. Amy noticed that was the first thing Rosie had said to him, and the smile on his face indicated he'd noticed that, too. With a few clicks, he had her unbuckled and lifted into his arms. Turning toward Amy, he said, "Let me carry her."

Rosie twisted her head around to keep her eyes on Amy but wasn't upset. Making a silly face at her daughter, she followed Liam as he walked into his house from the garage, entering a large laundry room.

He set Rosie down and turned to look at Amy.

"Um… let's see… I'll go back into the garage and get your suitcases so that you two can get into some dry clothes."

He hustled back through the door, and she looked around at the perfectly organized laundry room. A hamper stood in the corner, clothes neatly placed inside. Folded sweatpants and T-shirts were stacked on shelves next to the door. Looking down, her wet sneakers were creating a small puddle on the floor. Bending, she slipped them off just as he walked back in. His gaze raked over her, and she was aware of how bedraggled she appeared. He was just as wet, and yet, looked virile.

"I'll take these upstairs to one of the guest bedrooms and let you and Rosie get comfortable. There's a bathroom that connects, if you need a bath… or you might want a shower… or I guess she's too little for a shower."

She smiled, the competent Sheriff now appearing uncertain. "Liam, whatever you want to do is fine. I don't want us to intrude."

He gave his head a little shake. "Sorry, I guess I'm not quite sure what you need."

"If you can show us a place to dry off and get changed, that'll be fine." She reached down and took Rosie's hand. Bending, she tapped her finger on the end of her daughter's nose, eliciting a giggle. Following Liam, they walked through a large kitchen, equally as pristine as the laundry room. The open floor plan extended through the dining room and living area. As they headed toward the stairs, she noted no books or magazines were lying around, and the television remote was placed squarely in the middle of the coffee table.

Continuing to follow him upstairs into a wide hallway, he ushered them into one of the doors on the right. It opened into a beautifully appointed guest bedroom—queen-size oak bed with a pale blue comforter, an oak dresser and matching mirror, and a comfortable chair with a reading lamp in the corner.

He set the suitcases down and stood with his hands shoved into his pockets. Inclining his head toward the door on the side of the room, he said, "There's a bathroom through there. It connects on the other side to the other guest bedroom. Towels are already in there, but I'm not sure what else I have. To be honest, since my family lives close by, I never have overnight guests."

"We have everything we need. I'll take a bath with her, and we'll be fine. Thank you."

His mouth opened, then snapped closed quickly. After a few seconds, he cleared his throat. "Once you're ready, come downstairs, and we'll get something to eat."

Rosie slid behind Amy's legs and whispered, "I'm hungry."

His lips quirked upward just as he turned to leave, making him appear even more handsome. The door closed behind him, and she blew out a breath before turning her attention to Rosie, who was still looking around. "Come on, let's have a warm bath."

Rosie giggled and nodded. She turned on the bathwater, checked the temperature, then pulled Rosie's top and pants off. "Let's take off your big girl panties." Once

Rosie was undressed, she placed her into the tub and scrubbed her body, then added suds to her hair, making her giggle again.

Stripping, she climbed into the tub carefully, and without taking the time to luxuriate in the warm water, she rinsed off quickly.

She stepped out of the tub and dried off, noting the plush towels. Tucking an extra-long towel around her girth, she looked down. "Are you ready to get out? Mommy needs to get into some dry clothes and then we can find something to eat."

"I'm ready," Rosie said, her eyes bright as she held her arms up.

Lifting her over the edge of the tub, Amy quickly rubbed her daughter's little body with a thick, fluffy towel and slipped her into her pink pajamas. "Okay, sit here with Bubbie while Mommy gets ready." She grabbed her damp clothes and hung them over the towel bar, thinking of how soaked Liam had gotten while keeping them from taking the brunt of the rain. Digging into her suitcase, she pulled out stretchy pants and a big top, settling it over her stomach. Looking into the mirror, her hands moved to cup underneath her pregnant tummy, and she sighed. "What a story I'll have to tell you, Peanut." A puff of air slipped out, and she shook her head. "Along with all the other stories I'll have to tell."

"Mommy, I'm hungry."

Looking down, she smiled. "Well, then let's get the Rosie girl something to fill her belly." She held Rosie's hand as they walked out of the bedroom and down the wide staircase. Now that her mind was more focused on her surroundings and less on getting to safety, she was impressed with Liam's home. Beautifully decorated, it certainly didn't seem like a bachelor's residence. She jerked to a halt. *He's married! Oh, my goodness! He brought home a stranger, and his wife is probably fussing at him right now!* She continued to hold Rosie's hand, her daughter jumping down the last step, and heard his voice coming from the kitchen. Closing her eyes for a second, she let out a breath, preparing to meet an indignant wife who was now saddled with unexpected house guests.

Rosie stayed right with her, shy as usual. Walking into the kitchen, the scent of bacon sizzling greeting her, she was surprised to see Liam alone, his phone to his ear. He was in dry jeans and a T-shirt, his wet hair combed.

"Yeah, Mom, I've got her and her daughter here. We're in and fine, but how are you holding up? Okay, but call Corby, Lenny, or Harold if you need anything. Yeah, love you, too. Bye, Mom."

Before she could move, he'd tossed the phone to the counter and turned, his gaze moving over her before dropping to Rosie, hiding behind her legs. He lifted his gaze back to her and smiled. "You guys hungry? I've got bacon and scrambled eggs. I thought breakfast food sounded good."

"Oh, my, yes," she gushed. "After the time we've just had, comfort food sounds amazing." Stepping forward, she looked around. "What can I help with?"

"Nothing, I've got it. You and Rosie can sit down, and I'll get it plated in just a moment."

She looked over at the table, surprised to see a booster seat already in one of the chairs. Swinging her head around, she asked, "You have a booster seat?"

He chuckled. "Yeah, I've got nieces and nephews. They're not here often because I work so much, and when we get together, I tend to go to their houses or meet at my mom's, but a few things got left over the years. I remembered I had it and thought it might make things easier."

Smiling, she nodded and lifted Rosie into the seat. "Put Bubbie in the chair next to you."

Her daughter's eyes were wide as she leaned over to keep a watch on Liam. She whispered, "But Bubbie is hungry, too."

"I know, but Bubbie doesn't need to be on the table," she whispered in return. Once she had her daughter settled, Liam brought over the plates.

He set an empty one near hers. "I thought you could fix Rosie's the way you know she'll like it."

"This is lovely, thank you." She spooned some scrambled egg and a piece of bacon onto Rosie's plate and added a piece of buttered toast. Seeing that Liam had placed strawberry jam onto the table as well, she added a bit to Rosie's bread. "Okay, eat, munchkin." Kissing the top of her head, she sat down next to Rosie.

Sitting at a stranger's table after they'd rescued her, opened their home to her, and was now feeding her, she felt self-conscious. Chewing slowly, she then dabbed her mouth with the napkin. "Um… I really feel bad about intruding on your… um… family…"

"It's just me." Liam looked up from his plate. "I live alone. So, how do you know Tori?"

Smiling at having a familiar topic to share, she relaxed. "We met in college years ago. Jillian Evans, too. Well, I guess she's Jillian Wilder now that she's married. I know she runs a coffee shop in Baytown."

"Yes, I know Jillian and Grant Wilder, also. He's a police officer in Baytown with Mitch."

"Oh." She sighed. "I haven't been good about keeping up with them as often as I should, but when Tori heard I'd had some… um… difficulties, she called, and we've talked much more often in the last couple of months."

His eyes dropped to her hand where her wedding band gleamed. "Do you need to let your husband know where you are?"

She twisted the band slightly, the metal familiar, and yet, not comforting. Glancing down at Rosie, who was busy pretending to feed Bubbie, she shook her head. "I'm a widow."

His eyes widened for a second, and she felt sure her reply was not what he expected. "I'm sorry, Amy." His gaze dropped to Rosie before turning back to his food, and they finished eating in silence.

The quiet in the room was broken only by Rosie's soft babbling as she talked to Bubbie. As soon as her daughter was finished, she wiped Rosie's mouth and stood to carry their plates to the sink.

"Please, don't worry about those. I'll get them."

She glanced up at him and smiled. "It's no problem."

He walked over and stood next to her, shaking his head. "No, really. Let me put these into the dishwasher while you take care of Rosie."

It was earlier than Rosie normally went to bed, but her daughter was already yawning, tucking Bubbie under her chin. "I'll go put her to bed." He simply nodded, so she reached her hand out, her heart warming as it always did when Rosie looked up with a big smile. "Hey, sweetie, can you say goodnight to our new friend?"

Rosie pressed in close to her leg but peered up at Liam. Ducking her face, she said, "Night."

His lips curved, and Amy once again was struck with how handsome he was.

"Good night, Miss Rosie."

It took a few minutes to make it upstairs while Rosie insisted on holding onto the banister, hopping up each step. Once inside the guest room, she looked at the bed. She hoped Liam didn't mind as she turned the upholstered chair around and pressed its back to the side of the bed, creating a barrier to keep Rosie from rolling out of bed. With pillows on the other side, she was certain Rosie had a comfortable place to sleep safely. After she helped her brush her teeth and go to the bathroom, she settled Rosie into bed and climbed in with her. She only needed to sing lullabies for a moment before Rosie's breath deepened, and her daughter was fast asleep.

Sliding out, she stepped to the window, unable to see through the dark, and barely hearing the howling winds outside. It was obvious Liam's house was strong and well built, and a sense of complete safety moved through her. Sucking in a deep breath, she let it out slowly, peace filling her. As she walked back downstairs, it struck her that she hadn't felt peace in a long time. And it was found in a stranger's home in the middle of a raging hurricane.

6

Liam turned over what little he knew about Amy in his mind. *Met Tori years ago but they'd lost touch. A widow. Was that the 'difficulties' she'd mentioned? A child. Another one on the way.*

When she'd gone upstairs with Rosie, he assumed she'd gone to bed as well. He'd run the rental tags from her vehicle but that gave him no information about the woman spending the night in his house; probably not the smartest move for a Sheriff to make. *But in the middle of a hurricane, what the hell else was I going to do?*

Her purse was still on the kitchen counter where she'd set it when she came in. He walked over and looked down at the blue canvas, knowing her wallet and driver's license would be inside. *A quick look... a call to the station... a chance to find out where she's from and if she's wanted.* But he didn't move. It was one thing to think like a Sheriff, and no doubt he should have done that when they were both in the car, but he'd invited her here for safety. It was a line he wasn't going to cross unless she gave him reason to.

Turning away from the counter, he was startled to see her standing between the dining room and kitchen, her large, blue-eyed gaze pinned on him. She was still in the black pants that did nothing to hide her toned legs. Her shirt was large, hanging below her waist, loose enough to not stretch tightly over her stomach. Her thick, blonde hair was piled on top of her head and held in place with a clip, tendrils curling around her face. Barefoot, she was short, coming only to his chin.

Without speaking, she walked forward and stopped at the kitchen counter. Reaching inside her purse, she pulled out her wallet then dug inside for her license. Handing it to him, she said, "You can check up on me."

"Amy, I—"

"No, really, Liam. Please. You let me check you out by calling Tori. You need to know who you have staying in your house. I'm Amy Carruthers. Twenty-eight years old. I've been living in Ohio since I graduated from college. I went to college here in Virginia on a scholarship but am originally from Canton. My record is clean; no arrests, and believe it or not, no speeding tickets. I suppose if they gave out tickets for stupidly traveling in a hurricane, then you'd be giving me my first one."

He looked down at the license in her hand and shook his head, but she pushed it forward.

"Liam, it's not about trust. We just met, so there's no trust-breaking going on here. I'd feel so much better if you checked me out."

He held her gaze but only saw earnest pleading in her eyes. Nodding, he took the license in his hand and called dispatch. Reading off the name and number, he listened for a moment, his chin down to his chest, staring at his boots while he heard everything she'd had just told him. *Right down to the no speeding tickets.*

Disconnecting, he held her license out, her fingers grazing his as she took it back. "Your hands are cold."

"I'm fine," she said, replacing her wallet. "It's not your house that's too cold. It's just me. I've always had cold hands."

"I thought maybe you had gone to bed with Rosie."

She shook her head. "No, I have too much nervous energy from the storm, I suppose."

"How about some hot cocoa? My mom always said it helped her sleep, and I've always found her recipe to work for me."

She smiled, her face relaxing. "Sounds good."

He heated the milk and slowly stirred in the cocoa and sugar. Once mixed, he carried both mugs into the living room, nodding toward the coffee table. "Can you grab two coasters from the drawer?"

Amy smiled again, finding the coasters and placing them onto the table. He set the mugs down and waited to see where she preferred to sit. She took the comfortable chair, so he sat across from her on the sofa.

They sipped for a few minutes, the sound of the storm outside whistling as it went around the corner of the porch.

"Your house is amazingly quiet. I couldn't help but

notice when I was upstairs that the storm noise was not scary."

Looking up, he cocked his head to the side as though listening. Nodding, he set his mug onto the coaster. "I bought this house from a couple who was having it custom built. They wanted the best of everything, all kinds of upgrades, and then just before it was complete, he got transferred. They had to sell quickly, so while it was an investment for me, I still got a good deal." He nodded toward the windows. "They have hurricane shutters on the outside. It protects the glass, keeps leaks from happening, and definitely cuts down on the sound."

She laughed, looking over toward the dark window. "Oh, now I feel dumb. I looked outside the bedroom window and just thought it was dark. It didn't dawn on me that rain wasn't hitting the glass."

"Well, it is dark outside…" He smiled, enjoying her mirth. She appeared completely comfortable as she sat cross-legged in the wide chair. Her hair was now dry, but wavy tendrils framed her face. Her blue eyes were just as impressive as the first time he glimpsed at them staring up at him through her vehicle window.

Her gaze shifted around the room. "Your house really is beautiful."

"Thank you. I like it. I find that after the chaos of my job and family sometimes, it's nice to come home to this."

"You were talking to your mom earlier? I take it that she's in the area?"

He sipped more cocoa, licked his lips, and set the mug back down before settling against the comfortable cushions of the sofa. "Yeah. One of my brothers and one of my sisters live with their families next to her, so I knew they'd keep an eye on her."

"How many brothers and sisters do you have?"

"Two brothers and three sisters."

She startled, her head jerking. "Oh, my God! I was an only child so I can't imagine what six kids in the family would be like!"

"Total chaos is the best I can tell you."

She patted her tummy. "Well, I used to want to have a brother or sister and knew I didn't want Rosie to have that kind of loneliness."

"How far along are you?"

"Afraid I'll pop right here?" she quipped, laughing.

He chuckled in return. "Maybe. I thought you were shifting over to the passenger side to give yourself more room when I first saw you. I guess technically you were but only to get to Rosie."

"I'm eight months. Don't worry… I've got four weeks to go."

They were silent again for another moment, and he had so many questions he wanted to ask but wasn't sure what would be intrusive or not. She surprised him when she looked over and cocked her head to the side, saying, "I suppose you want to know what on earth I was doing on the road, traveling in a hurricane with a child, pregnant, and a trailer full of my possessions behind me."

"I'd be a liar if I said I wasn't interested."

Smiling, she asked, "Do you want the short version or the longer one that gives more explanation?"

Staring at her beautiful, expressive face, it struck him how interested he was in learning more about her. "Truthfully, I'd love to know anything about you that you want to tell me. And since we're in the middle of a hurricane and can't go anywhere, you can make it as detailed as you'd like it to be."

She shifted around in her seat. "As I said earlier, I was born and raised in Ohio. My parents were hard workers, but while we were always comfortable, we didn't have a lot of money. I wasn't sure I'd be able to go to college but was surprised when I started getting letters from out-of-state universities because of my test scores. One of them was from a college in Virginia, and when I looked at their brochure, I thought it was beautiful. Their offer was for a full ride, including room and board. My parents hated for me to be gone for four years, only coming home for holidays and summers, but they were very excited for me to have the opportunity. So, I came, and that's where I met Tori. While I loved being in Virginia, it was always my plan to go back and settle in Ohio to be near my parents."

He nodded his agreement. "I can understand that. I joined the Army after I graduated from high school. Did a tour as an MP… um, military police. I came back home into the area as soon as I got out of the Army and finished my civilian police academy training. I wanted to serve close to home and wanted to be near my family."

She licked her lips, her gaze dropping to her hands that had slowly been rubbing her pregnant belly. He remembered her saying that she'd gotten in contact with Tori after having some difficulties and was now wondering if she was going to share what those difficulties were. *Obviously, one must have been losing her husband.*

As though she could hear his thoughts, she lifted her face and sadness moved through her blue eyes. "Sometimes, I feel as though a lifetime has happened in the past six years. When I got home from college, my parents informed me that my mom had been diagnosed with ovarian cancer. There was nothing I could have done so they didn't want to worry me, interrupting my education. She died a few months later, and I've always regretted not having those extra years with her. Two years later, my dad died of a heart attack. I was alone and lonely when I met my husband. We were married and had Rosie, but I'd just found out I was pregnant again when I lost him."

"Shit, Amy." His heart clenched at her words, not being able to imagine how her heart ached. *Fuck, if I lost my mom and didn't have my siblings... I can't imagine. It was hard enough when I lost my dad.* "I'm so sorry."

"It sounds horrible when I say it all at once… Well, it is horrible. I had a job in Ohio but no family. My husband had been in foster care, so he had no family."

"So, nothing to hold you to Ohio." He thought of his deep ties to the Eastern Shore and couldn't imagine having nothing as an anchor.

Her lips curved slightly. "I needed a change. I didn't

handle things well when my husband died. Not for the reasons you might expect. But… well, anyway, I wanted to make a life change."

They were quiet for another moment, and he wondered if she was finished sharing. She leaned her head back and held his gaze. The intensity in her stare was fierce. Finally, she sucked in a deep breath before letting it out slowly.

"I met my husband at a time when I was very lonely. I normally don't hang out at bars, but some of the women I worked with at the time wanted to go, so I went. There was a group of firefighters there. I saw Marty and thought he was cute. Acting goofy, hogging for attention as he talked loudly while playing pool, but as it turns out, he saw me, too. We flirted, danced, and he asked me out. We dated for a while, and even though we were opposites in personalities, he was fun. Then, I'm embarrassed to admit, I got pregnant. I thought we'd been careful, but, well…" Her voice grew soft, her lips curving. "I'd never call Rosie a mistake; more like a happy little unplanned surprise. But I never expected to get married. If there was one thing I knew about Marty, he liked to have a good time."

"What changed?"

She shrugged, a little snort slipping out. "He was excited about having a baby. Insisted we get married. I think perhaps the fact that he didn't have a family while growing up made him happy about the idea of having one. The problem was that he didn't really know how to." She sighed. "He was just as much of a hotdog as a firefighter, always needing attention. For a long time, I thought he was just extroverted and enjoyed having fun. It was a while before I realized he craved being the center of attention—to the detriment of everyone else around. I even overheard a few of his friends say that he'd been warned by their Captain on more than one occasion to be more careful. He'd take risks, and that put the rest of them at risk, also. I think he was also an adrenaline junkie. Loved to go rock climbing, racing motorcycles. He was desperately looking for something that he never found, whether with his friends, or at a fire, or in our marriage."

He leaned forward, his attention riveted on her. "That doesn't sound much like a partnership."

Her head moved back and forth slowly. "No, it wasn't. I mean, he was a nice man, a kind man. As far as I know, he was faithful, but we were more friends and roommates than deeply committed lovers and partners. As a father, he loved Rosie but spent little time playing with her, not so much caring for her. One night, he was at the station when a call came in. Big industrial fire at a warehouse. I remember all night staying awake because something didn't feel right. I can't explain it, but the next morning, the station Chaplain and Captain came to see me. He'd been killed when wooden beams fell on him. It was a few days later that I found out he'd gone in when he shouldn't have—before the area was cleared. He just charged in, acting like a fool, and look what happened."

"Christ, Amy, I'm so sorry." He shook his head, lifting his hands to the side, palms up. "I feel like that's all I keep saying, but I don't know what else to say."

"This might sound terrible, Liam, but my first thought was I was so thankful that his unsafe behavior hadn't caused anyone else to be harmed. And then my second thought? I was so angry. Angry at a man who couldn't seem to grow up. Angry that he never learned from his past mistakes. Angry that he could be so cavalier with his own safety, the safety of his friends, and not seeming to give a damn about me or Rosie." She shrugged again, taking another big breath. "A few weeks after the funeral I discovered I was pregnant. To be honest, I was so angry at him over his death, I sought counseling for a while. And it was actually the counselor that suggested I make a change in my life."

He cocked his head to the side. "This is quite a big change at this time of your life."

Chuckling, she nodded. "She didn't exactly tell me that I should pack up everything and move to another state, but that's what happened."

"And Tori?"

Her lips curved upward, her beauty once again shining through. "Tori had heard through a mutual friend about Marty. She called to express her condolences, and we started talking weekly. She knew I was in counseling and knew I needed to make a change. She told me about Baytown and how her husband was part of an American Legion that tried to get the news out to other veterans who were looking for a good home. She wondered if that would be something for me to do. A chance to make a huge change in my life since I was no longer tied to Ohio. A chance to start over. A chance to raise my children in a peaceful area.

Since my job can be done from home, it seemed perfect."

She shifted forward in the chair and then stood, her hands resting on her lower back, and stretched.

Jumping up from the sofa, he reached toward her. "Are you okay? Are you in pain?"

"No, believe me, I would let you know. I just get stiff and need to move around." She bent and picked up her mug, grabbing his as well. As she moved toward the kitchen, he followed. Once there, she washed the mugs, and he dried them. She turned and leaned her hip against the counter, and he mimicked her behavior.

"So, that's how you ended up on the Eastern Shore, heading to Baytown with your possessions in a trailer. I'm curious, though, what were your plans when you got here?"

"I looked online and found a small rental house outside of Baytown, but the landlord said it wouldn't be ready for another week. My house had sold in Ohio, and the new owners weren't able to extend the closing. Tori offered me a large room in her B&B until the rental was available."

"You mentioned you can work from home?"

"Yes, after college, I worked in a large medical office for a group of orthopedic surgeons, first as an office manager. After Rosie, I wanted to cut back on my hours, and with my experience, I became their medical transcriptionist. I later took a job for a medical transcription company once Rosie was in pre-school. I can do the job from home, but it's best if she's not around to take away my concentration. Being pregnant again, my boss knew I was cutting back my hours. I had a continuing account with an orthopedic surgeon that just happens to practice here in this area. Dr. James Malcolm. His practice includes a telemedicine component as well. My boss said it would be nice for me to just keep that account to work on. He thought that if I ever wanted to go back to being an office manager, I might be able to work for Dr. Malcolm since I'd already be familiar with his practice."

"Oh, so you've met the doctor?"

She laughed and shook her head. "No, actually, he has no idea who I am. Well, technically he knows his transcriptionist is Amy C. That's how we're identified, no full names. But I can contact him sometime and let him know that I'm here if I want to."

"Wow, you had it all planned out."

"Well, I thought so. I left Ohio two days ago, wanting to drive slowly since I had the trailer and not wanting Rosie stuck in her car seat for too long at a time." She laughed and rubbed her belly again. "Plus, I knew I needed lots of potty breaks. I simply wasn't paying attention to the weather. Believe me, I wasn't being *Marty*," she said, her fingers making air quotes around his name. "I would never be cavalier with my daughter or my baby's life. I've never had to be concerned about a hurricane before. And instead of the radio, we were playing children's music to keep Rosie entertained. It wasn't until the rain started when we were coming from Maryland that I knew something was happening." She sucked in her lips, her gaze on him. "And now you know just about everything there is to know about me."

He stared, knowing it might appear rude, but couldn't seem to stop. There was something refreshing about her. She was so open and candid. Here she was, in a new place, planning a new future, and a hurricane had stepped into the way. *But it brought her into my path.* When that thought hit him, he smiled.

7

Oh, my God. I've just blurted out my whole life to a complete stranger. A man. A Sheriff. A man who looks like he's never made a goof in his life. Blowing out a breath, she decided running away was the only way to preserve what little dignity she had left. "Um… you'll have to excuse me, Liam. I guess it's pregnancy brain that's made me keep blabbing. I'll say goodnight and head to bed."

"Please, don't apologize." His hand reached out toward her then settled onto the counter, close but not touching. "I'm glad to hear about you."

She lifted her brows to her hairline. "Then you must be bored and craving any company to make it through my whole dissertation."

His shoulders shook as he laughed. "No, really. I had wondered what made a pregnant woman with a small child get on the road during a hurricane. You explained and it makes sense."

"Well, that explains today. You hardly needed to know about the past ten years of my life."

Now it was his turn to shrug. "Well, you are staying in my home. To be honest, it feels nice to know more about you. And this is a bit belated, but welcome to the Eastern Shore."

Laughter erupted from deep within, and her hand went to the bottom of her belly, offering support. She wiped a tear from her eye, saying, "Thank you. I hope for your sake you don't have to show every newcomer such hospitality, but I'm glad you came to my rescue."

The sound of the wind whipped past the house's defenses, and her gaze shot to the window even though she couldn't see outside. "I confess to being very ignorant about hurricanes, Liam. Will this be over by the time we wake up?"

He shook his head. "No, I'm afraid not. This is the biggest hurricane we've had out here in my lifetime. It's hitting as one of the most ferocious ones with the highest sustained winds. We're just on the outskirts of it now."

Blinking, she jerked her head toward him, wondering if he was joking. His face was serious. "Really?"

"I'm sorry, Amy, but the hardest will hit us tomorrow. And if it stalls, then it could be with us for two whole days."

She sucked in a gasp. "My trailer… it's got everything we own in it."

He reached his hand farther over the counter, this time laying it over hers, and she relished the feel.

"You parked near some trees so that created a buffer. But honestly, the most important thing is that you and

Rosie are safe. The trailer's contents can be replaced if necessary."

"God, you're right. I'm sorry—"

"Don't apologize. You've had a harrowing time."

The warm feel of his large hand on her moved through her. She looked down, surprised at how comforting it felt. *When was the last time a man touched me in concern to offer comfort?* She hated to admit it had been many years since Marty had done that. Oh, sure, they'd had a decent sex life, and he'd been a fun lover. But that was always it with him—fun. Never giving of himself when she needed it.

Blinking out of her thoughts, heat filled her face. "I can't thank you enough for your generosity." He smiled, but before he replied, she pulled her hand back. "Well, I really should go check on Rosie."

"Yeah, I'm ready to turn in also."

He flipped off the lights as they walked through the house and stopped in the upstairs hall. "Goodnight, Liam."

"Goodnight, Amy. If you need anything, anything at all, don't hesitate to ask."

She smiled, nodded, and turned to go into her bedroom, closing the door with a soft click. Stepping over to the bed, her smile widened at the sight of Rosie, curled with Bubbie held tightly in her arms, sleeping soundly.

"What a crazy day, sweetheart," she whispered. Climbing into the bed, snuggling with her daughter, she closed her eyes, but instead of seeing the raging storm rocking their vehicle, Liam's face filled her mind. *What a crazy day.*

Amy opened her eyes, blinking at the darkness in the room but easily able to see Rosie's grinning face right in front of hers. Her daughter was leaning over, her little hands clutching Amy's cheeks.

"Mommy, it's morning!"

Blinking some more in the dark room, the muffled sounds of the storm outside, she yawned widely. "How can you tell, baby girl?"

"I knows 'cause I woke."

"Oh, so if you wake up, then it's morning?"

"Yep. I knows."

She leaned forward, kissed Rosie's cheek, and stretched her arms up. Rosie mimicked her stretch, and Amy tickled her under her arms.

"No, Mommy! I gotta pee!"

"Then let's go. We don't want to pee in Mr. Liam's bed!"

Rosie giggled as she slid down off the bed and raced into the connecting bathroom. Still blinking the sleep from her eyes, Amy followed her daughter. "Wash your hands," she said between yawns.

"Can we have cereal?"

"I don't know what Mr. Liam has, honey, but we need to be quiet when we go downstairs. I'll find something for us to eat."

Finishing in the bathroom, they moved into the

bedroom where Rosie began to look for something to wear. After digging through most of her clothes, she settled on pink leggings and a t-shirt with a sparkly unicorn on the front.

Amy looked at the exploded suitcase and shook her head. "You made a mess."

"I needed clothes."

"Did you have to scatter all of them around to choose an outfit?"

"I needed *these* clothes."

Her daughter's almost-four-year-old logic was a good enough answer for Amy. Finding matching pink leggings, she chose a tunic top of pale pink.

Rosie looked her over. "You need a unicorn, Mommy."

Stifling another yawn, she thought of the rental SUV, trailer, the hurricane, no home at the moment, and nodded. "You got that right, Rosie. I need a unicorn." Taking her daughter's hand, they quietly stepped into the hall, and she noted Liam's door was still shut. It struck her that with everything that had gone wrong, being rescued by a Sheriff who happened to be as kind as he was easy on the eyes was incredibly fortuitous, and she chuckled at the thought of Liam as a lucky unicorn. A pull on her hand brought her attention back to Rosie's empty stomach.

Tiptoeing downstairs, she saw the time on the stove clock. Just after six a.m. *Another hour of sleep would have been nice.* While it was comforting to know the hurricane shutters on the windows were helping to keep them safe, she wanted to see outside. "Stay here, sweetie. I'll be right back." She walked to the front door and turned the knob, opening it slowly. Her eyes widened at the sheets of rain coming down sideways as the winds whipped the tops of the few trees she could see. Gasping, she shut the door quickly, glad to be somewhere safe.

Turning, she noted the pictures on the mantle and walked over. There were multiple framed photographs of Liam from childhood with his large family, him as a teen with his arms around a group of guys all wearing Baytown Boys baseball shirts, and him in his Army uniform. Set amongst the pictures were jars filled with green, blue, clear, and brown broken glass.

"Pancakes. I want pancakes."

Looking down at Rosie's bright eyes, she grinned and stepped away from the living room. Touching her daughter's nose with the end of her finger, she reached out her hand. "Tell you what… let's see if we can find what we need and then we'll make pancakes for Mr. Liam, too."

"Yes!" Her small fist shot into the air.

Amy was glad to see Rosie appeared to not have suffered from the storm last night. She turned to the cabinets, pantry, and refrigerator, finding what she needed, including a tub of strawberries. Pulling a stool over to the counter, she helped Rosie up so that she would be able to participate. Soon, pancake mix was mostly in the bowl with the eggs and milk, only a bit sloshed onto the counter along with the eggshells. Ladling the batter onto the hot griddle, she warned, "Stay back, baby."

It only took a few minutes to plate the fluffy pancakes, drench them with syrup, and cover them with strawberries. Since Liam had not come down, she put his on warm. Sitting at the table with Rosie, they dove into the deliciousness.

Rosie picked up her glass of milk with sticky hands, drinking most of it before it tipped when she put it back down. "Uh oh," she said, eyes wide. "Sorry."

Before Amy had a chance to grab a paper towel, Liam walked into the kitchen, his eyes wide at his guests before they shifted to look at the mess.

8

Liam couldn't believe he'd slept later than normal, but then, he'd been exhausted from hurricane preparation in the county, getting his house ready to withstand the storm, and unexpected house guests that completely caught him off guard. Plus, his thoughts about Amy and her life story had rolled around his mind long into the night.

Now, it was only six-thirty in the morning, and he'd planned on a cup of coffee in solitude while checking in with the deputies and other law enforcement to see how the county had withstood the night. Instead, there was flour, gobs of batter, broken eggshells, multiple bowls, spoons, and wads of paper towels on the counter, not to mention a very sticky-fingered little girl staring at him with strawberry-red juice on her chin and milk on the table. He blinked, his feet glued to the floor.

Amy jumped from the table, her smile wide. "Good morning. We made some pancakes for you, too. I hope you don't mind. I know I should have asked if I could use your kitchen, but Rosie wanted pancakes, and—"

"No, no, you're fine." He started for the coffee pot, but she managed to get there before him.

"Have a seat, and I'll get it for you." She was already plating a stack of pancakes, topping them with more syrup than he'd ever used before. Then, she added sliced strawberries—the ones he'd planned on using in a protein shake later. She set the plate on the table across from Rosie who was grinning at him shyly, her sticky fingers poking in her syrup.

"How do you take your coffee?"

Jerking his head over, he had to think for a second. "Um… black. Just black." Almost immediately, a cup was placed in front of him. "You don't have to serve me, Amy." The words had barely left his mouth when the scent of the pancakes called to him, and he took a bite of the lightest, fluffiest, pancakes he'd ever tasted.

He closed his eyes for a moment and allowed the buttery goodness combined with the sweet maple syrup and strawberries to settle over him. A little giggle met his ears, and he opened his eyes to see Rosie smiling as she stared at him.

Licking his lips, he swallowed. "They're good. Did you like them, too?"

She nodded, shyly looking over at her mom. Amy walked over with a wet paper towel in her hands and began cleaning the sticky mess off Rosie's hands and mouth. She bent to kiss the top of her head. "Come on, munchkin. We need to clean the kitchen."

Swallowing another bite, Liam shook his head. "No, it's okay—"

"She always helps me in the kitchen when we cook but also knows we have to clean our messes." Amy plopped Rosie back onto the stool and handed her daughter another wet paper towel. While Amy washed the bowls and utensils, tossing the trash, Rosie wiped the counters.

Liam was impressed seeing Rosie manage to get most of the mess cleaned up. Amy went back over the counter with another wet cloth and then dried the surface before helping Rosie down from the stool. By the time he had wolfed down the pancakes, Amy was sliding the plate away from him. He stood and followed her, placing his hand on her shoulder. "Seriously, Amy, please, don't wait on me."

She smiled and shrugged. "It's not a big deal, Liam. After all, I used your kitchen and made myself at home. The least I can do is make sure you're fed during this storm and ready to do whatever you need to do."

"Well, I appreciate it."

"Speaking of the storm," she said, folding the cloth and turning to face him, her back leaning against the counter. "What happens now?"

He cocked his head to the side. "I'm sorry. What do you mean what happens now?"

"With the hurricane? I know you're the Sheriff, so I don't want to load you down with more responsibilities considering the whole county is probably needing you."

"I appreciate your concern, but the whole county's

hurricane response isn't resting just on my shoulders, thank God."

She smiled and nodded. "Well, good. Although, you seem more than capable of handling whatever needs to be handled."

Her easy acceptance of what he might need to do along with her confidence in him kept the smile on his face. "I do need to check in with my staff and the county emergency response team to see what's greeting us this morning."

"Do you mind if I turn on the TV? I wanted to see what was happening and I confess I peeked out your front door. Holy moly, it was scary!"

"Yeah, and the worst hasn't hit yet." He nodded toward the living room. "Go ahead and turn on the TV. I'll just be in my office for a while." She smiled but hesitated. He realized he was in her way when she turned sideways to get between him and the counter. "Sorry. I didn't even ask how you and Rosie slept."

"She was out all night. I slept okay, all things considered."

His gaze dropped to her stomach. "Baby keep you up?"

Nodding, her hand smoothed over her baby bump. "Of course. Just like every night. This one is active."

"I… um…" He wanted to ask more. *How was she? Did she have a doctor in mind? Was she still having some pains? Did she know the sex of the baby? What were her plans when the baby came?* But he stumbled over the words, not wanting to seem as though he was quizzing her. "Um… I guess I'll head to my office." Feeling self-conscious, he turned and walked into the office that was just off the kitchen. Closing the door behind him, he moved to his desk and settled into the chair.

He talked to dispatch first, pleased to find out that there had been no major incidents in the county during the night. *But then, the worst of the storm will be hitting in a few hours.* Tom reported that the jail was secure, and no problems had arisen. Checking in with the deputies that were on duty at the two emergency shelters, the all-clear was another bonus report. *So far, so good.* The county's emergency response coordinator was next, and other than downed trees, a few of them on vehicles, and one roof that had blown off a vacant, already-dilapidated house and ended up in the neighbor's yard, there was no other destruction to report.

He sat for a moment, then moved to the window and raised the hurricane shutter enough to peer out. Strong winds, pummeling rain. But so far, not as horrible as it was going to get. *I wonder...*

He sat back down and made a call. "Corby? How's it going?"

"Good, bro. What's up with you? Mom said you had house guests."

"Yeah. I came across a pregnant woman and her daughter who needed some assistance. They were trying to get to Baytown but were never going to make it. We managed to get here, so they'll be safe during the storm."

"You said *pregnant*? Is there a chance she's gonna have the baby anytime soon?"

"No, but if she was, you'd be the first person I'd

call." His brother was one of the volunteers for the fire and rescue squad. "I got a favor to ask but say no if you want to. I know it's bad out there, but right now it's not as bad as it's going to get. We had to leave her SUV that was pulling a small trailer out on Highway Thirteen about four miles from my house. It's got everything she owns in it, and I was thinking of trying to get it back to my house before things get even worse."

"No problem, you know I can help."

"Then we better do this now. If you can get to my house, we can get out there, and I'll drive it back."

"Shouldn't be a problem." His brother laughed. "Of course, the Sheriff has said that vehicles need to stay off the road. I'm assuming since I'm going to have the Sheriff in my vehicle, I won't get a ticket."

"Very funny, Corby. Just pick me up as soon as you can." Chuckling, he disconnected, then closed the hurricane shutter once again. After checking in with the other law enforcement leaders, finding their areas were much the same as his, he walked into the living room, finding Rosie playing with her stuffed rabbit and Amy's attention riveted to the weather station.

She appeared enthralled by the drama from some of the meteorologists, seeing a young man standing on the shore of Virginia Beach, his rain jacket flapping in the wind, his hat long gone, his hair plastered to his head as the rain pelted his body, and his legs spread to help give him a stable foothold. Holding a microphone, he talked of the wind velocity, the inches of rain falling per hour, and warned people to stay indoors.

Amy looked over at him, shaking her head, her brow lowered. "Why is he standing out in the rain?"

"It's not enough for the weather stations to just tell us how bad things are going to be, they have to put somebody out there in the middle of it to show us as well."

"They do this for every hurricane?" she asked, her eyes wide. "I guess I should know this, but I've never spent much time watching the weather station. And since I've never had to be concerned about a hurricane coming in, this is my first time paying attention."

Before he had a chance to respond, his phone vibrated and he glanced down. "I'm going to go out for just a bit. There's something I need to get."

Amy's chin jerked back, and her eyes widened even more. "You have to go out in this?" She sighed, slowly shaking her head. "Of course you do. You're the Sheriff."

"This isn't exactly Sheriff business, but it's something that needs to be taken care of. My brother is picking me up. He's just pulled up to the garage, so I'll go out that way. Do you have your phone? I want to give you my number."

She moved over to her purse and pulled out her phone. Tapping in the number he gave her, she called him so that he'd have her number as well. While Rosie continued to play, she walked him through the house and into the laundry room. "Please, be careful, Liam."

"I wouldn't be doing this if I didn't think the trip would be successful and I'd be safe. The storm is going to get worse in several hours, but it's slowed down right now. I should be back in about an hour at the most."

His hands started to reach out, the desire to touch her arm strong, but instead, he held back.

She obviously had no such resistance as she reached out and placed her hand on his forearm. She gave a little squeeze and said, "Come back safe, and Rosie and I will fix lunch."

It was on the tip of his tongue to tell her not to worry about cooking for him, but he had the feeling she was going to do what she wanted. "Make yourself at home, but make sure you stay off your feet as much as possible."

With that, he turned and headed through the garage and out the side door. Racing through the rain, he climbed into Corby's truck. As Corby started down the driveway slowly, he asked, "Are you sure you know what you're doing? I'm not the only one who knows you've got a pregnant woman and little girl staying in your house. With mom stuck in her house during the storm, I think she spent an hour on the phone with the rest of us."

"There's nothing to wonder about. There was no way I could get her to an emergency shelter, and even if I could, I hated the idea of her and the little girl sleeping on a cot. I've got the room, so I might as well make use of it."

"You always liked your life kinda neat, Liam. Seems like you just invited a little bit of the chaos that the rest of us deal with right into your home."

He thought of the mess he discovered in his kitchen when he came down this morning, but he could hardly complain because it was quickly cleaned up. "It won't be chaos because they'll only be here for a couple of days. Now, stop asking me questions and focus on the drive. I want us to get there in one piece and back home in one piece."

Corby laughed, and with his focus on the windshield where his wipers were swishing furiously and the visibility was still only a few feet ahead, he drove out onto the highway.

It took almost fifteen minutes to get to the place where Liam had discovered Amy the evening before, and Liam breathed a sigh of relief at the sight of her SUV and trailer intact as they pulled along beside it.

"Ohio? A rental pulling a trailer? And she was driving in this last night?"

Glancing toward Corby, Liam nodded. "She left Ohio a couple of days ago, not wanting to drive for a long time with a little child, plus needing to make a lot of pit stops. She admits she didn't have the radio on because she was trying to keep Rosie entertained. By the time she realized the hurricane was coming, she was sure she could make it all the way into Baytown. She wasn't actually stranded when I found her. She'd just stopped to take care of her daughter."

"She's still lucky you came along." Corby stopped his truck as close to Amy's SUV as he could get, still allowing room for Liam to get out his door. "You going to be okay going back with that trailer?"

"Yeah. The winds are strong, but as soon as I turn off the highway, I'm going to be where trees will provide a buffer. Thanks for doing this, bro. I owe you one."

"Next time we're at the pub, I'll collect." Just as Liam

was getting ready to climb out, Corby added, "As soon as the storm passes, expect Mom to come over. Hell, you'll probably get Ellen, Marie, and Sue, and your sisters-in-law as well. They're all pretty curious about you having a woman and child in your house."

Liam snorted. "Believe me, there's nothing to see or tell. She's a widow with a four-year-old child getting ready to have a baby. All I'm doing is giving her a place to stay for a couple of nights until she can get to Baytown."

"Damn, that's gotta be hard on her. You're a good Samaritan, but you know Mom. If she thinks this woman needs help, she'll be right there ready to supply it."

Liam thanked his brother again, then threw open the door and climbed out, his face immediately stinging from the rain hitting him with the gale-force winds. He had snatched Amy's keys from her purse, feeling bad for taking them without her permission, and yet, not wanting to get her hopes up that he might be able to get her possessions closer to her. The rental door clicked open easily, and he climbed inside. Waving to Corby, he started her SUV and slowly pulled out onto the road.

Immediately, the wind made steering difficult, especially with the trailer pulled behind. He was glad it wasn't a huge trailer, giving the wind less of a target to blast, but its lighter size was still pummeled by the rains and winds causing it to sway. *Christ, Amy would never have been able to hold onto this vehicle for the next twenty miles to Baytown.* Now, he saw it as fortuitous that Rosie's juice box had spilled and she'd gotten upset, and was very grateful that Amy was concerned enough for her daughter's distress to pull to the side of the road. *And thank God I found them.*

He wondered about his sanity when he'd made the offer to take them to his house, having never invited a stranger over before. He sometimes felt guilty when his family almost always met at his mom's house or one of his siblings' homes. It wasn't a question of having enough room considering his house was large. He just found that he liked his peace and quiet. He liked knowing where things were, not having to search for items, not having to clean up other people's messes. He loved his siblings and their kids and enjoyed his friends and get-togethers. But the truth was he liked his solitude.

These thoughts filled his mind as he clung to the steering wheel tightly, slowly creeping down the road, glad no other vehicles were out. Making the turn into his drive, he ascertained the best way to park to not only shelter the SUV but more importantly to shelter the U-Haul containing Amy and Rosie's possessions. He pulled to the side of his garage, leaving the back of the trailer closest to the garage door. Once again jumping from the driver's seat, he raced into the garage, heaving a sigh of relief that he'd been successful in his endeavors. As soon as he stepped into the laundry room, Amy hurried from the kitchen, relief also written on her expressive face.

"Oh, Liam, I'm so glad you're home! I couldn't help but worry. The news is displaying charts that show the hurricane center getting closer, and they're still calling it a Category 5. I feel so safe here, but I'm so afraid for other people's homes that aren't nearly as secure as yours. I can't imagine what the damage might be like."

It dawned on him that her first concern was for other people's homes, not even mentioning her trailer. He lifted his hand and dangled her keys in front of her face. Her brow scrunched, and she cocked her head to the side. "My keys! How did you get them? Did they fall out of my purse?"

"I'm afraid I was sneaky, Amy, and should apologize. They were laying at the top of your purse, and I admit that I took them."

Her chin jerked back slightly. "You took my keys? Why?"

"That was my brother who came to pick me up because I'd asked him if he would take me to your vehicle."

"You're kidding!"

"The news was that the winds had slowed ever so slightly, and if we were going to try to get it to safety, it was our only window during the daylight. We made it out there, it was fine, and I brought it back."

She gasped, her hands clenched together as they pressed against her chest. "My trailer? You got my trailer back here?"

"It's parked right next to the garage with your rental SUV. So, anything that you might need from it, it'll be safe right where it is." Her smile was gratitude enough, but she caught him off guard when her hands flung out to the side as she jumped forward. She threw her arms around his neck and hugged him tightly, her belly pressed against him.

"Oh, my God, Liam! I can't believe you went out in the storm to get our things! I should be so upset that you put yourself in danger but all I can think of is that you're back here safely, and Rosie and I won't lose what we brought!"

His arms wound naturally around her waist as though he'd known her for much longer than just meeting the previous night, and he laughed at her delight. A kick moved against his stomach and he jolted. "What... wow."

She let loose of him, her arms dropping, her face pink with blush. "Oh, I'm sorry. I hope I didn't embarrass you." With her hands on her stomach, she smiled. "Peanut wanted to say thank you as well."

He dropped his gaze, staring at her stomach, wondering if the baby would move again. Amy reached over and took both his hands in hers, bringing them forward so that they rested on her stomach. After just a moment, the baby kicked again, right where his hand was. Jolting again, he grinned. "Does it hurt?"

She shook her head. "No, it's just letting us know they're getting ready to come out and greet the world."

"Is it a boy or girl?"

Sucking in her lips for a few seconds, she shrugged. "I don't know. I told the doctor that I didn't want to know." Brows lowered, she sighed. "I'm not sure why. But, whatever it is, Rosie and I'll be ready to welcome it into our little family."

He'd been around his sisters and sisters-in-law when

they were pregnant, and a lot of his friends had babies, but it dawned on him that he'd never had his hands on a pregnant belly before. And all of those women had husbands that were dedicated to them, excited about the baby, and ready to share in the event. *And Amy doesn't.* His gaze lifted, seeing a sadness move through her eyes. He couldn't understand why it affected him so, but her sadness cut right through him.

9

He walked out of his bedroom, having checked the upstairs windows to make sure there were no leaks. Needing to look at the windows in the guest room where Amy and Rosie were staying, he stopped outside, heard their soft voices downstairs, and entered the room. His feet stumbled to a halt at the spread of clothing scattered all about. Two suitcases were open, and little girl clothes had been tossed around as though Rosie had attempted to look at every outfit before deciding. While the adult clothes were not quite so haphazardly displayed, there were quite a few that were hanging on the footboard of the bed and in the open suitcase, and the chair was now turned and pressed against the mattress. Stepping over the items carefully but with some difficulty, he checked the window, glad that it was holding steady against the wind and rain.

Moving into the bathroom, his brows raised to his hairline at the explosion of toiletries covering the vanity. Lotion, deodorant, shampoo, toothpaste, toothbrushes, hairbrushes, little barrettes with pink sparkly hearts, and a bag with makeup spilling out of the top. With three sisters, it wasn't as though he'd never seen a bathroom covered in female toiletries, but having lived on his own for years, he'd gotten in the habit of seeing more of the counter and less… *stuff.*

Walking past the mess, he checked the bathroom window, once again pleased that there was no sign of a leak. Feeling as though he had intruded on Amy and Rosie's space, he quickly left their room and checked the other guestroom. It was a mirror image of the room the girls had slept in but with no clothes, suitcases, or toys. Neat. Clean. *Bland.* He jolted at the last descriptive word that moved through his mind. *No, not bland! Just neat.*

As he walked down the stairs, he halted, glancing into the living room and seeing Rosie playing with several toys, Bubbie being front and center. A coloring book and crayons were on his coffee table, and as he watched, it appeared she was *teaching* Bubbie how to color.

"Use blue for sky and green for grass. The duck is yellow and the dog is brown."

A miniature dollhouse sat on the floor near the coffee table, several small pieces of furniture and toys scattered about. He hoped he didn't step on one and break anything. He didn't have to wonder where Amy was, considering the scent of garlic and tomato sauce wafted past. Just as he was getting ready to come down the last few steps, he heard Amy walking out of the kitchen.

"Oh, Rosie! Remember, I told you to keep your toys neat. Liam's house is super clean, and we don't want to make a mess."

"But I'm not making a mess, Mommy. I'm playing."

"I know, sweetie, but sometimes when you play you make a mess."

"You make a mess in the kitchen."

Amy laughed, and Rosie giggled. "You're right about that. Sometimes we do make a mess in the kitchen! But I always clean it up, don't I?"

"How come Mr. Le-Um doesn't make any messes in his house?"

"It's Liam, one word, not two. And I'm sure he's messy sometimes, but we want to make sure that we keep his house as clean as he does."

Just then, Amy came around the bottom of the stairs and saw him standing there. Eyes wide, she jumped slightly. "Oh, I'm sorry." An adorable blush crossed her cheeks. "I was just coming to help Rosie clean up."

"No, she's fine. Really."

Amy looked at him, her gaze appraising. Leaning closer, she spoke softly. "Liam, your beautiful house is spotless. It's easy to see that's the way you like it, and I want to keep it that way, too. You're so kind to let Rosie and me stay, and even though she's a little girl and doesn't understand how to keep things quite so neat, I want to make sure that you don't regret our being here."

He stepped forward, close enough that the distance was polite, and yet, he could see the darker blue rimming the pale blue of her irises. "I want you to be comfortable here. I don't expect Rosie to not play and enjoy herself. Truly, it's fine."

She continued to stare for a moment, thoughts moving behind her eyes, but he wasn't sure what conclusion she came to. While it was true he liked his life to be orderly, he didn't want to be unyielding. She finally smiled, and he felt a weight lift off his chest as though he'd been waiting for her response.

"And even though I told you that you shouldn't cook for me, I smell something delicious coming from the kitchen."

"It's the least I can do. Plus, I love to cook, and I haven't ever been in a kitchen that's as beautiful and well-equipped as yours. I used to do a lot of baking in my little kitchen and would even sell bakery items at a local coffee shop. But I never had a space like this to cook in."

"I'm impressed," he said. "While I don't want you to feel indebted, if you truly enjoy cooking, then please, make use of my kitchen."

She smiled, and it struck him how often she did despite her situation. He'd spent less than twenty-four hours in her presence and already found that he craved her gentle smile.

She glanced back into the living room. "Rosie, start picking up. I'm going to have lunch ready soon."

Rosie's head popped up. "I want to help."

"You can come into the kitchen and butter the bread but only when your crayons and coloring books are put away and you've straightened the dollhouse."

He watched as Rosie's face fell, her shoulders

slumping as though her mother had just placed the weight of the world on them. "I'll give her a little help and then bring her into the kitchen." Amy opened her mouth as though to protest, and he jumped in. "I won't do it for her, but I'm pretty adept at helping my nephews and nieces."

Another smile greeted him before she turned and went back into the kitchen. He walked over and looked down as Rosie's large, blue eyes stared up at him. Her chin quivered ever so slightly, and he smiled. "Would you like a little help? If we work together, we can get into the kitchen quicker."

Her eyes held suspicion, and he held his breath, waiting for her decision. She nodded shyly and picked up a bright pink mesh bag. Unzipping it, she gently placed her crayons in carefully.

Unlike his siblings' kids, she was so reserved, her gaze continually moving to him before she ducked her head, her focus on the crayon cleanup. He squatted next to the coffee table and her eyes widened. Picking up a crayon, he handed it to her. "Here's the blue one."

Her brows lifted as she moved her gaze between his face and the crayon. Slowly, she shook her head. "No, it's yellow," she whispered.

"Oh," he said, speaking as softly as she, and picked up another. "What color is this?"

She sucked in her lips, pulling her chin in. "Orange."

It only took a moment for them to collect the crayons. She'd been so shy around him at first but now seemed to be willing to at least speak. Once the crayons and coloring books were stacked neatly, he watched as she carefully placed the tiny furniture and dolls into the small dollhouse, closed the two sides together, and snapped the latch. Twisting her head, she glanced between him and the kitchen as though he might renege on his allowing her to help in the kitchen.

Standing, he held out his hand. "Ready to cook?" She stared at his hand for a long moment before nodding. "Let's go see what we can help your mom with. I'm hungry." She didn't take his hand but walked beside him into the kitchen, Bubbie in her arms.

Amy looked up from the stove where she was stirring a pot of spiced tomato sauce and watching over a pot of boiling pasta. Her gaze dropped to Rosie. "Hey, sweetie. Did you and Mr. Liam get the toys cleaned up?"

Rosie nodded, skipping to her mother's side. "Can I butter the bread?"

"Did you thank him for his help?"

Rosie's eyes cut up to him as she moved closer to her mother's legs. Shaking her head, she tightened her grip on Bubbie.

"Well, say, '*Thank you,*' and then you can butter the bread."

Her eyes now cut over to the bread on the counter, the tub of butter next to it. "Thank you," she said softly.

"You're welcome, Miss Rosie."

Her smile widened and a little giggle slipped out. Looking up at Amy, she said, "He called me Miss Rosie."

"He must think you're a very special little girl." Rosie giggled again and then she climbed up onto the stool, took the butter knife, and began slathering butter on the bread slices. Her movements were uncoordinated, some pieces with big gobs and others where the butter was smeared thin.

Amy looked over and winked. "That looks good, sweetie."

Rosie smiled, and Liam agreed, "It sure does." Rosie jerked her head around as though in surprise, her smile still in place. It was strange how he wanted the shy little girl's approval, taking her smile as proof that she was no longer afraid of him.

Soon, they sat down to homemade spaghetti with toasted garlic buttered bread. The food was delicious, and when Amy presented dessert of feather-light sugar cookies, his mouth watered. "I keep wanting to say that you shouldn't be feeding me, but this is too good to deny myself the treat."

After eating, Rosie helped them both clean the kitchen, her shy smiles growing more plentiful. Settling back in the living room, they turned on the weather channel and watched the news reports of the storm as the winds increased outside. Now, despite the hurricane shutters, the sound of the screaming wind could be heard. Rosie looked over occasionally, her gaze seeking her mom, gaining reassurances that they were fine. It didn't take long for her to look over at him, nodding when he told her that his house was safe. "It's like the brick house in the Three Little Pigs. The huffing and puffing won't blow it down." That elicited another smile.

While Amy took her upstairs for a nap, he moved into his office, making another round of calls. The jail was secure. The emergency calls that had come in had been handled, resulting in two rescue calls for possible heart attacks, both transported successfully to the hospital. There were already power outages reported in the Manteague area, but Wyatt had those residents at the emergency center in the local elementary school that was closest. He figured it was only a matter of time before more power was lost all over the Shore. When he checked in with Colt, Mitch, Hannah, and Dylan, they reported much of the same: the residents had heeded the warnings, the roads were clear, and the emergency response teams were responding to the few incidents that had occurred. So far, there were no residents without housing, but multiple trees were down, roads blocked, and older outbuildings were demolished.

He leaned back in his chair, blowing out a long breath as his mind was filled with what would need to be done when the storm passed. While he'd told Amy that the whole county's hurricane response wasn't resting just on his shoulders, being the Sheriff carried a heavy burden. Roads would need to be cleared so that his deputies could check on all residents and the rescue squads could get to anyone injured. The elderly that lived alone in the county were on a call list and would need to be contacted or visited. He knew he could count on the numerous churches in the area to provide manpower and assistance, but those efforts would have to be coordinated. He scrubbed his hand over his face, fatigue pulling at him as the winds howled outside.

As he left his office, he met Amy coming from the kitchen, two hot cups of coffee in her hand, one black and one light tan with milk and what he had already discovered would be at least three teaspoons of sugar. So used to being by himself, he grinned at the knowledge someone was there to share the load. He leaned over, sniffing the strong brew in appreciation. "Hope one of those is for me, Ms. Carruthers."

Lifting a brow, she glanced down at the two cups and grinned. "I can assure you, Sheriff Sullivan, I never drink black coffee." She shrugged and added, "Plus, I'm not supposed to have caffeine, so mine is just a tad of coffee in the milk."

He took his cup from her hand and led her into the living room, placing them on the coasters. Settling on the sofa facing her in the chair, much like their positions last night, he was surprised at how comfortable the familiar scene felt.

The wind could now be heard as it rushed around the corner of the house, causing a few creaks and shudders. Her gaze jumped to the window even though they were unable to see outside.

"How is Rosie? Was she able to go to sleep?"

Bringing her attention back to him, she nodded. "Yes. I was surprised considering the noise is more ferocious upstairs, but she's tired. It's been a difficult few days for her. Lots of changes."

"Can I ask how she's doing… um… you know, with everything?" As soon as the words left his mouth, he wished he could snatch them back. It was such a personal question, one that went beyond the bounds of what she might want to share. He opened his mouth to tell her to ignore him when she leaned forward, placed her cup back onto the coffee table, and held his gaze.

"Between the loss of her dad, the upcoming birth of this sibling, the move, and now the storm, she's actually doing pretty well. The storm doesn't frighten her because she doesn't understand the threat. Now, if there was a lot of lightning and thunder, she'd be much more scared. The move is also something that she doesn't really understand, but I've been telling her how much fun she'll have with new friends, so I think she's picked up on my outlook." Chuckling, she smoothed her palm over her belly. "She also acts like she's excited about having a sibling, but I think she's more excited about having a real-life baby doll she thinks she can play with."

He took a sip of the hot coffee, enjoying the way Amy made the brew strong, the way he liked. It was strange how quickly she picked up on little things like that.

She shifted in the chair, something he noticed she did often, probably to find a more comfortable position, and he was struck once again with the realization that she was close to her delivery date. Just when he was going to ask her if she needed to lay down with Rosie and take a nap, she continued to answer his original question.

"And as far as the death of her father, it was shocking to me how little Rosie's day-to-day life changed. I know that sounds horrible but it's true. Being at home with us was not something Marty sought to do. When he wasn't on shift at the firehouse or on-call, he and his buddies would go out rock climbing, motorcycle racing, anything that would give him that adrenaline rush. He'd walk into the house, pick her up and hug her, calling her his Rosie girl, walk over and kiss me, and then go out the door again. If he was home when she went to bed, he might read her a story, but that was it. I fixed the food and fed her. I sat and played with her. She went with me when I went shopping. When Marty died, his larger-than-life presence was gone, but considering he wasn't around much..."

Her voice trailed off, and the two of them sat quietly for a moment before she added, "I sometimes think children are much more resilient than adults are. As long as their basic needs are met and they are loved, they seem to be able to move forward, at least at this age."

He nodded slowly, turning her words over in his mind. He was much older than Rosie when he'd suffered the loss of his father, but his youngest sister, Marie had only been a little older than Rosie. Marie's memories of their father were fuzzier, mostly planted because of stories the others told in photographs.

"What about you, Liam?"

Her question jarred him out of his musings about his own family, and he looked up sharply. "Me?"

She laughed, her head thrown back. She wasn't tall, and yet, with her head back, the column of her pale throat and smooth skin caught his eye. As she dropped her chin, her pale blue eyes continued to twinkle, and he was struck once again with the realization that she was quite beautiful.

"Yes, you," she said. "You know so much about me, which is strange. I'm not usually such a blabbermouth with people I don't know. But maybe it's everything I've been through recently and the fact that we're stuck together that made me give you my life story. But I'd really like to know more about you."

"I'm not sure there's much to tell."

"Oh, I don't believe that. I think waters run very deep in you, Liam Sullivan."

Her words struck him, and his breath caught in his throat, but no words came forth.

She leaned forward, her voice soft. "A man who serves not only his family but his country, and now this county. A man who worries about his mom and siblings yet prefers to visit them on their territory. A man who has a beautiful house but keeps it pristine, almost sterile. A man who deals with criminals yet opened his house to a stranger." Leaning back against the cushion of the chair, she nodded slowly. "Oh, yes, Liam. I think there is much to you."

10

He sucked in a deep breath and picked up his coffee cup for another sip, feeling the need to occupy his hands while his mind tried to wrap around everything she'd said. Unused to talking about himself, he hesitated, but a crack had been exposed in his armor. Things his family hinted at now being brought out by someone he'd known for less than a day.

Lifting his gaze, his eyes bored deeply into hers but found no malice or even teasing. Her calm expression of interest simply called to him. Setting his cup back down, he lifted his hand and ran it over his face.

"I look back on my childhood, and there was an exact point in time when everything changed. It's as though you could draw a straight line and say here was my childhood before my father died, and here was the rest of my childhood after he died. It wasn't a slow change or a subtle change. It was instant. Everything I was before that wasn't what I was after that." He winced as the words left his mouth, wondering how they sounded to someone else, but Amy simply nodded as though she understood exactly what he meant.

Now that he'd started, it seemed that the floodgates were opening, and while the storm raged outside, words spilled forth from him.

"Dad worked hard, but my parents were at every ballgame that I or my brothers played in. I had chores at home and was expected to help out with my siblings, but I was a regular kid. Probably typical oldest child syndrome, I was certainly more serious than my brothers, but like most kids, there was a certain self-centeredness about me. When I think of the *before,* I remember laughing at meals, picnics, playing games, having friends over, and at thirteen, noticing the changes in the girls that I went to school with."

Amy smiled, crinkling her nose. "If you were as cute at that age as I imagine you were, I'd say the girls were noticing the changes in you as well."

He chuckled, and it struck him as odd that he was able to talk about those painful days long gone by with a lightheartedness that he had never felt. "You're probably right. I was on the verge of becoming one of those jocks, like many of my friends. I'm sure if things had been different, I'd have been cocky and probably looking to score under the bleachers." They both laughed, and he finished his coffee. Leaning forward, he was about to set it on the coaster when he stopped, his hand holding the cup an inch off the table. Giving his head a little shake, he set it down. Looking up, he was not surprised to see her watching him carefully, but she said nothing.

"My mom's a strong woman, but it's not hard to imagine that losing the love of her life hit her hard. It hit us all hard, but she was lost for a while. She never told me that the kids were now my responsibility, but the moment I learned my dad had died, I knew I needed to step up." As he spoke, a memory came back, one that he hadn't thought of in years. "Funny, I just remembered something. Church women were sitting with and comforting Mom, food was pouring into the house, some of the neighbor kids were playing with my siblings, and I was standing in the backyard trying to figure out how Dad could've died so suddenly without any warning. A couple of the men came over, and one clapped me on the back and said, *'Liam, son, you're now the man of the family. It's up to you to take care of everyone like your dad would've wanted.'* Damn, I guess from that moment on, I felt like everything changed."

"Oh, Liam, I'm so sorry. I understand the man was just trying to offer his condolences, but to be honest, that was a crappy thing for him to say."

Nodding slowly, he shrugged, his hands lifting to the side slightly, palms up. "Well, I took those words to heart. From then on, I tried to be the man of the family. I got up early every morning so that I could make sure my siblings were ready for school. I was fourteen years old, Ellen was twelve, Lenny was ten, Sue was nine, Corby was seven, and Marie had just turned five."

Eyes bugging, Amy blew out a huge breath. "Oh, my God, I can't imagine."

"I got them up, made sure they were dressed, made sure they had their backpacks, made sure they had breakfast. At first, it was because Mom was having some problems with day-to-day living, but even when she came back to herself, it had become ingrained in me. I didn't want the kids to make a mess that I knew I'd have to clean up, so I started drilling things into them like don't leave a wet glass on the table, wipe down the counter as soon as you make a mess, keep your toys picked up so that Mom doesn't have to trip over them. I stopped playing ball and hanging out with my friends as much because I needed to make sure my siblings were getting their homework done, and as soon as I was fifteen, I got a part-time job at the grocery store. I didn't have time to always be picking up after them and didn't want Mom to have to deal. So, I became a neat freak and, looking back, pretty demanding."

"Your before and after moment."

Her words were spoken softly but understanding permeated every syllable. He continued to nod slowly, glad that this woman who was virtually a stranger *got* him. "I know it might seem strange that I joined the military right after high school. That seems like I turned my back on those responsibilities." His mother had been proud, but he remembered a few comments from others in the community, questioning his desire to go off and fight *foreigners* when his own family needed him.

Amy stood, and he thought she was going to stretch her back again, but instead, she walked around the coffee table and sat on the sofa with him. Shifting so that she was facing him, she reached over and placed her hand on his arm, squeezing gently before letting go. "I don't think you turned your back on those responsibilities at all, did you? I have a feeling you sent a lot of your paycheck home."

The rasp of the quick inhalation sounded out in the room despite the wind howling outside. His family knew but no one else did. Or maybe even if his friends did, no one had ever spoken of it. The Eastern Shore was a poor area, and without further education, he was never going to have a job that would pay enough for him to help his family. By the time he joined the Army, Ellen and Lenny were in high school, both with part-time jobs. Sue was getting ready to start high school and Corby and Marie were in middle school. His mom went to work, and his siblings were old enough to now be able to take care of themselves. Swallowing deeply, he glanced down at his arm and wished that Amy's hand was still on his.

"You're right. My siblings were older, taking care of things themselves, and my mom was working. The Army gave me a full-time job with pay and benefits and a chance to learn how to be a policeman. I spent very little and had plenty to send home for the family, plus, I saved the rest." He chuckled as another memory hit him. "I had an uncle who thought I should go into mechanics, but Mom told him to hush up. She knew my dream of being a police officer and supported me following that dream."

"And look at you. You followed your dream while

still helping your family. I think you're absolutely amazing, Liam."

He rolled his eyes. "I wouldn't call me amazing. I just did what I had to do because it's what needed to be done."

She shook her head, her honey blonde hair flying back and forth with the force. "That's where you're wrong. There are a lot of people who would've been in your position who would not have made the same choices. They would've put their own desires, needs, and wants ahead of everyone else. You were still a child when you stepped up, taking on responsibilities."

"But I now think that I've become stuck."

Blinking, she cocked her head to the side. "Stuck?"

"Stuck in my ways, stuck in my life. The Army was great but it also appealed to my orderly need for having things a certain way." Shaking his head, he grunted. "I love my nieces and nephews, but we always visit at their houses or Mom's place because they hate feeling like they have to be so careful at Uncle Liam's place."

She placed her hand over her heart, her gaze penetrating. "Look at me and Rosie. You didn't have to invite us here to be safe. But you've opened up your home to a little girl and a pregnant woman who make messes in your kitchen. I think you're a man who always goes above and beyond."

A peaceful silence settled over them for a moment even as the sounds from the hurricane swept around the house. His gaze dropped to where her hand now rested on her stomach.

"Do you have a doctor picked out?"

She jerked slightly, then smiled. "Tori had given me the name of her doctor, and I'd contacted them before deciding to move. I have an appointment next week and then will be ready to tour the hospital. Not exactly ideal, but the pregnancy is normal so there shouldn't be any problems."

"It's probably the same group my sisters and sisters-in-law have used. They've never had any complaints."

"Good to hear." After another moment of silence, with her elbow on the back of the sofa cushion, she propped her head in her hand and sighed. "I hate that Marty's missing this, but he wasn't with me the last time. He was on duty and managed to race in after the delivery was over. I do remember his face as he held Rosie. Such awe… For a moment, he was struck silent, something that had never happened before. Then, he had the nurses take pictures, and started sending them out to his buddies. It was endearing at the time, but looking back, I now see it was a way for him to stay in the spotlight. He simply couldn't just bond with his wife and newborn daughter. He had to turn it into something about him."

She looked up, sucking in a sharp breath. "I'm sorry, Liam. I know it sounds callous to speak of him when he can't defend himself—"

He waved away her concern. "Hey, you say whatever you feel. And, for what it's worth, I'm sorry you lost your husband and Rosie lost her father. That sucks, and I totally get it, and I'll never say you're better off, that's not what I'm thinking. I admire how you're taking charge of your life, making changes, moving forward.

You're creating a wonderful childhood for Rosie, giving her love and support. And this child won't know their biological father but they'll know love." He chuckled, adding, "And now that you're here, you'll be surrounded by people who will make sure you never feel alone. Hell, my family is ready to adopt you and Rosie. Throw in Tori and her entire gang, you won't be alone."

"Her gang?"

Grinning, he asked, "She mentioned her husband was involved in the American Legion, right?" Seeing her nod, he continued. "Well, Mitch came back to Baytown after the military and after working for the FBI. Much like me, he had family and old friends here. It turned out that there was a group of us from high school that knew we had a great place to come back to. So, we started the American Legion chapter, and one of the things we did was throw out the invite to some of our buddies who didn't really have a place to call home. Now, there's a lot of fresh faces in the area, and most of them have paired off. Tori and Mitch were just the beginning. She's big with the Legion Auxiliary, and believe me, her posse is formidable in taking care of each other. You'll fit right in."

A wide smile crossed her face. "That sounds divine."

"And Rosie will have a whole group of new friends, too."

"Oh, now that sounds even better!"

A loud whistling sound swept past the house and the sound of a crack in the distance hit their ears.

"The storm sounds louder."

Nodding, he agreed. "Yeah. Today will be the worst.

Well, today and tonight. By tomorrow, we'll still have wind and rain but it should be moving inland."

"Do you expect much damage?"

He scrubbed his hand over his face. "I don't know how much. Hopefully, the damage is just to property and not to lives."

"Mommy?"

He and Amy swung their heads toward the stairs, seeing Rosie sitting on a step halfway down, her Bubbie clutched in her hands. Amy shifted her girth around, but he had already jumped up and stalked toward the stairs. "Hey, Rosie, did you have a good nap?"

She looked up, blue eyes wide, her blonde hair waving about her head. For a few seconds, she simply stared, then slowly nodded. He held his hands toward her, waiting to see if she would want only her mom to come to her. After another few seconds of holding his gaze, she lifted her arms. He bent, carefully picked her up, and tucked her in close as he turned back to the living room. He'd held children before but there was something about gaining the trust of someone so small, who obviously didn't trust easily. With his arms wrapped securely around her, his heart squeezed as she encircled her arms around his neck. A small sound nearby caused him to look over. Amy stood by the coffee table, her fingers pressed against her lips, blinking away the moisture that had visibly gathered.

He walked to her, and she leaned over to kiss her daughter's cheek, pleased to see that Rosie didn't try to lunge toward her. Amy's gaze met his and she smiled.

"I'll make sure she takes a trip to the potty and then we can have a snack."

He lowered Rosie to the floor and watched as mother and daughter held hands as they walked down the hall. Something warm swept over him, a feeling he couldn't define, and honestly didn't want to. But he relished the sense of peace, nonetheless.

11

Amy assisted Rosie as she washed her hands in the powder room, her mind racing with all she had learned of Liam in the past day, especially in the past hour, as well as surprise at all she'd shared with him. Talking through her tumultuous feelings about Marty had never been easy but with Liam it was simple.

"Mommy, are you sad?"

Blinking, she looked down. "No, baby. Sorry, I was just lost in thought. But how on earth can I be sad with such a darling daughter as you?"

Rosie giggled as they walked into the kitchen. "What can we make for Mr. Le-Um?"

"Mr. Liam. How about brownies?"

"Ooh, yeah!"

"What's this I hear?" He walked into the kitchen, a smile on his face.

Scrunching her nose, she winced. "I really need to ask before I assume I can use your kitchen."

He gave her a look that quelled her arguments.

"Girls, you are free to use my kitchen, even if you want to make something yukky. But I know I heard brownies, which are definitely not yukky!"

Rosie leaned closer to him, something she hadn't done before, and gently touched his arm. He knelt to her level, and she whispered, "Mommy makes 'em good."

"I bet she does." He stood, held his arms out, and she reached up. He lifted her and placed her on the stool at the counter.

"We'll try not to make too much of a mess," Amy said, grinning.

A blush rose over his cheeks, and he shook his head. "Do whatever you gotta do to make those brownies. I think I'm learning to survive some mess."

His phone vibrated, and he checked the screen. "I need to head to my office for a bit." Tapping Rosie on the nose gently, he turned and walked away.

Amy stared at his retreating back, and if she was honest, she noticed his ass as well. *Get a hold of yourself, woman. But then, a little eye candy doesn't hurt anyone and has no calories!*

Soon, the scent of chocolate filled the kitchen, and she wiped the counters as Rosie went into the living room to play. The winds were howling, and she hoped Liam's house was as sturdy as it seemed. Curious about her rental and trailer, she moved through the laundry room and into the garage. There, the sounds of the storm intensified. Blowing out a breath, she stopped in her tracks, wondering how the roof could stay on with the ferocious wind pummeling it. *And how many of the smaller houses in the area that aren't so reinforced can withstand it?*

Moving to the side door with a window but no hurricane shutter, she was shocked at the lack of visibility. The rain fell so hard that she was only able to see a short distance, but it was evident the rental SUV and trailer were right there next to the house in perfect condition. *I can't believe he went out to bring my things here.* Biting her lip, she thought of all she had learned about Liam. Dropping her chin to her chest, she glanced down at her belly, her hands cupping the weight. "Oh, Peanut, I'm so sorry you won't meet your father. But I promise to try to give you good men in your life to help you along."

With another blast of wind slamming rain against the window, she walked around Liam's SUV and his Sheriff's vehicle and moved into the kitchen just as the oven timer sounded.

She was soon joined by Rosie and Liam, both sniffing the air in exaggerated appreciation. "Got to let them cool first," she admonished, laughing at both of their pouts. Rosie headed to play more in the living room, and he stayed, his back to the counter, his arms on the edge behind him.

"She seems to be warming to me a little."

Nodding, she hung the dishtowel on the oven handle and turned to face him. If his face graced a law enforcement magazine, every woman looking at it would want to break the law just to be arrested by him. His dark brown hair was brushed to the side as though his fingers were his comb. His eyes never seemed to miss much that went on around him. She wondered if that came from being the oldest of six children. Tall and muscular, his T-shirt stretched over his chest and his jeans did wonderful things to her sex-starved-pregnancy-hormones libido.

She cleared her throat, turning her mind to what he said. "She's quiet. She's a watcher. When she gets with other children, she'll watch them first before joining in. When she's around loud adults, she tends to cling to me."

"Is this something since her dad died?"

Shaking her head, she sighed. "No. Well, maybe more clingy since Marty died, but she's always been a more quiet, introspective child." Sucking in her lips, she winced. "He didn't understand that."

Her gaze had dropped, but Liam stepped closer, his sock-encased feet stopping in front of her slippers. Lifting her head, she stared into his face, his eyes so expressive, a mixture of uncertainty and irritation. She tilted her head to the side and waited.

"I don't get what you're saying, Amy. What didn't her dad understand about his own daughter?"

Swallowing deeply, she felt more exposed than with her previous divulges. Her shoulders hefted slightly. "I think he wanted her to be a mirror image of himself. He wanted her to be the little charmer when we went places, and instead, she would cling to me. She was a bit slow in learning to talk, and for a big talker, that frustrated him. He was gone so much, but when he came in, he'd swoop her up into his arms, loudly exclaiming how much he'd missed her. Then, he'd set her down and that was it. Little playing, little reading, certainly no help at meals or bedtime." Shrugging again, she added, "I guess I tried to compensate. Telling her how much her daddy thought she was wonderful."

"Kids can tell."

She sucked in a hasty breath, his words hitting her with their heavy force of truth. "Yeah."

"But she'll have the image of her dad that you give her now. The one that lets her know she was loved."

"You're good at this, you know. Always saying the right thing. Rescuing damsels in distress."

He barked out a laugh. "You were not a damsel in distress. You were a mom who was trying to get her daughter to safety while taking care of a spilled juice box."

Laughter erupted, joining his. Their combined mirth moved through her, the pleasure so real. "How can I have only known you for less than twenty-four hours, and yet, feel like we know so much about each other?"

"It's like the military."

"Huh?"

"Throw strangers together in an extreme situation and camaraderie is born."

"Well, Lord knows I need camaraderie right now," she laughed.

He reached up and tucked a wayward strand of hair behind her ear, and her breath caught in her throat. It was such an intimate act, and she fought the desire to lean her cheek against his palm.

"Mommy?"

Jerking slightly, she straightened. "Coming, sweetie."

With a smile toward Liam, she nodded toward the pan of brownies. "Don't eat any before we get back." She hoped her quip hid the tremor in her voice. *Damn. Pregnancy hormones need to take a break!*

The afternoon passed much like the morning for Liam, but now that dinner was over, he hid away in his office, telling himself he needed to work. He'd called his mom, each sibling, his staff, the emergency response team, the emergency centers, and his friends, and now sat at his desk, having covered the county and not able to think of anyone else to call. *Coward.*

While he did need to find out everything he could about the damage from Hurricane Ivy, it was a different woman that filled his mind. Amy. Well, two women. Amy and Rosie.

He had wanted to close the distance between him and Amy and kiss her earlier. Where the hell that thought had come from, he had no idea. He rarely went out on dates, finding the needs of his job and family to take up most of his time. What was left, he enjoyed with his friends and the American Legion activities. *Or maybe I just use them to fill my time since I have no one else.*

On that sobering thought, he knew he needed to remain cautious around his house guests, making sure to not take advantage of them. Stepping out of his office, he heard their laughter coming from the living room, and a grin slipped over his face.

"You have streaming." Amy looked up at him, excitement in her voice.

"Beauty and the Beastie!" Rosie cried out, the most animated he'd seen other than her obvious delight at the brownies they'd devoured earlier. Now, it was after another delicious dinner, and Amy had a movie ready to go.

An idea struck him. "Hang on a moment. I'll be back." Turning, he headed into the kitchen and popped two bags of microwave popcorn. Pouring them into two big bowls, he walked back into the room where Rosie was reclined against pillows on the floor and Amy was sitting behind her on the sofa.

"Popcorn!" Rosie exclaimed, and Amy's brows shot up.

"Liam, you have no idea how much of a mess a four-year-old can make with popcorn."

"I'm not four," Rosie corrected.

"No, but you will be soon. And that's not the point. The point is that you need to be very careful—"

"And have a good time with the movie and your snack," Liam interrupted. He grinned at Amy's shaking head and sat on the sofa next to her, handing her a bowl.

She glanced at her belly and laughed. "You'd better hold the bowl on your lap since I have no lap at all."

The next hour and a half passed in a way that he hadn't experienced in his house. Sure, he'd spent lots of time with his siblings' kids but never kicked back on his own sofa watching Disney and eating popcorn. Relaxed, he glanced down to see Rosie's eyes riveted to the screen, her mouth moving as she softly sang along with the characters. Amy's head had drooped to the side and ended up on his shoulder, her deep breaths letting him know she was snoozing. He didn't want to move, glad she could sleep. He knew she'd wake and be embarrassed, but he liked the feeling that this competent woman could lean on him.

The movie ended and Rosie sat up, looked around, and grinned as she whispered, "Mommy's asleep."

He nodded just as Amy blinked her eyes open, then sat up quickly, a blush hitting her face. "Oh, my goodness—"

"Don't even say it," he admonished. "You were sleepy and needed to rest."

She swiped her hair back from her face and looked at the TV. "The movie is over. Wow, I was out." She looked down at Rosie. "It's time for bed, sweetie."

"You already slept."

"Yes, I know, but you need to get ready to go to sleep."

Rosie giggled and stood. She bent and picked up her half-eaten bowl of popcorn and held it gingerly in her hand. Taking a few steps toward Liam, she looked up at him. "I didn't spill."

He took the bowl from her and smiled. "You did great, Rosie, but here's a secret. Even if it had spilled, we could have cleaned it up."

He was rewarded with a smile that warmed his heart, more than he could remember in many years. Amy walked by, winking at him as she took her daughter's hand, and he stared as the two of them went up the stairs.

Now alone with pillows and a blanket scattered on the floor with a few kernels around, bowls of popcorn and cups on the coffee table, and a bit of drool on his shoulder, he sucked in a deep breath, realizing his house felt more like a home in the past twenty-four hours than it ever had.

12

Once again Amy was on the sofa with Liam while Rosie was tucked in bed fast asleep. She inclined her head toward the jars of glass on his mantle. "Rosie asked me about those. I wondered but didn't know what to tell her."

"It's sea glass."

Her gaze cut from his face up to the mantle and back again. "Sea glass?"

"It's bits and pieces of glass that you find on the beach."

A chortle slipped out. "I'm sorry, but I don't understand. Isn't glass on the beach a bad thing?"

He smiled, and she pushed down the attraction that she felt but was unable to ignore the peace that moved through her.

"Sea glass isn't just where someone broke a glass and put it on the beach. Sea glass originates from the ships in the ocean, or in our case, the Bay. Ships come from all over the world and drop anchor off the

Eastern Shore as they wait to get the all-clear to travel up the Chesapeake Bay to Baltimore. They're not supposed to dump their trash in the ocean, but we know that can happen. Glass bottles of all types and colors, dishes, and cups get tossed overboard and into the deep water. But the water is constantly moving, and the glass gets broken into many pieces as it's ground down into the sand and the waves. Eventually, it's washed up on shore, but by that time, the edges are smooth."

Standing, Amy walked over, her curiosity now at an all-time high. Looking over her shoulder, she asked, "Do you mind if I look at it closer?"

"Not at all." He stood and walked over to stand next to her.

She lifted down one of the jars filled with bits and pieces of dark green glass. "It's so beautiful."

"Pick up a piece. Roll it around in your fingers and feel how smooth it is. All the sharp edges have been ground down by the sand."

She reached into the wide-mouthed jar, pulling out several pieces. She ran her fingers over the surfaces, finding them to be as smooth as he said. Looking up, she realized how close he was standing and smiled. "It's amazing. The pieces are smooth as silk."

"It's life."

His words made no sense to her, but the look on his face was pensive. She wanted to ask what he meant but hated to interrupt whatever thoughts were going through his head. He gave a little shake as though pulling himself from whatever rabbit hole he'd traveled down and said, "That's what my grandmother used to say. It's what my mom tells her grandchildren, too."

"That sea glass is life?"

He nodded. "Life can be hard, my grandmother would say. We can feel broken and tossed to the sea. We can get churned by the waves and scraped by the sand. But we persevere. And at some point, we'll be gently laid upon the shore, all our rough edges smooth. So, even in our brokenness, we become beautiful."

Her breath halted in her lungs as his words bored deep within her soul. Swallowing deeply, she finally managed to suck in air but was unable to stop the moisture gathering in her eyes. "I think that's the most beautiful thing I've ever heard. Certainly the most inspiring."

"My grandmother used to take me for walks on the beach, and she'd say that her eyesight wasn't so good and her arthritis kept her from bending over so I needed to collect the sea glass for her. The funny thing was, though, she had jars and jars of it at home, so what I picked up, she put into a jar and would give it to me. As a teenager, I hid it in my closet, not wanting any friends to see but not wanting to get rid of it. As soon as I bought this house, my mom handed me a box that was filled with all these jars that I'd forgotten about. My grandmother is long gone, so these jars and her words mean a lot."

She handed the jar to him, and he lifted the heavy pottery from her hands and placed it back onto the mantle. She reached up to drop the few pieces that were in her hand back into the jar, but he stilled her movements. "No, keep those. I'll show you and Rosie how to look for sea glass and you can start your own collection, telling the story to her. But those, your first pieces of sea glass, can be your reminder of all the things you thought had broken you but really just made you more beautiful."

She tried to stifle the gasp that slid out, nonetheless. "Thank you. I'll treasure them, honestly. It'll always remind me of my time here with you." She'd only been in his presence for a day but felt more of a connection with him than she ever had with anyone. She had no idea how that could be but refused to deny her feelings.

He held her gaze, so close his breath whispered warm across her face. "And when I look at these jars, they will now always remind me of you."

She licked her lips, noticing his eyes dropped to her mouth. Dragging in a ragged breath, she stepped back, needing the distance to clear her head. She didn't want their time together to end but knew that as the storm passed over during the night, the morning would bring change.

Liam took the travel container of coffee from Amy's hand, both thanking and admonishing her. "You didn't have to do this; breakfast cooked when I got downstairs and now coffee to go."

"Hush," she fussed.

A giggle met their ears, and they turned to look at the table where Rosie smiled up at them. "Mommy told you to hush."

Opening his mouth in mock surprise, he asked, "Do you think I should hush?"

Rosie shook her head, her pigtails bouncing on top of her head. "No, I like you, Mr. Le-Um."

Something moved inside him, and he locked his knees to keep from rocking back a step. Something tangible. Something warm. He stared into Rosie's owl-eyes with the smile gracing her sweet face, and a fist squeezed his heart. A grin from the adorable little girl had been hard-won. But earning more was a true gift. One he couldn't believe her own father ignored. Blowing out his breath, he smiled and winked, immediately gifted with a larger grin.

Turning back to Amy, he opted for a haughty expression before walking over to Rosie and bent to kiss the top of her head. "You take care of Mommy today." As the words left his mouth, it struck him how easy they were to say and how much he meant them. Turning back to Amy, he noted her wide-eyed look of surprise. "I'll have my phone with me all day if you need anything. Remember that I don't want you to go anywhere. I know that residents are going to get out and about, but we want to keep the roads as free from vehicles as we can so that our deputies can get around to assess the damage and see if anyone needs assistance."

"I promise that Rosie and I will be here. I need to talk to Tori as well as my landlord. And I haven't checked my email since we got here, so I need to pull that up and see if the hospital's orthopedist has anything he wants me to work on."

He nodded his agreement and for a second hesitated, the desire to walk over and hug her so strong. Clearing his throat, he simply nodded. "It may be a long day, but I'll be back as soon as I can. Also, wait on me before you try to get to anything in your trailer. The contents may have shifted, and I don't think you should be straining yourself right now." With those final words, he ignored the rolling of her eyes and headed out the door. *Jesus, if my friends and family could hear me now, they'd be laughing out their asses.*

The drive to the Sheriff's Department Station took longer this morning as he made several side trips to check on the damage along roads off the main highway. The rain was still pouring down and the winds were still blowing, but it was more like a spring rainstorm than a hurricane. Ivy, at last, had mostly moved over the Eastern Shore, but it was evident she'd left a trail of destruction in her path.

Many trees were bent over, some were uprooted, branches down. Several houses in lower areas had water right to the door and he didn't doubt that others on the more back roads may have water inside the house. Billboards were down, signs were blown over, and an old, abandoned trailer had been tossed into a ditch. The image of that happening to Amy's trailer when it was connected to her SUV with her and Rosie inside made his gut clench.

Residents were already outside, sawing downed trees to clear roads. He stopped at one house, a tree having landed on the porch, blocking the entrance.

Neighbors had already assisted the man who lived inside.

Once at the station, he quickly called his top staff together for a briefing. Overall, the news was mixed. Tom reported that the jail had lost power for only a few hours but the generator had kicked in. The jail staff that had stayed during the storm had been released as soon as replacement staff had come in that morning. Terrence, his Lieutenant of Patrol, reported the same with the deputies that had volunteered to ride out the storm in the station.

Ross was coordinating with the Fire Chiefs in the County as well as the EMT Captains. "People are getting out and helping neighbors, which is good. The Fire and Rescue have already made several trips transporting people to the hospital. Mostly elderly but a few who got out and tried to take care of something with their house and got hit by tree limbs or flying debris. More and more deputies are on the road, reporting damage to houses. Some are flattened."

Liam nodded. "I want to thank each of you for your dedication during this time, and we must get the same message down to every single member of our staff. I'll have my assistant type up a memo, but I want you to verbally give my thanks as you go about seeing everyone." He closed his laptop and sighed. "Now, I need to head to the emergency shelters and meet with the emergency response team. I expect the Red Cross to come in to assist as well."

"How are things to the south?" Ross asked.

"Colt reports that North Heron suffered about the

same as us. He's been able to get to some of their coastal areas and see the coastal flooding that occurred. A few million-dollar homes on the bay had flooding and wind damage, but I'm more concerned about our citizens who barely had housing to begin with and now have nothing."

The others nodded their agreement, and with the first of his meetings over with, he headed out of the conference room, stopped by Margaret's voice.

"Sheriff Sullivan."

Stopping in his tracks, he sucked in a deep breath and turned slowly. "Yes, ma'am?"

Margaret was not a stranger to lifting her voice over the wide space when needed but today walked straight up to him and held his gaze. "I understand that you stopped to help a stranded motorist on your way home the other evening."

"Yes, ma'am."

"You radioed that she was pregnant and had a child with her."

"Yes, ma'am."

She lifted her chin, holding his gaze despite his great height advantage. "Husband?"

While Margaret was one to gather gossip, she wasn't one to spread it all over the place, a trait he greatly appreciated. "A widow."

He watched her brow furrow slightly, her lips pinched together. "An emergency shelter can be difficult in those circumstances. I thought I might check in on them to see if they had what they needed."

"Thank you, Margaret, but that won't be necessary.

It would have taken too long to get them to the emergency shelter, and I agree that it wasn't the best place for them. She knew Tori, Mitch Evans' wife, and we called them so that she could be assured I was reliable. And since I was only a few miles away, I brought them to my house to stay."

If Margaret was surprised, she gave no reaction but continued to hold his gaze. Finally, with a chin dip, she patted his arm. "You're a good Sheriff, but more importantly, you're a good man. You always did take responsibility to heart." Cocking her head to the side, her lips curved ever so slightly. "I confess you have a happy look today. Perhaps your houseguests are good for you." Without giving him a chance to say anything else, she turned and walked back toward reception.

He chuckled and walked out to his car. Several hours later, exhaustion pulled at him. The good news was that other than one elderly man who'd had a heart attack, there was no loss of life during the storm. The emergency shelters had allowed travelers and vacationers to get back onto the roads, and while residents were going back to check on their houses, the shelters would have to continue for those who'd lost their homes.

The bad news was that while parts of the county came through without suffering too much from Ivy, her rage had taken its toll on some of the residents. There were pockets of residences where the houses were irrevocably damaged by falling trees, roofs blown off, and flooding. Many vehicles were damaged, and a few farmers reported animals that had died when their barns collapsed.

But, like most rural counties, the residents pulled together. Even though it was still raining, neighbors were helping neighbors, offering shelter and food. He'd driven by his mom's house, grateful to see it standing unharmed with just multiple tree limbs scattered about the yard. Checking in with all his siblings, he discovered much the same, except Ellen's husband's truck had the windshield smashed from a fallen tree limb. Other than that, his family came through unscathed.

He started the almost forty-minute drive to get home from the northern part of the county when thoughts of Amy and Rosie flooded his mind. Truthfully, they'd been on his mind all day. But now, a sudden fear moved through him that they would have already left.

He called her, not wanting to wait another moment to hear her voice. She picked up on the first ring, and he smiled. "I wanted to see how you and Rosie were doing."

"We're fine but we wondered when you might get home. Have you eaten at all today?"

"I had a sandwich at the emergency shelter during lunch when I was checking on people."

"We fixed dinner. It's something that we knew could heat up easily whenever you got home."

"Damn, you and Rosie are spoiling me. I almost hate to ask, but are there any brownies left?" She laughed, and he loved the sound.

"Yes. I have to tell you that Rosie was the one who wanted to make sure that there were brownies left for you. I think she's been worried about you."

He smiled, and much of the tension he'd felt during

the day began to ease off his shoulders. "It'll take me a while to get home, but I'll get there as soon as I can."

She asked how his day had gone and how the county had fared from the storm. He told her what he could, glad she cared enough to inquire and glad that he had someone to share with. By the time they finished, he realized he only had a few more miles to go. "I should be pulling in soon."

"Then dinner will be ready."

They disconnected, and for the last few minutes of his drive, his heart felt lighter than it had in years. Was it just that he now had someone to share the burdens of the day? As Sheriff, he had to be the strong one. The one in charge. The one whose shoulders needed to be wide enough to handle the pressures of the job. But that thread of connection with someone else who cared... *How can I have these feelings about a woman I've known for such a short time?* But with a beautiful woman, a cute little girl, and a dinner he knew was going to be delicious waiting for him, he didn't worry about why he was asking the question—or the elusive answer.

13

"Tori, don't worry. Seriously, please, don't feel bad. Let me get hold of my landlord tomorrow, and I'll bet he'll let me move in a few days early. If not, then I can take you up on your offer. Okay, I'll talk to you tomorrow after I've gotten hold of my landlord. Bye."

She stood in the kitchen, her hands on the counter, her mind in turmoil as she went over her options. Glad that Rosie had already had a bath and was in the living room with Liam, she rubbed her forehead.

"What's up?"

She startled. "For a big guy, you move very quietly."

He walked in, stopping at the counter. It hit her how often they had stood this way in the past several days. Both leaning against the counter, close but not touching. He'd gotten home, and they sat down to a dinner of homemade chicken pot pie which he declared to be as good as any he'd ever had, much to Rosie's delight. The meal had been so pleasant, and Amy listened with great interest as he talked about how the rest of the county had survived the hurricane, glad for the good news and sorrowful for those who'd suffered any loss. And as much as she wanted to give Liam his privacy back, she was already dreading having to leave. Now, with Tori's news, she wasn't sure what to do.

"Hey, what did Tori say that's got such a conflicted look on your face?"

She forced a smile. "Well, because they had flooding in a few of the rooms, she's had to shift some of her guests around, so the room that was for me and Rosie isn't available. I told her that I'd call my landlord to find out if I can go ahead and move into the rental house a few days early. If not, then she wants me and Rosie to just come and stay with her and Mitch and their little boy."

"Oh."

She stared, his grunted one-word reply giving her little indication of what he was thinking.

"But Mommy, I want to stay with Mr. Le-um."

Glancing over, she realized how often Rosie had been listening to her conversations lately. Wondering if that was from curiosity or anxiety, she decided she needed to be more careful with what she said. "I know you like it here, Rosie, but Liam has already been super sweet to let us stay while the storm was outside. And I can find out tomorrow if our new house is ready for us."

"But if it's not, I don't want to stay with anyone else."

"My friend Tori has a little boy about your age. His name is Eddie."

"But I don't know him. He might try to take Bubbie."

Recognizing the signs that Rosie was close to a meltdown, she sucked in a deep breath and let it out slowly, her fingers rubbing her forehead. "Sweetheart, nobody's going to take Bubbie. And I don't know what we're doing right now, but you've got to let Mommy figure it out, and I promise you'll be with me no matter where we go."

"Stay. Stay here with me," Liam said, his gaze moving from Rosie's quivering chin up to Amy's wide-eyed stare. He lowered his voice, mouthing, "Please."

She opened and closed her mouth several times, her mind racing even more than it had before. Caught between the desire to throw her arms around him and cry, 'Yes, yes', she was also concerned that he'd stepped in before she had a chance to deal with Rosie. "Well… um… we'll see what the landlord says tomorrow and then we'll talk about it."

It seemed that the only thing Rosie focused on was that Liam wanted them to stay. She threw her little arms into the air, shouting, "Yay!", and ran back into the living room.

She dropped her chin to her chest and shook her head slowly. Opening her eyes, she saw his socked feet right in front of hers, and she was struck with déjà vu from the previous evening when they stood in the kitchen so close together.

"Am I in the doghouse?"

A chuckle erupted from deep inside, and she lifted her head to see the competent, confident Sheriff look like a little boy who might be in trouble. "Of course, you're not in the doghouse. You've done nothing but take care of us since the moment you saw us on the side of the road."

"As soon as I spoke, I realized I shouldn't have said anything with Rosie here but I hated for her to look so sad. My only thought was that it didn't make sense for you to have to pack up everything and drive to Tori and Mitch's house to stay in their guest room when you're already comfortable here. But I'm sure you want to see your friend, and their son could be a ready playmate for Rosie. I'm sorry, I screwed up."

She shook her head and reached out, placing her fingers around his wrist. "Liam, you couldn't screw up if you tried. I just feel bad because I don't want to tread on your kindness. I called the landlord several times but never got him to pick up the phone. I'll try again tomorrow morning. I'm looking forward to seeing Tori and Jillian again, and she's already got plans for me to meet some of her other friends, quite a few who also have children. But packing up to live in her guest room wasn't high on my list of things I wanted to do."

"So you'll stay? Until you can get into the rental?"

"I'd love to if you're sure you don't mind. Anyway, the rental was going to be available in about five days, so we wouldn't be in your hair too much longer even if he can't let me move in early."

He smiled and nodded. "Okay, but even if your landlord says you can move in, don't leave unless I'm here. I want to go with you. I want to check it out since you rented it sight-unseen. I want to make sure it's secure and has everything you need."

Amy cocked her hip and huffed. "You don't have to

do that. I'm perfectly capable of taking care of things myself."

"I know."

His words were so soft, almost reverent, and her bluster fled immediately.

He continued, "I've only known you a few days, but I'm a damn good judge of character. And you, Amy Carruthers, are one of the best people I've met. I might have helped you during the storm, but you've helped me by just being here. So, I'd like you to stay. Not because of what I can do for you, but for what you and Rosie are adding to my life."

Her heart pounded, and her chest heaved as the air rushed from her lungs. "I think that's the nicest thing anyone has ever said to me." She almost added *and that includes Marty* but didn't want to mar the moment.

Just then, her phone rang. "Oh, it's my landlord." She answered, but the only thing he could tell her was that he hadn't had a chance to visit the house today to see if there was any damage. She arranged to meet him at the house in the morning, and they could make sure it was fine for her to go ahead and move in.

Delivering that news to Liam, he nodded. "We'll go together. All three of us, and we can check it out."

"Don't you have to go to the station?"

"Yes, but one of the perks of being the Sheriff is that I can make a change in my schedule if I want to. Anyway, it'll give me a chance to see the streets around where you're going to be living. We haven't had a chance to have deputies get out onto every single street today, so we'll take a look at it."

She couldn't think of a reason why they shouldn't go together, and honestly, she was thrilled. "Okay, I'll take you up on that."

She finished in the kitchen while Liam headed into the living room. A few minutes later, she watched Liam sit on the floor, playing with Rosie. Her abdomen squeezed, and she winced. *Now, just hang on, Peanut. Let me get your sister settled, and then we'll get ready for your grand entrance.* Rubbing her stomach, she hoped Liam would stay in their lives even after she was no longer living there.

"You've got to be fu—friggin' kidding me."

Liam's growl was almost drowned out by Amy's cry of, "Oh, my God."

He heard a small whimper from the back and twisted around to force a smile onto his face. "Hey, Rosie girl. It's all good. You hang here for a moment while your mom and I go chat with the man standing over there, okay? Can you do that for me?"

Gaining her nod, he placed his hand on Amy's arm, drawing her wide-eyed, open-mouthed attention from the windshield over to him. "Let's go talk to Mr. Porter."

"Talk… but…"

"Amy." He spoke her name soft and low, but with authority, needing to gain her focus. "Rosie is going to wait here with Bubbie."

She stared for a few seconds, visibly struggling to gain control of herself before she nodded. "Yeah, sure."

Twisting around, she smiled at her daughter. "I'll stay in sight, sweetie, so you and Bubbie can see me."

"After we talk to the man, we'll go get a donut, okay, Rosie?" Liam asked.

Rosie agreed eagerly, and he hoped his promise was not going to upset Amy more than she was already. He looked at her pale face. "I'll come around. Stay put and let me help 'cause the ground is soaked and soft, making it hard to walk on."

He wasn't sure if she heard him, but she was still seated when he opened her door. Taking her hand, he helped her down. Once her feet were settled onto the ground, he wrapped his arm around her shoulders and led her over to the man standing in front of the house. It was a mid-sized house, all on one floor with three bedrooms, giving Rosie her own space separate from the nursery. Red brick, fenced-in yard for Rosie to play in. Sitting back from the tree-lined street, making it safe from passing traffic. An attached one-car garage was connected to the kitchen. It all looked like the pictures Amy had shown him last night.

Except for one major thing.

The roof was completely crushed from a massive, uprooted tree. It appeared that over a third of the house was now without a roof and the water damage on the inside would probably require the entire house to be demolished.

Her feet stumbled, and he tightened his grip. "Come on, let's get this over with."

As they approached, the owner of the house, Mr. Porter, the older, tall, thin man, stood looking at them, his gaze moving from Amy up to Liam in his full Sheriff's uniform. Shaking his head, he began talking before they stopped.

"Ms. Carruthers, Sheriff… as you can see, the house can't be rented."

Liam thought that statement had to qualify as one of the most obvious comments in history. "We can see that, Mr. Porter. What we need to know is what are Mrs. Carruthers' options?"

Mr. Porter sighed, his face pinched. "Well, this is the only rental that I've got. You can check with some rental websites to see what else you can find—"

"This was the only house listed for rent." Amy's voice shook, and Liam clutched her tighter, hoping she would lean on him.

"Well, I'm just as sorry as I can be." Mr. Porter turned back and looked at his house, another heavy sigh leaving his chest.

"I'm sorry, too, Mr. Porter. I'm sorry for your loss."

Liam looked down at Amy, stunned that a pregnant woman with a small child who just found out she had no home was offering sympathy to someone else.

Before he had a chance to speak, Mr. Porter nodded. "That's real kind of you. I guess we're both out of luck. But I'll return your deposit and the first month's rent you paid in advance. I'll have my secretary cut you a check today. Where should I send it, or do you want to come to get it?"

"Have her deliver it to the Sheriff's office. Make sure my name is on the envelope."

"Uh, yes, sir, Sheriff Sullivan. I'll get right on that. I'll have her bring it over this morning. Right away."

"That'd be good, Mr. Porter. Like Mrs. Carruthers said, we're sorry for the loss of your property. Contact your insurance company, and the emergency response team has a hotline for helping county residents to clean up from the storm."

With Mr. Porter's thanks, he turned a silent Amy around and began walking her to the Sheriff's SUV. She was so pale and quiet he wanted to get her home as soon as he could. Assisting her back into the passenger seat, he smiled and winked at Rosie, whose wide eyes were pinned on the house with the massive tree laying on top.

Hustling around to the driver's side, he hauled himself up behind the wheel. Starting the engine, he turned on the heat even though the temperature outside was warm. Twisting around in his seat, he first looked back toward Rosie and winked.

"Mr. Le-Um, that man's house is broken."

Despite his worry for Amy, he couldn't help but chuckle. "You've got that right, Rosie. That man's house is broken."

A strange-sounding chortle burst out next to him, and his gaze jerked around to Amy. Her fingers were to her mouth, and for a few seconds, he wasn't sure if she was laughing or crying. He reached out, barely touching her shoulder, when she turned toward him, pressing her lips together. She shifted a little bit more, looked into the back seat, and smiled. Laughter burst forth as she nodded. "Oh, Rosie, that's the perfect description of that house. It's broken."

The three of them laughed for a moment before a heavy sigh fell from Amy's lips. She sucked in a deep breath before letting it out slowly. "Okay, well, I've got some reevaluation to do. Drop us off at your house before you go to work, Liam, and I'll start looking to see what rentals are available."

He opened his mouth, then closed it quickly. She was right. First things first. He wanted to get her home, away from the sight of the *broken house,* and then they could plan. Whether or not she'd agree to the plan that had settled firmly in his mind he had no idea. But maybe, just maybe, she'd see things his way.

Starting the engine, he winked at Rosie before glancing toward Amy. "Sure thing… right after we get a donut."

14

Amy stared out of the kitchen window, stunned at the difference it made to have the hurricane shutters no longer covering the glass. Liam's house was bright with sunshine and the natural light went a long way to helping her mood.

She had no idea what he thought about her current housing situation. Once they'd gotten home, he'd opened all the hurricane windows to let the sunshine flood into the house, kissed the top of Rosie's head, then stopped in front of her. "Talk to your boss, chat with friends, use the kitchen if you want, but do not make any housing plans. Not until I get home and we have a chance to talk. Please, promise me that."

Not having any idea what they needed to talk about, she hoped he might have an idea for possible housing. *Maybe he knows someone who is looking to rent a house or large apartment.* Considering her mind was in a whirl from seeing a large tree through the house she thought she, Rosie, and the new baby would be living in, it was easy enough to acquiesce to his request.

After he left for work, Rosie had wanted to stare out of each window, equally as excited about the light pouring in. Amy could now see that his house sat back from the road with a wide, white gravel driveway. The sliding glass door in the dining room led to a wide deck that overlooked a flat lawn with sparse trees in the background, and she knew beyond that was the Bay.

Once Rosie had dragged her to every window to peer out, she managed to get her daughter settled in the living room with crayons and paper, her dolls, and books. "Mommy is going to sit at the dining room table and check her emails and start looking for a new house."

"I still want to live here," Rosie declared.

"I agree it's nice, but we have to have a place of our own. But when we find it, Mr. Liam can come to visit us there." That seemed to have the effect Rosie needed, and Amy smiled as her daughter's attention returned to her toys.

She opened her laptop for the first time since she'd arrived at Liam's and began scrolling through emails. Most were junk or spam, and she deleted those quickly. One was from a friend in Ohio, checking to see that she'd survived the hurricane. *Good grief, even she knew there was a hurricane coming, which was more than I did!*

Her boss had sent several emails indicating that he knew she had been traveling but to let him know when she was ready, and he'd start sending the orthopedic surgeon's records to be transcribed again. She responded, and it was only a few minutes later when she received emails with the first audio record sent from Dr. Malcolm. Chuckling, she assumed her boss had been desperate and waiting for her to get back with him.

Glancing over at Rosie playing quietly, she decided to spend as much time as she could starting to work. An hour later, she was finishing the first two records just as Rosie wandered over and looked up. Amy held up a finger to indicate that she should wait, then quickly sent the transcription back to her boss. Pulling off her earphones, she smiled down at Rosie. "Thank you for playing so quietly while Mommy worked. Are you ready for lunch?"

With a resounding 'yes' ringing out, she smiled as she pushed herself from her chair and walked into the kitchen. As she fixed sandwiches, she thought of the transcription she'd just completed. The terms were familiar since she'd worked in an orthopedic office when she was an office manager in Ohio. *Finally, something is going right.*

She and Rosie walked outside after lunch, glad for her daughter to have a chance to run and play in the yard. Her lower back was aching, and with her hands pressed just above her ass, she slowly stretched from side to side. *Four weeks to go, Peanut.* She winced as her abdomen tightened, wondering if this baby was going to wait for full-term before arriving. Calling Rosie back inside, they settled in the living room and read stories before she allowed Rosie to watch educational shows on TV.

Rosie was excited with what she was viewing, and glancing at the clock, Amy knew she'd have at least an hour before she needed to get ready for Liam to come home. She'd already spent time that morning glancing through rental options, not finding anything that would suit. But, with her free hour, she could get started on another transcription.

By the time she finished, she was well acquainted with Medical Supply of the Shore from the multiple referrals that Dr. Malcolm sent their way. In larger areas, doctors might have a favorite medical supply business they'd refer patients to but usually left it up to the patient. The doctor just provided the prescription. From what she was seeing in Dr. Malcolm's practice, she assumed this particular medical supply company was probably the only one around. *Curious that he uses it for his telemedicine clients as well.*

Returning her transcription to her boss who would forward it on to Dr. Malcolm's office records manager, she logged out and closed her computer. Rosie's TV show was just going off, and they headed into the kitchen together. Just as she started dinner, her phone rang. She connected, glad to see Tori's name on the screen. "Hey, Tori."

"Oh, Amy, ever since you let me know this morning that your rental house was broken, as Rosie proclaimed, I've had you on my mind. I've talked with a bunch of my friends, and no one has a house to rent, but offers to stay with them flooded in. Of course, I want you here with me! Rose, a friend who owns an ice cream shop in town, had an idea. She and her husband own two apartments in town. One is over the ice cream shop, and the other is over his mechanic's shop. The one over the ice cream shop has a renter, but the other one is empty since another friend of ours moved out. It's large but only has two bedrooms, and the worst is that they are on the second floor, and unfortunately, there's no good place for Rosie to go outside and play since it's right on the street. I promised Rose that I would mention it to you, but I think you'd be happier staying with us. I've put a call out to the American Legion Auxiliary to see if anyone knows of a house to rent. Obviously, there are vacation homes in Baytown, but they are rather expensive."

"Oh, Tori, I don't want you spending your time worrying about me. I don't know what we're going to do, but Liam made me promise to not make any plans until he gets home and we have a chance to talk. I have a feeling he was going to be calling some friends and relatives today to see if anyone has a house to rent."

Silence ensued, and she wondered if Tori was still on the line. Just as she was about to ask, Tori said, "Well, it sounds like Liam has plans. By the way, how are the two of you getting along?"

"Fine, just fine. He's been incredibly accommodating and nice. More than nice, really. We have a good time together. He's asked about Marty, and I've been honest with him. We talked about his family as well. And he's great with Rosie. She adores him. So, yeah, it's been good... uh... he's been a good friend..." Her voice trailed off as she realized she was babbling, wondering what Tori must think.

It didn't take long for laughter to burst from Tori. "I've known Liam for about four years, and I have to tell you that he's an interesting blend of fun and serious, laid-back and uptight. But even Mitch said that it's unlike Liam to invite anyone into his home, much less to stay. So, I'd say, it's more than just fine. And it sounds like he's more than just a good friend."

Before she had a chance to retort, Tori said, "Oh, sorry to call and run, but Mitch just got home. I'll keep asking at the Auxiliary to see if anyone has info on a house to rent. Also, I'll come by Liam's tomorrow and bring my son, Eddie. That'll give Rosie someone to play with."

Thanking her, they disconnected and she sighed. She could always agree to rent someone's basement or rooms but hated to move in with strangers. Snorting, she had to admit that was exactly what she'd done with Liam. But somehow, deciding at night in a hurricane was easier than taking the time to think of all the reasons why she didn't want to move.

Tired of trying to think of her next plan, she turned to the stove when the front doorbell rang. Surprised, she hesitated, uncertain if she should open the door. *Oh, good grief, this is the Sheriff's house. I hardly think anyone bad would be trying to see him.* She walked through the living room, seeing Rosie's face turned up to her, glad that she had instilled in her daughter the rule that only a grown-up answered the door.

Pulling it open, she stared through the glass storm door at a tall, statuesque, beautiful blonde standing on the front porch with a covered dish in her hand. The woman startled, her chin jerking back slightly as her gaze raked over Amy, landing on her protruding belly.

"May I help you?" Amy asked, feeling Rosie slip up beside her, her little hand reaching for the back of Amy's shirt.

The blonde remained silent as her gaze now took in Rosie before moving back to Amy's face. "Who are you?"

Considering Liam's family had been told about her and Rosie, she assumed this woman wasn't a relative. It didn't take much to figure out that whoever this woman was, she'd like to be a lot more to Liam. "I'm Amy, and this is Rosie. And you are?"

"What are you still doing in Liam's house?"

"Still?"

"I'd heard he'd rescued someone but the storm is over. It seems strange that you're still here."

"Well, we are, but I don't believe that's any of your business. If you're looking for Liam, he's not home yet." She inclined her head toward the covered dish. "If you brought something for him, you can certainly leave it, and I'll be sure to let him know you came by."

The blonde drew herself up, so tall it was easy for her to look down her nose at Amy. Her lips pinched tightly together. "I won't leave it. Just tell him that Rachel came by. I'll stop by the station tomorrow and give it to him *personally*."

"You do that. Goodbye, Rachel." Not caring if she was rude, she closed the door, her heart pounding. The tug on her shirt brought her gaze back down to Rosie.

"I didn't like her, Mommy."

Chuckling, she admitted, "I wasn't too crazy about her myself."

"She was ugly. Is she Mr. Le-Um's friend?"

"Probably not as close a friend as she'd like to be. And I thought she was pretty. Why did you think she was ugly?"

Rosie wrinkled her nose. "Because she didn't smile." She looked up at Amy. "You smile a lot and you're pretty."

Laughing, she bent, clutched Rosie's cheeks in her hands, and gave her a smacking kiss. Rosie giggled and ran ahead of her into the kitchen. She couldn't help but wonder why Liam was keeping her and Rosie around when he could obviously have Rachel. *Well, as soon as I find a house, we'll be out from under his feet.* Sighing, that thought didn't make her feel any better.

Deciding to make biscuits from scratch to go with their pork chops, Rosie was soon elbow-deep in flour and having a blast. That was how Liam found them when he walked in.

With a grin on his face, he kissed Rosie's head and walked straight to Amy, tucking a strand of hair behind her ear.

"Hey," she said, her gaze searching his face, looking to see how his day had gone, noting he looked exhausted.

"Hey, back." A smile played about his lips, but instead of speaking, he looked past her and sniffed. "Damn, that smells good."

"I hope it is, although it probably won't be as good as the dish that someone was bringing to you today."

His eyes widened for a few seconds, then he dropped his head and cursed under his breath. "Damn. Tell me the pie and casserole brigade didn't come marching to the door."

"Brigade? Oh, my goodness, you've got more tall blondes bringing you food?"

His hands rested on his hips as his head dropped back and he stared at the ceiling. "God give me strength." Another sigh slipped out. "Rachel."

"Yep," she said, popping the 'p' on the end. "I don't think she was too happy to see me."

He dropped his chin and stared directly into her eyes. "I have no idea what that woman may have said to you, but please, ignore anything that comes out of her mouth. She's trolling for husband number three. I think it's three, but maybe it's four—"

"Three? Oh, my God!"

"She's only one of the brigade. The others are older women in the area who are trying to marry off their daughters, nieces, and granddaughters. They do this with just about every eligible bachelor around."

"Well, I hate to be the bearer of bad news, but she wouldn't give the food to me, so you're just going to have to eat what I fixed."

Barking out a laugh, he shook his head. "Rachel can't cook worth shi… uh… worth anything. She goes to the grocery store and buys something frozen, heats it in the microwave, puts it in a dish, and then tries to bring it to the station. I leave hers and all the other brigades' offerings for everyone to eat during lunch. This is the first time she's stopped by the house."

"Probably because she heard you'd helped someone and wanted to see if that someone was still here."

He started to curse again, but she placed her finger on his lips, cutting her eyes over to Rosie. He mumbled his apology with her finger still in place before playfully nipping at it. She jerked her hand back and shook her finger at him. "Go change, do whatever you need to do to take your mind off your day, and dinner will be ready in a few minutes."

He stayed in place, his expression softening. "It used to involve hanging with friends when they were single, but as life moves on, it's mostly been me, a beer, and sitting on my deck." He nodded toward Rosie and smiled. "This is nice. Really, it's nice."

He winked and walked out of the room, and it struck her once again how easy it felt here with him. But instead of giving her peace, she realized that soon, playing house with Liam would have to end. She couldn't stay here forever, and she desperately needed to get settled before the baby came.

After dinner, he looked at Rosie and asked, "How would you like to take a walk to the beach?"

Her eyes brightened and she bounced in her chair. Looking over at Amy, she whispered as though in awe. "Oh, Mommy, can we?"

"Of course, if Liam says we can."

"Absolutely." He dropped his gaze as she absent-mindedly rubbed her stomach before glancing back to her plate. "You didn't eat a lot, are you feeling okay?"

"Just very full," she laughed. "A walk would do me good."

It didn't take long for them to walk to the end of his grassy yard, through the trees, and down a short lane to come to the Bay. Rosie clapped her hands and ran over the sand toward the water, stopping well short of the edge.

"Oh, my!" Amy stood and looked out onto the Chesapeake Bay. "I haven't seen the ocean since I was in college and we'd drive to Virginia Beach on Saturdays."

"Well, technically, this isn't the ocean. That's why the waves aren't as high, and there isn't the riptide that you can get with the ocean."

"It's beautiful. I used to think that the Bay was smaller, that you could see from one side to the other."

"Here, it's about twenty miles long."

She let out a deep breath, her hand cupping underneath her tummy, taking in the fresh air. "I'm so glad I decided to move here, even if my first few days were nothing like I thought they'd be."

He stepped closer, catching a tendril of hair that was blowing in the breeze, his fingers rubbing the strands before tucking it behind her ear. "I'm glad you decided to move here, too. And I'm not sorry that I found you that first night."

She wanted to lean into his hand, clutch his shirt, and pull him close. But instead, she gave herself the gift of simply staring into his eyes.

"Mommy! Mr. Le-Um! Look!"

They both turned at the same time, seeing Rosie run on her little legs toward them, clutching something in her hand. For a second, she hoped it wasn't a crab, then immediately knew if it had been, her daughter wouldn't be clutching it. As Rosie opened her fingers, a beautiful green piece of sea glass lay in her palm.

"It's like yours," Rosie said, staring up at Liam. "Here, I founded it for you."

Squatting, he appeared to be studying it carefully before declaring, "I think that's the prettiest piece of sea glass I've ever seen in my life. You keep it. You can start your own jar."

Rosie's little fingers closed around the sea glass, clutching it to her chest. "Mommy, it's the prettiest piece he's ever seen."

She swallowed deeply, determined not to let an errant tear fall down her cheeks. She knew Marty had loved Rosie but he never seemed to know how to show it. She couldn't remember a time when he'd been excited about anything she'd done, drawn, or discovered. Clearing her throat, she smiled. "I know, baby. Let's see if we can find some more."

They walked along the beach for a little while, finding so much sea glass. "Is it always like this?"

"You can almost always find some, but after a storm, there's more. The waves and currents have churned up more from the bay and dumped them onto the beach."

After bending a few times, she became winded, and Liam insisted that she point to the pieces she wanted, and he'd pick them up. Normally, she would've scoffed at the idea that she couldn't bend, but the twinges she felt in her lower back gave her pause. Soon, his pockets were full of sea glass, and they started back to his house.

She was breathing heavier, moving much slower than she had been earlier. As soon as all the pieces of sea glass were rinsed off and placed into a jar, she looked down at her daughter. "Okay, Rosie, it's bath time."

Liam stepped closer, his gaze roving over her, his brows lowered in concern. "I know I can't give her a bath, but I hate that you're going to have to bend over. You seem a lot more fatigued than normal. Are you sure you're okay?"

"I'm fine. This little one is just making their presence known. I'll run just a little bit of water into the tub, and I won't lift her. I'll just hold her hand as she climbs in and out." Calling out to Rosie again, the two made their way upstairs.

15

Liam paced downstairs for a few moments, then finally jogged up the stairs, wanting to be close in case Amy needed him. Their bedroom door was open but the bathroom door closed. He could hear the sound of splashing and Rosie chattering about the sea glass and the ocean, answered occasionally by Amy. His ears perked up as he heard Amy tell her it was time to get out of the tub. Ready to spring forward if needed, he breathed a sigh of relief as he could tell Rosie must have been dried off and was now in her pajamas. He started to turn to go back downstairs when Rosie's voice carried clearly.

"Mommy, can we stay here forever?"

"We're going to stay in this area, sweetheart. We'll get a house, you can start preschool, Mommy will have the baby, and we're going to stay."

"No, I mean can we stay here with Mr. Le-Um in this house? He'll be lonely if we go away."

"We can't stay here, Rosie. This is his house. But we can stay friends with him. I'm sure he'd like to do that."

"Don't you want to stay here with him?"

"Oh, honey, it's not a question of what I want to do. But people don't just live in other people's houses. It's like you have your own dolls and sometimes you can let a friend play with them but they're still your dolls."

"I didn't like it when Chrissie tried to take my dolls!"

"That's right. And this is Liam's house, and he invited us to stay for just a little while. This can't be our forever home."

Their voices grew softer, and he could no longer discern what they were saying. He'd already planned on talking to Amy that evening when Rosie went to bed, but nerves had him wondering what to say. Now, with Rosie's honesty, he smiled as he jogged down the stairs.

After Rosie was sound asleep, he sat with Amy on the sofa, sipping hot cocoa as had become their habit.

"I started working today."

So deep in his thoughts of how to bring up what he wanted to say, her words caught him off guard. Blinking, he repeated, "Working?"

Laughing, she nodded. "I couldn't have done transcription from home when Rosie was little, and certainly can't when the baby comes, but she was playing so quietly earlier that I was able to get over an hour of transcription from Dr. Malcolm at the hospital. He sends his patient notes to the hospital, and they send them to my secure portal."

"You mentioned an orthopedic surgeon earlier, and I didn't even think about it being him."

"Oh, do you know him?"

He shook his head. "No, not really. I just know of a few veterans in the area that have seen him. Mostly some of the older men that I know from the American Legion. Hips, knees, those kinds of surgeries."

"Oh, yes, he seems to have a lot of elderly patients and keeps the local medical supply store with plenty of clients."

"You'll find that a lot here. The area doesn't have a lot of competition for certain businesses, so there may just be one."

The silence settled, and once again, she spoke before he managed to get his thoughts together.

"Liam, we need to talk about this morning. I managed to keep busy most of the day with Rosie, some work, and even offending your casserole brigade by my presence—" She stopped to giggle as he rolled his eyes. "But I've also done some thinking and planning. There are very few homes listed right now for rent. A couple of them are old, and I'm afraid maintenance would be too difficult. Some are more for beach rentals, and they are too expensive. With Mr. Porter giving me back my security deposit and first month's rent, that helps, but I still need to find a place that fits my budget. I talked to Tori, and she offered for me and Rosie to come live with them. I hate that idea, though, because she's getting ready to have a baby in a few months. It just doesn't seem right to crowd in with my brood at this time. She also mentioned that several other friends have houses large enough that Rosie and I could stay with them, but I feel like it's the same problem. Almost all of them have babies or are getting ready to have babies. She's going to check with the Auxiliary to see if any members have rental property, but with so much damage across the area from the hurricane, that will be hard to find. She also mentioned Mitch's parents have room, and so do Jillian's. I met Jillian's parents many years ago in college, so I suppose that's a possibility. But the idea of bringing a preschooler and a newborn into a retired couple's home makes me want to break out in hives."

His hand landed on her leg, and she stopped babbling. But, instead of looking at him, she dropped her head into her hands and groaned.

"Oh, I'm so sorry. None of this is your concern, so just ignore my ramblings. I'm sure that I can move in with someone temporarily until a house becomes available."

"Amy." He waited until her head snapped up, her gaze finally focusing on him. "Shush."

She blinked. "Sheriff Sullivan, did you just shush me?"

Grinning, he lifted a brow and nodded. "Ms. Carruthers, I believe I did."

Her lips slammed together and stayed pressed for only a few seconds until she burst into laughter. "Oh, I can hardly blame you for shushing me considering I was blabbing incessantly."

"Look, Amy, in the few days that we've been together, I can tell that you're practical and think through your plans. I know it seems like everything's gotten derailed, first with the hurricane, then with Tori's Sea Glass Inn having some water damage, and now with your rental house completely *broken,* as Rosie says. I'm sure between Tori and the other friends, family, and Auxiliary, they could come up with someplace for you to stay, but it wouldn't be optimum. Not with a small child and a baby coming in a month. But the last thing you need right now in your life—or Rosie's life—is added stress."

"Okay, Liam. I agree with everything you just said about what's happened to me, but it doesn't move me closer to having a place to live."

"I'm not finished." She blinked, and he grinned again. "My suggestion is for you to not rush into a situation that would make you uncomfortable. Take time to find the right place for you and Rosie. And, until then, you already have a place to live. A place with room, a yard, a big kitchen that you love to cook in, and someone that you've become familiar with."

She blinked again, giving her head a little shake. "Are you... are you suggesting here? Are you suggesting that Rosie and I stay here?"

"Humph," he groused, now doubting her desire to stay. "Is that such a bad thing?"

"No! No, it's not a bad thing at all, but Liam, you've only known me a few days."

His arms stretched over the back of the sofa, his fingers landing lightly on her shoulder. "Amy, if you move into anyone else's house, you're going to know them even fewer days than me."

She closed her eyes slowly and dropped her chin, and he watched as her chest lifted as she took a deep breath. As she blew it out, she raised her head and held his gaze. "Liam, you've adapted very well to us, but I know you like your peace and quiet. I know you like your coffee table without crayons, your kitchen counter without messes, and your windows without any little sticky fingerprints."

Shaking his head, he heard the pleading in his voice. "My house was that way because it was the only way I knew. But the last couple of days when I came home, I couldn't wait to get here to see you and Rosie. I want to find out what she's been doing, I want to see your smile and check to make sure you and the baby are okay. You haven't taken advantage of my hospitality. Instead, you've given me a reason to think of my house as a home."

She sat quietly, but he could swear he saw hope in her eyes. Or maybe it was just the hope in his own eyes that he saw reflected.

She dropped her gaze, her hands fiddling with her maternity shirt stretched over her stomach. Finally lifting her head, she sighed heavily. "Liam, a couple of days is very different than even a couple of weeks. One of the reasons I wanted to go ahead and move into our home was so I could get into the trailer and dig out some more of Rosie's things, puzzles and toys, a few more of her favorite dolls." Wrinkling her nose, she added, "But if I move into someone else's house, I wouldn't want to drag those things out there, either."

"I've got plenty of room here for you to bring Rosie's things in. Monday through Friday, I'm gone to work all day and there's no reason why she can't enjoy her things here in the house. I'm generally not in the office on weekends—one of the perks of being the Sheriff, although I can get called in at any time. You can work from here when Rosie's napping or on weekends when I'm here to help out. There's the extra guest room upstairs that's just sitting empty if you want her to have her own bedroom with a shared bathroom with yours."

Shaking her head quickly, Amy said, "Oh, no. She and I together in one room are perfectly fine."

He grinned widely. "That sounds to me like you're considering it."

"I guess I am." She winced and shifted her position on the cushion.

"Are you okay? I'm worried about you."

"I'm sure you've seen this with your sisters, sisters-in-law, and friends who've had babies. Everything just starts feeling uncomfortable in the last trimester."

He shook his head slowly. "I hate to admit this, but I've never paid attention. I mean, I always wanted them to be healthy and have healthy babies, but I've never been that involved. Damn, that makes me really sound like a selfish prick, doesn't it?"

She laughed, and he loved the sound. "No, that doesn't make you sound like a selfish prick. To be perfectly honest, I don't think most single men think a whole lot about pregnancy, other than how to avoid it."

"You're probably right."

Another silence settled over them, and he waited, knowing enough about Amy already that she needed to run through the idea in her mind. She finally looked up and said, "Everything you said makes sense. If Rosie and I moved into another person's house, they would be strangers, and here, at least we already know you and you know us. I admit the fact that Rosie loves it here is a big bonus. She feels comfortable with you and that doesn't happen easily."

He wanted to crow but kept a gentle smile firmly on his face. "All good reasons, Amy."

"But…"

His brows lifted in surprise. "But?"

"But if we stay, then I'll be actively looking for a house to rent before the baby comes. Plus, we need to come to an understanding about the rent. I can easily pay you what I was going to pay Mr. Porter—"

"Whoa! I'm not having you pay rent!" She blinked, and he hated that his words came out harsher than he meant, but there was no fucking way he would take her money.

"Liam, of course, I'll pay. I can't stay here and not pay!"

Straightening his back, he shook his head. "You're not renting a whole house here. You're just in one bedroom that was sitting empty."

"We use your kitchen and your food. We use the water and electricity and internet."

"You cook meals for me. Hell, having you here is like having my own personal chef! I don't expect that either, but it surely is a reason for you not paying rent!" They both stared at each other, their faces tight, each arguing their opposing positions.

"Liam, if I don't pay for me and Rosie being here, I can't in good conscience stay here."

"If you think Mitch or Jillian's parents will let you

pay, you're gravely mistaken." He sucked in a deep breath through his nose before huffing. They remained silent for another moment, but as soon as she winced again, he capitulated, not wanting to add to her stress. "Okay, look. When you can get out, then you can buy some groceries, especially for the things you know you and Rosie like to eat. But you cannot pay full house rent. That makes no sense."

Slowly, she nodded. "Okay, but I have to pay something. We can figure out a percentage and split utilities." Sighing, she added, "I don't want you to ever regret asking us to stay or be terrified that I won't leave. As soon as a decent house becomes available, we'll move out. That way, we won't lose your friendship from too much familiarity."

His fingers reached over to her shoulder again, gently rubbing the tension he felt in her tight muscles. "Turn around."

He was surprised when she gave him her back with only the barest mumble of, *'bossy.'* He began to massage her neck and shoulders. "You shouldn't be this tense. It's not good for you or the baby."

She snickered. "I didn't think you kept up with pregnancy."

"Common sense tells me that. Plus, I've gotten very interested in one pregnant woman in the last couple of days."

She looked over her shoulder, her eyes wide. Not wanting to have to delve into his confusing and confused emotions at the moment, he ordered, "Turn around," again. She acquiesced, then began groaning as his fingers dug into her muscles.

"God, your hands are magic."

He slowly finished the massage. "When's your appointment to see the obstetrician?"

"I'll go in two days."

"Do you need someone to watch Rosie?"

She shook her head as she shifted back around on the sofa. "No, Tori said she could come by."

He nodded, hesitating for just a few seconds, then asked, "Can I come with you?"

"You want to come with me?" Her eyes widened as she shifted further around to face him directly.

"Yeah… it just seems like a good idea to have someone with you…" He dragged his hand through his hair, exhaling audibly. "Fuckin' hell, Amy. I really want to be with you when you go. I can't explain it, I just know what I want. But I don't want to crowd you or make you uncomfortable—"

"No, no, that's not it. You just surprised me. Marty never wanted to go to the doctor with me."

"I think we've already established that, at times, Marty was an idiot."

Her eyes widened even further, and her mouth dropped open. Just as he thought she might be angry and was kicking himself over having said something rude about her deceased husband, she clapped her hand over her mouth, stifling a giggle that ended up being a belly laugh.

"Oh, I shouldn't laugh, but you're right. He was my husband and the father of my children and could be a good man. But he could also be a real idiot. I always tried to excuse it by saying he didn't have a real childhood himself, but lots of people came from his background and managed to grow up." Still smiling, she said, "Thank you for your honesty. I needed that. And sure, you can come if you really want to. But don't worry if your job interferes and keeps you from coming. Just knowing that you want to is nice."

Their cocoa was long finished, and she yawned widely. "We've covered a lot of ground tonight, and I'm exhausted."

He nodded, stood, and took her hand to gently pull her up from the sofa. They took their cups to the kitchen and rinsed them out, and he walked around and checked the doors. It didn't miss his attention that she waited at the bottom of the stairs for him so they could walk up together.

Standing outside their bedroom doors, her face lit by the nightlight in the hall, her beauty struck him once again. Without thinking about what he was doing, he leaned forward and kissed her forehead, whispering against her soft skin. "I'm really glad you're staying. You, Rosie, and the Peanut." Leaning back, he was almost afraid to witness her reaction, but her smile said it all.

"Good night, Liam. We'll see you in the morning."

He met her smile with one of his own and nodded. That night, lying in bed, he thought of Amy and Rosie staying in his house and smiled again.

16

Ugh! I've got to concentrate! Normally, when Amy put on her headphones to transcribe, she had no problem blocking out the world. But then, that's why she used to go into an office to work, and when she worked from home only did when Rosie was in preschool. *I can't blame this on Rosie.*

Her daughter had woken up so excited to find out that they were going to stay at Liam's house. After he left to go to the station, Rosie had been playing quietly for most of the morning. Now, she was having her break, playing a game on Amy's iPad nearby so that Amy could keep an eye on her.

No, this is all on me. Her mind was filled with the vision of Liam standing so close at the top of the stairs last night, then leaning forward and kissing her forehead. She blamed her tumultuous hormones on the fact that she had to fight the desire to jump him. *God, what a disaster that would've been. We're friends, that's all. Plus, I'm as big as a whale, carrying another man's baby. Yep, I'm sure he's tempted!* Her last thought was followed by an eye roll, then she shook her head, breathed deeply for a moment to clear her mind, and turned back to the next file needing to be transcribed.

She'd made it through Dr. Malcolm's surgery notes and was now entering dictated recommendations and prescriptions for physical therapy as well as medical devices. *As much as he refers clients to Medical Supply of the Shore, I'm not surprised he dictates these orders.*

After another fifteen minutes of transcribing orders, she was surprised to open a file that appeared to be a phone message as opposed to medical orders. Checking to confirm that it came from Dr. Malcolm and had been sent to her for transcription, she continued typing.

Much of medical transcription didn't make sense to the typical transcriber, but her skill was not only typing quickly but in knowing the terminology used. But the more she typed, the more confused she became. Looking down, she reread the notes. Client names with birthdates. Medical diagnosis next to each one. Then, a prescription for various splints to be filled by the medical supply store here on the shore. What confused her was his voice saying, *"—then, make sure you duplicate patient names. Change birth date and prescription. Charge both. File under Medicare, as usual. Same for Johnson and Trabelle."*

Her fingers hovered over the laptop keys, a snake of unease slithering through her. She couldn't understand why he needed to have the store duplicate a name but change the birthdates. If he wanted the same patient to have more than one prescription for supplies, then their birthdate would stay the same. She replayed the dictated message. The very first part was cut off but the rest of the message was as clear as she'd heard the first time.

Johnson was a common last name, but Trabelle wasn't. Since both were the names of the two doctors he had in his telemedical practice, it was easy to conclude that whatever he was instructing, he wanted the other two to do the same.

Still filled with unease over the message, she glanced at the clock and realized it was almost time for Tori and some of her friends to stop by. Saving her transcription, she decided not to send that file in until she had a chance to listen to it again. *And do a little research!*

She'd just put away her laptop when she looked out and saw Tori pulling into the driveway followed by a caravan of other vehicles.

"Mommy! Who are all these people?"

She moved to Rosie quickly, knowing Rosie's aversion to being thrust into a group of strangers. Taking her hand, she said, "That's Mommy's friend Tori, and she's brought a few other people to say hi to us. But I promise I'll stay right here with you." Gaining Rosie's nod, they walked to the door together.

Soon, Liam's house was filled with a large group of women, most with children or babies, and several more pregnant. She hugged Tori, not believing how many years had passed since they'd been in college together. Jillian rushed in, throwing her arms around her as well.

"Liam was bragging to the others about the delicious goodies you bake. I'm desperate to have some more things I can sell at my coffee shop," Jillian said. "I know with the baby you can't think about that now, but promise me that in the future I might convince you to do some baking for the shop as an extra way for you to make money."

The idea thrilled her, but she barely had time to nod before she was being introduced to so many other women that their names began to run together. Maddie, Belle, Jade, Sophia, Lia, Katelyn, and Carrie. The women gathered in the living room, giving Rosie a chance to get to know the other kids with her mom nearby.

Tori leaned over and said, "Liam called to let me know that Rosie was shy and would feel more comfortable if she was able to see you."

Touched that he had ensured that Rosie would have playmates but still be comfortable, she smiled. Tori's son, Eddie, and Katelyn's son, Finn, were almost the same age as Rosie. Jillian, Maddie, Carrie, and Jade all had newborns in their arms. Belle and Tori were pregnant but not as far along as Amy was.

Tori knelt to greet Rosie and said, "You'll have to come into Baytown and stop at Sweet Rose's Ice Cream Shop. It's run by my friend, Rose, who was excited that you have a name just like hers. She said she'll give you a special ice cream cone when you come."

"I was named for my grandma," Rosie pronounced, then looked up at her mom, her eyes wide. "Can we go sometime?"

"Absolutely, baby."

It didn't take long for Rosie to warm up to Eddie and Finn, and they soon went into Liam's backyard to play.

Carrie sat next to her and smiled. "My husband is Colt. He's the North Heron County Sheriff, basically Liam's counterpart. They're good friends, so I'm sure you and I will see a lot of each other."

It was on the tip of Amy's tongue to deny that she should be considered on par with Carrie who was married to a Sheriff, but with all the other women around, she hated to make it a point. Instead, she simply smiled, secretly thinking how nice it would be to actually *be* with Liam.

The next hour passed easily, with wonderful conversation and lots of laughs. She looked across the room at Tori, glad that her friend had found happiness, both with her husband and friends. It seemed that Baytown had been very good to her. Wanting the same for herself and Rosie, she listened as the other women talked about childcare, preschools, playdates, get-togethers, and the Auxiliary.

"I'm asking if anyone knows of a rental house," Tori began.

As Tori spoke, her gaze darted around at the other women, and Amy caught what seemed like a secret vibe moving between them. Not understanding what their silent code was about, she looked back at Tori.

"As soon as I find out anything, I'll let you know," Tori continued, smiling. "But you seem to be very happy here…"

"Oh, Liam's just being very accommodating for me and Rosie. But I do need to find a place for us to live. I'm due in another month, and I really want to get settled before this baby comes."

"Well, we'll all keep our ears open and let you know as soon as we hear of something," Tori promised.

Before she had a chance to say more, the others changed the subject, and she was drawn into another conversation.

Liam drove down his driveway, not even pretending that his nerves weren't taut. He didn't normally come home at lunch but knowing that Tori was going to be not just visiting but bringing a bunch of her friends had him on edge. *What if Amy feels overwhelmed? What if they ask questions that put her on the spot? What if they question why she's still there and make her think she should leave? What if one of them has already found a rental home for her? What if Rosie gets nervous and Amy isn't close?* These concerns pounded through his head, and as he spied the large group of vehicles parked in front of his house, he gripped the steering wheel tighter. *Fuck!*

Climbing from his Sheriff's SUV, he stalked toward the front door when Rosie came flying around the corner of the house with two little boys fast on her heels.

"Mr. Liam! Mr. Liam! I've got friends!"

The smile on her face caused the air to rush from his lungs as he bent and swooped her into his arms just as she threw herself at him. Hugging her tightly, he smiled, realizing she didn't stumble over his name. He looked down at the two boys grinning up at him. One was the spitting image of Mitch, and if memory served him correctly, Katelyn and Gareth's son, Finn, was about the same age.

Just then, the front door opened, and Amy smiled as soon as her gaze landed on him. "I had no idea you were coming home." Suddenly, her smile dropped, and she glanced over her shoulder. "Um… there's kind of a lot of people here."

Inclining his head toward the line of cars parked out front, he laughed. "No kidding."

She was still biting her lip as though concerned that he might be upset. With Rosie still in his arms, he stepped close. He could see a multitude of smiling women's faces pointed his way from the living room, but he leaned in close to whisper in Amy's ear. "It's fine. I want you to have friends. I came home because I just wanted to make sure that you and Rosie were okay."

Looking up, relief flooded her face and she smiled. The urge to lean over and kiss her was so strong, it took all of his willpower to step back. Hearing another vehicle come into the driveway, he turned, wondering who else was left to greet Amy. Mitch was climbing down from a Baytown Police Department vehicle, barely out of the door before his son raced to him, Finn close on his heels. Colt was alighting from his Sheriff's Department SUV.

"You might as well come join the party," he said as the two men walked up to the front porch. Both men greeted him, then smiled at Rosie, who stared in awe.

"I'd like you to meet Amy Carruthers and her daughter, Rosie. This is Mitch Evans, Tori's husband."

"Oh, it's so nice to meet you, Mitch," she said, her smile wide.

"Same to you, Amy. I've heard a lot about you from Tori. She's thrilled that you moved to the area."

"And this is Carrie's husband, Colt," Liam introduced.

Carrie stepped out onto the porch as Colt greeted Amy before reaching over to take his son from Carrie's outstretched arms. They all moved into the living room together. Liam nodded toward the women as he set Rosie's feet onto the floor, and soon, the group began gathering the baby carriers, diaper bags, and saying their goodbyes.

"I hope I'm not chasing you out," he said. "I just stopped by to check on Amy and Rosie."

The women all assured him that they needed to get home but were glad that Amy and Rosie were staying with him. The smiles and glances they passed amongst themselves did not go unnoticed by him. As the others hugged Amy and promised to get with her soon, Tori and Carrie held back with their husbands.

"I'm so sorry that my Inn didn't work out for you to stay in, but I'm so glad that you're here on the Eastern Shore," Tori said, wrapping her arms around Amy. "I can't believe it's been so long since we've been together. Now that you're here, we'll see each other all the time." Corralling Eddie who was still playing with Rosie, Tori and Mitch managed to get out the door.

Carrie hugged Amy and said, "I work at the diner up the road. It's not fancy, but if you ever want good food and would like to give Rosie one of the world's greatest milkshakes, come on by. If you ever just need someone to talk to, let me know. There are enough of us that are pregnant or just had babies that we know how this stage is."

Liam smiled, his mood better now that he knew that Amy had the support of a big group of good women and Rosie had found a couple of playmates. He walked Colt and Carrie out to their vehicles to say goodbye.

"I'll tell you what everyone told me when I got with Carrie," Colt said. "It looks good on you."

Shaking his head, he sighed. "Right now, we're just good friends. Amy's had a rough time and has a lot on her plate."

"Nothing wrong with starting as good friends," Colt continued. "And if you think it's not more, you're lying to yourself. If there's one thing I know, Liam, you've never lied to yourself."

Before he had a chance to retort, Colt buckled his baby into the car seat and assisted his wife into her vehicle before climbing into his. Liam waved them down the road before he went back into his house. Rosie was still excited but Amy managed to get her to sit at the table to eat a sandwich. She turned to Liam, offering him homemade chicken salad on a croissant.

He looked down and shook his head. "I wasn't expecting lunch, Amy. You need to stay off your feet."

"I made these right after you left this morning before I started transcribing. I like to bake."

"Well, your enjoyment is going to put pounds on my middle!"

She lifted a brow and stared at his abs. "Uh-huh.

When you've got a watermelon in your middle, then we can talk."

He laughed but continued to eat, loving every bite. Her face grew serious, and he turned his full attention back to her. "What's on your mind?"

"Remember how I said that I was doing medical transcriptions for Dr. Malcolm? Well, I was working this morning and came across something that sounded suspicious to me. It's probably nothing, but I just wondered what you thought."

"Hit me with it."

"He not only has his local practice, he has patients from all over the country with his telemedical business. There are two other orthopedic surgeons, him being the owner of the business."

"Telemedical?" He finished his sandwich and pushed his plate away. "I think you mentioned this the first night you were here, but I'm not familiar with that term."

"It's becoming more and more prevalent in the industry, especially in remote areas where medical care is hard to get to or with the elderly who have difficulty getting in to see someone. There's been a lot of tele-health, which is the distribution of information and health-related services, but telemedicine is specifically where medical personnel diagnose and monitor. It allows the doctor to check in with the patient, actually diagnose and give prescriptions. Certainly, there are limits but it has greatly increased the medical care that many people can receive."

"So, you seem concerned. It doesn't sound like a bad thing to me."

"No, actually it's not. And I've done a lot of transcribing for telemedical doctors. It also doesn't surprise me that he prescribes a lot of medical supplies, such as splints, braces, crutches, wheelchairs, walkers, even hospital beds and lift chairs. What does surprise me is that he only seems to have his clients go through the medical supply store that's here on the Eastern Shore, even when the client is on the other side of the country. That seems like a huge expense, and it also seems like it's always for Medicare patients."

Cocking his head to the side, he held her gaze, then lifted his hand and smoothed the creases in her forehead. "And you're suspicious of this?"

As soon as his hand fell away, the crinkle reappeared. "Sort of. But it's more. He sent a message that I'm not sure I was supposed to receive. It involved changing names and birthdates for clients and gaining approval through Medicare. I mean, I don't have anything specific to go on, but since you're the Sheriff in this area, I thought I'd mention it just in case you ever heard of anything. I don't want to make a big deal out of nothing, but I can't just ignore it."

He listened with concern, more for her than for what she was describing. "Amy, you're the professional in this. You do whatever you need to do to settle your mind. I just hate to see you so stressed."

She waved her hand and laughed. "Doing a little internet digging while sitting in a chair on my computer is hardly stressed." Inclining her head back toward the living room where it had been crowded with people just an hour before, she laughed. "Now *that* had me stressed."

"I was so worried about everybody coming in here, that's why I came home for lunch. I just had to check on you and Rosie."

He held his breath as something moved through her eyes that he couldn't define. She lifted her hand and placed it on his arm, giving a little squeeze. "Thank you for that. It turned out fine. I loved seeing Tori and meeting her friends. They've invited me to an Auxiliary meeting, and I'm looking forward to that, too."

"Well, if you're okay, I've got to get back to work. There's a lot of cleanup going on in the county, and I need to make sure that the Sheriff's Department is available where needed." He leaned down and kissed her cheek, the gesture so natural that he hadn't even given it a thought until he felt her smooth skin underneath his lips. Jerking slightly, he leaned back, ready to apologize if she was upset. Instead, her eyes sparkled and her smile widened.

Driving back to the station, that expression on her beautiful face stayed with him the rest of the afternoon.

17

After Liam left, Rosie took a nap, crashing after lunch and having run and played so hard with her new friends. While Rosie was upstairs in bed, Amy fired up her laptop, her curiosity overriding wanting to get a new transcription done.

It was not hard to find Dr. Malcolm's telemedicine website. He and two other orthopedic surgeons, Dr. Johnson and Dr. Trabelle, provided diagnosis, monitoring, prescriptions, and medical recommendations for orthopedic patients all over the country. As she scoured the website, she was fascinated with what telemedicine could do. If a patient already had x-rays, Dr. Malcolm could access them and make his own diagnosis. He could have regular phone calls with them, and where available, internet appointments.

Scrolling down to the bottom of the website where it listed associated businesses, the Medical Supply Company of the Shore was the only one available.

While that made sense for Dr. Malcolm since he was here, it didn't make any sense for the other doctors who were located elsewhere. Dr. Johnson practiced in Mississippi and Dr. Trabelle in North Dakota. *Maybe the medical supply store here is the cheapest? But only with Medicare patients?*

She then went to the other doctors' websites, seeing if she could find any other similarities. Something caught her attention, and she went back to Dr. Malcolm. He'd obtained his medical degree in the Caribbean before coming back to the United States and finishing his education at several other medical schools. Going back to search, she easily discovered both of his partner doctors had also completed their initial medical degree from the same Caribbean medical college. *Three doctors, all graduating at the same time from the same university. All knowing each other. Going their separate ways, and yet, coming back together to create their business led by Dr. Malcolm. An orthopedic telemedical business that only uses a small medical supply store in the far reaches of the Eastern Shore.*

Her suspicions continued to be aroused. When she'd worked as an office manager, she had been diligent to make sure their medical office was accurate with all records, including financial as well as medical. Even the hint of medical fraud was to be avoided.

But before she had a chance to research further, a knock on the door interrupted. With all the visitors she'd had that morning, she couldn't imagine who it would be and hoped it wasn't Rachel coming to see if she was still there.

She peeked out, seeing an attractive woman that appeared to be in her fifties standing on the front porch. Sighing, she wondered if this was more of the casserole brigade that Liam had mentioned. *If this continues, I'm really going to get the gossip tongues wagging. Just what I need after moving to a new place.*

Plastering a smile on her face, she opened the door. Before she had a chance to speak, the woman's gaze moved over her face, dropped to her pregnant belly, and then moved back to her face before smiling widely.

"Oh, my! You must be Amy. And just as beautiful as I was told. It's so nice to meet you. I'm Carolyn Sullivan, Liam's mom."

Blinking in stunned silence, she unlatched the storm door. She stood back, welcoming Liam's mom into the house, trying to smooth her hair back into its ponytail, glad that she'd put on a little makeup before her earlier guests had visited. "Please, come in. Well, you hardly need me to invite you into your son's house. It's nice to meet you, too. Can I get you something to eat or drink?"

"No, no, my dear. Please, let's just sit down to get a chance to get to know each other. You should take a load off anyway. Liam says you're getting close to delivery, but he's a man who doesn't have a clue, so I can't trust him on that."

"I still have a month to go, even though I'm sure I look as big as a house."

Waving her hand dismissively, Carolyn sat on the sofa and smiled. "You look exactly like a pregnant woman should look. Happy and healthy."

Sitting in the chair facing the sofa, she linked her

hands in her lap, uncertain of the reason for Carolyn's visit other than to scope out what strange person her son had invited into his home. Wishing she could think of something clever, or at the very least appropriate, her mind blanked. If his mother was going to accuse her of taking advantage of her son's good nature, she was glad Rosie was upstairs asleep.

"I confess I was quite surprised when Liam told me that he'd brought someone stranded in the storm to his house." Carolyn's brow crinkled as she shook her head slightly. "No, that's not true. Liam has always had a very responsible nature, sometimes to his detriment."

"I'm sure, Mrs. Sullivan, that you have concerns about him bringing us here and taking advantage of his responsible nature, but I have feelers out in all directions for another rental home to become available—"

"Oh, my dear, I don't have any concerns at all. Quite the contrary! I was thrilled."

Amy's chin jerked back slightly. "Thrilled?"

"Liam checks in with me almost every day, which I hope doesn't make him look like a mama's boy. But that's part of his responsible nature, even though he has five siblings that check on me also." She laughed and shook her head. "Some days, I wish my children would stop calling, and I might get something done."

Her lips twitched at Carolyn's profession of wishing her children left her alone when it was obvious by the affection in her voice how glad she was that they were there for her.

"I know that Liam has told you of his father's death

and how it affected him. He was only thirteen and took so much on himself. I'm afraid I wasn't aware initially. There wasn't much in the way of insurance, so I went back to work, and Liam took on the burden of helping to raise his five siblings. He became the man of the house, taking on responsibilities far above what he should have. I'm embarrassed to say I didn't realize how much burden he'd taken off my shoulders until it had become ingrained in him."

"Mrs. Sullivan, I've only known Liam for a very short while, but I think I can truthfully say he has no regrets. Life experiences change all of us, and I know he'd hate for you to think you were anything other than the best mother."

Carolyn's eyes sparkled as she blinked furiously for a moment. "Oh, my dear, that is such a lovely thing for you to say. And please, call me Carolyn."

Nodding, she allowed herself to relax ever so slightly. Clearing her throat, she said, "I know that Liam stopped to check out what was happening during the storm because that was his duty. And I'm completely aware that his insisting on Rosie and me coming to his home was a huge step away from that professional duty. She and I appreciated it more than you can imagine. I do feel like it's a rather auspicious way to start my life here on the Shore. I hate for everyone to assume we're taking advantage of his kind heart."

Once more surprising her, Carolyn burst out into laughter. "I assure you, Amy, that my son does take his professional responsibilities very seriously. But if he'd had any doubts about you at all, he would never have brought you to his home. He would have taken you to an emergency shelter even if that meant he was going to have to stay the night himself. Oh, no. The fact that he brought you here meant he already trusted you."

"But we'd just met!"

"My eldest is an excellent judge of character. That's why I didn't worry when he told me that you were here. Now, as to why you are still here..." Her eyes twinkled before she finished her thought. "That tells me that he wants you here. I'd suggested that you and Rosie come live with me."

Amy's mouth opened but no words came forth, something that Carolyn had no problem with.

"I told him that I have a big house and was around and would make sure that you and Rosie were fine. But he insisted that he wanted the two of you to stay here." She leaned forward, her eyes still twinkling. "And that definitely told me that he wants the two of you." Settling back against the sofa cushions, she looked like a cat with a bowl of cream. "So, I wanted to see with my own eyes who this beautiful woman and sweet child were that have enraptured my son."

Glancing down at her eight-month pregnant belly, Amy snorted. "I'm not sure enraptured is the right word, Carolyn."

"Oh, my dear. Enraptured is exactly the right word."

Just then, a little sound was heard on the stairs, and the two women turned their heads to see Rosie peeking around the corner, eyes wide on their visitor.

"You must be the adorable Rosie!" Carolyn's smile widened even more. "I'm Liam's mom, and he's told me so much about this sweet little girl that's in his house. I just had to come to meet her for myself!"

Rosie looked toward Amy, who smiled and nodded. "Come on in, sweetheart. Did you have a good nap?" Rosie skipped into the room, climbing up on Amy's lap, Bubbie clutched in her hand, her gaze never leaving Carolyn's face.

She leaned up and whispered, "Is she mean, too?"

Blushing, knowing that Carolyn could hear Rosie's question, she shook her head. "No, Liam's mom is very nice."

"Was someone mean to you, sweetheart?" Carolyn asked.

"We had a visitor yesterday. I don't think she was very happy to find us here."

Carolyn rolled her eyes and nodded. "Well, I can only imagine that most of the casserole committee has already discovered that he's off the market. But for someone to be *mean,* I can also assume that was Rachel." She shook her head, her nose scrunched as though she was smelling something unpleasant. "Good riddance to bad rubbish, I say."

A giggle slipped from Amy's mouth, joined by Rosie, who had no idea what she was laughing at. Rosie, feeling more at ease, climbed from Amy's lap and sat on the floor, playing. Amy's gaze stayed lovingly on her daughter, finally looking back up toward Carolyn.

The two women chatted for several more minutes,

Carolyn not seeming at all concerned that others might think Liam was off the market. Every time she tried to mention that she was looking for a place to live, Carolyn's hand waved dismissively as though she'd be wasting her time.

"You'll have to meet my middle daughter, Sue. She's pregnant as well but has two more months to go. Also, my Ellen is dying to meet you. She's my oldest girl and has two children. Her youngest should be about the same age as Rosie. I know you'd already looked into the area when you decided to move here, but please, take advantage of all the people here that want to help. I know you're friends with Tori and met some of her posse this morning. Definitely come to the next Auxiliary meeting, and I'll have a big Sunday dinner at my house at the end of the month."

Carolyn stood, and Amy followed suit, walking her to the door. By now, she wasn't surprised when Carolyn wrapped her in a hug, then held her hands as she leaned back. "You are very welcome here, Amy. Not just to the Eastern Shore, but with my family as well. If you need anything, give me a call."

Waving as Carolyn left, she realized that between her morning visitors and the entire family's cell phone numbers that Carolyn left, she'd gained a huge number of local contacts. *And friends.*

She looked down at Rosie working on her new puzzle. "Sweetie, Mommy needs to make a phone call while you play a few more minutes. Okay?" Gaining Rosie's distracted nod, she moved back over to her laptop, pulling out her phone, calling her boss.

"Mike? It's Amy. I had a question about the latest transcriptions that you sent to me. You said that Dr. Malcolm has only been using your company for several months?"

"That's right. It's my understanding that he used to have the hospital transcriptionist handle everything. He hired us about six months ago to do all of his record transcribing when his telemedical business began."

"And am I the only person that has been assigned to him?

"Yeah. When you cut back your hours, it made sense to give you just one account. What's going on? Is there a problem?"

"No, no. There were just a few things that didn't make a lot of sense, and I was trying to get a feel for his medical practice. I've come to realize he does a lot of telemedicine, so I was just trying to figure out some of his needs." Her lower back was beginning to ache, and she squirmed in her seat. "That was all, Mike. Just a few things about his practice that made me curious, so I thought I'd check."

"Well, let me know when you go on maternity leave, and I can send his records to someone else."

Saying goodbye quickly, she disconnected, grimacing as the pain intensified. Pushing up and standing, she glanced down at her belly, the baby pressing on her bladder. Walking to the bathroom, she rubbed her belly. "Peanut, I wish you'd settle down until I can get moved into a house."

Finishing in the bathroom, she washed her hands and walked out to see Rosie still playing. "Hey, girl. How would you like to make some cookies before Liam comes home this evening?"

Rose's reply was to throw her arms into the air, run around in a circle, then head straight into the kitchen. Laughing, Amy followed, her hands still rubbing her back.

18

DR. JAMES MALCOLM'S OFFICE

"Dr. Malcolm?"

He looked up and smiled, seeing his efficient records office manager at his doorway. "Benita, come in, come in. What do you need?"

"I have several forms for you to sign."

He quickly dispatched with the signatures. Looking up when she continued to stand, he lifted his brow. "Anything more?"

"Well, I received your transcriptions back from the company and entered them into our digital records, but there was one that didn't come back. When I went to look for it, I didn't have any record of sending something else. I assume you must have sent one yourself and wanted to know if you needed me to enter that record if the transcription came back to your email address."

He shook his head slowly, confusion filling him. "I don't recall sending anything… but I'll check. I'll let you know if I need you to enter a record."

"Excellent, Dr. Malcolm. I'm leaving now, so you have a nice evening."

Wishing her the same, he turned to his computer, trying to discern what record he could have sent to the transcription company. He remembered when Benita was out last week for two days, and he forwarded the records to be transcribed by the company he used. *But what extra record could Benita be referring to?*

The company offered a secure portal for the sending and receiving of confidential patient records. Finding the date in question, he glanced through the list of what he'd sent. One without a patient name caught his eye, and he clicked on it, allowing him to listen to his dictation. With each passing second, his heart threatened to beat out of his chest as he heard his voice give instructions to his partner, ending with, "Nathan, make sure you duplicate patient names. Change birth date and prescription. Charge both. File under Medicare, as usual. Same for Johnson and Trabelle."

Swallowing with difficulty, he tried to steady his breathing. *How the hell did I send the phone recording?* In slow motion, those moments came to the forefront of his memory. The dictation machine on. His partner, Nathan, at the supply store calling.

His mind raced as he tried to figure out a way to fix the complete fuck up. Moving back to the transcriptions, all he could determine was Amy C. is who always received his records. *But she didn't send it back. Why not? Is she suspicious?*

Picking up his phone, he called the transcription

company. "Mike? Hello, it's Dr. James Malcolm. I had a question about my transcriber, Amy C."

"What a coincidence. She was asking about you today, too."

His heart dropped. "Oh, really. Did she say why?"

"No. She wanted a better understanding of your telemedical business, I think. But you're very lucky. Not only is she one of our best transcribers, she lives near you."

Trying to steady his voice, he focused on breathing. "Oh, that is interesting. Is there a way I can find out her name?"

"Only if she agrees. Our transcribers are protected by our company. But I'll let her know you're interested in meeting with her."

"Oh, no, that won't be necessary. I just wanted to check over something with her, but I'll have my office manager do that. Thank you." Disconnecting, he leaned back in his chair, his mind still racing. *Did she listen to it? Did she attempt to transcribe since it wasn't attached to a patient record? And she lives near here?* He couldn't believe the odds of that considering his account could have gone to any transcriber in the country.

Picking up the phone again, he called his partner. "Nathan? I need you to do something for me. See if you can find a resident in the area whose first name is Amy and their last name begins with a C."

"Are you serious? Is it a patient? Client?"

"No, neither, but you're better at this sort of thing."

"What the hell is wrong, James?"

"No, no, nothing's wrong. I just need to locate this

person as soon as possible. They might have an idea of things we don't want them to know."

"Goddamnit! Okay, fine. And when I find them, then what?"

"We might need your nephews to pay her a visit."

"If you've done something to jeopardize what we have—"

"Don't threaten me, Nathan. We're in this together. So, protect what's ours and find that woman!"

19

Liam woke suddenly, blinking in the dark of the night, trying to figure out what jarred him from sleep. Swinging his legs over the side of the bed, he sat for a moment. Hearing a moan coming from across the hall, he leaped forward, throwing open his door and racing into Amy's room, not bothering to knock.

Her bed was rumpled, the sheets on one side thrown back, and he could clearly see Rosie's sleeping form on her side from the light emanating from the bathroom. With the door already open, he hurried inside, seeing Amy gripping the edge of the vanity counter between the double sinks. Her pale face was contorted in a grimace as her eyes sought his in the mirror.

"Thought it… was just… a… backache," she panted, standing in a puddle.

"Christ, what's wrong?"

"It's… time."

"Time?"

"Time, Liam. Peanut… time."

"Now? Shit, Amy… it's too early!" Her face contorted again, and he lifted his hands toward her, desperate to assist but clueless. "I don't know what you need!" Before she could answer, he barked, "Hospital! I need to get you to the hospital!"

"Rosie… I need someone—"

"Mom! I'll call Mom!" Not waiting to see if that was okay with Amy, he raced back through her bedroom and into his, grabbing his phone from the nightstand.

A cry coming from Amy sent him flying back across the hall. She was kneeling on the bathroom floor. "There's no time to get to the hospital," she said between groans.

"Oh, fuck!" he growled, dropping to the floor next to her. Dialing 9-1-1, he quickly gave his location and need to the operator. "Can't stay on the line." Disconnecting, he called his mom, letting her know what was happening, gaining her assurance that she would be there in fifteen minutes. "And Mom, call Corby!"

He'd just disconnected when the dispatcher called back, wanting an update while giving him the ETA for the ambulance.

"Sheriff Sullivan, this is Roberta. Tell me what's going on."

"Amy… the woman that's staying with me, has gone into labor."

"Okay, the ambulance is about twelve minutes away."

"Roberta, I don't know if that's enough time."

"Okay, stay calm. Are you in your house?"

"Yes, we're upstairs in the bathroom."

"Can she get to a bed?"

"Let me see." Shoving the phone into his pocket, he leaned over to be directly in her face. "Amy, honey, let's get off the bathroom floor." When she didn't object, he slid one arm under her back and the other under her knees and stood. Obviously, her bed with Rosie wasn't the right choice, and eschewing the other guest room, he stalked back into his room, laying her on his bed. Pulling the phone back out, he said, "I've got her on a bed."

Following more instructions, he grabbed pillows and placed them under her knees, raced to his linen closet and slid extra towels and sheets underneath her, and worked her panties off. *Less than nine minutes until the ambulance gets here, we can do this.*

Suddenly, she raised up, her face red and contorted, her hand reaching out and latching onto his, squeezing tightly. He held on, ignoring the pain in his fingers. An animalistic noise came from deep within her throat, and he looked down between her open legs, seeing the crown of the baby's head. Gasping, he put the phone on speaker. "Oh, my God, I can see the top of the head!"

"Sheriff, tell her to keep breathing. And while you're at it, you keep breathing, too."

The operator kept asking questions, and he fired back the answers as quickly as he could, asking Amy for the answers he didn't know, passing along her grunted responses. Second pregnancy. The first delivery was normal. Thirty-six weeks pregnant. Twenty-eight years old.

Another primal growl erupted, and she began to

push. The head partially moved out, then seemed to go back in. Describing what he saw, the operator assured him it was normal, but his heart was pounding so hard he barely heard her.

"Amy, honey, keep breathing. She says you gotta keep breathing."

Her eyes popped open, holding his, fire shooting from them. "Don't tell me to fuckin' breathe!"

Sucking in a deep breath, he let it out slowly, rubbing her leg gently. "Come on, Amy. You're doing great." Glancing at the clock, he knew the ambulance should be there in about six minutes. *Christ, Almighty, hurry the fuck up!*

Another scream from her lips, and he saw the head come out toward his hands. With sweat dripping down his face, he gasped to the dispatcher, "Head is out, but, oh… Christ, it's purple!" Amy's fingers clutched the sheets, her knuckles white, and her wide-eyed, desperate stare causing his heart to stumble.

"Liam, calm down," the operator said. "Support the baby's head, and don't worry about it being purple, that's normal. Have her keep breathing because there will be more contractions."

"It looks stuck. Should I pull?"

"No, absolutely not. Don't pull. Just support her and the baby. Let the shoulders ease out. Don't pull, just let the shoulders ease out with the next contraction."

Looking up at Amy, he tried to force a smile onto his face but knew his expression was probably frozen in fright. "Gotta breathe, sweetie, gotta breathe."

"I need to push!" she cried, gripping the sheets again as her upper body lifted, her abdomen tightening.

One shoulder slid out but then stopped. Reporting to the dispatcher, he continued to follow her instructions but could feel Amy's distress combining with his own.

"Mommy?"

He jerked his head around, seeing Rosie standing in her nightgown with Bubbie in her arms. Pulling the sheet up a little bit, he said, "Hey, Rosie girl. I need you to stay out there, okay?"

"What's wrong with Mommy?"

"She's getting ready to have the baby, and I need to help her until the doctors get here. My mom's coming in just a minute to play with you. You remember her, right? You just met her yesterday?"

Rosie nodded, and just then, he heard his mom's voice call out from downstairs, thanking God that she had a spare key. "Mom, we're upstairs. Please, come get Rosie!"

His mother must have flown up the stairs because she was there instantly. She smiled at Rosie before offering an encouraging smile to him. "Let's go downstairs with your sweet bunny and see what we can find to eat. Liam is going to take good care of your mommy and the doctors will be here in a few minutes, so we can stay out of their way."

He glanced back to the bed, seeing Amy trying so hard not to cry out through her next contraction, and knew she didn't want to scare Rosie. When Rosie slipped her little hand into his mom's and they moved out of sight, he could have wept with relief.

Right on cue, Amy cried out once again, clawing at the sheet as she tried to gain leverage. She pushed, her face red, hair slicked back, and mouth open in a silent scream.

"Oh, my God, there's the other shoulder!" He kept his eyes on the baby's upper body in his hands.

Amy kept pushing, and he cried out again, "I can see an arm!"

With the dispatcher's encouragement, his hands gently cradled as the baby slid the rest of the way out. Terrified of its purplish color, he wrapped it in a clean towel. His entire body began to shake as he carefully held the baby close, his breathing erratic as he peered down at the tiny miracle in his arms. "Oh, God, oh, God, it's a girl," he chanted.

Amy flopped back onto the bed, her chest heaving, her arms limp beside her body. The operator announced that the ambulance had arrived, but he barely heard anything over the pounding of his heart. Amy leaned up, soaked in sweat, her gown still bunched around her waist, and stretched out her arms. "My baby. Is she alright?"

"Hang on, Amy, they say I need to wipe the nose." Her eyes followed his every movement as he obeyed each instruction given to him. Her fingers began to fumble with the buttons at the top of her gown, and just before he placed the baby on her chest, he kissed the tiny head.

Noise came from the stairs and the rescue members

rushed into the room. Looking up, he spied Corby leading the crew. His brother's gaze hit the bed with Amy cradling the baby and then over to Liam's bloodied hands, and he smiled.

"Damn, bro, you did all the work for us."

Shaking his head, unable to speak, he looked down at Amy as she cooed and nuzzled the tiny baby before lifting her tear-filled eyes to him. Letting out a heavy breath with his gaze still pinned on her, he shook his head. "No, she did it… Amy did all the work. She's amazing. Amazing."

Amy lay in the hospital bed, cradling the baby. Once they'd arrived at the hospital with Liam following in his Sheriff's SUV right behind the rescue squad with his lights flashing, she'd been whisked away to the maternity ward where she and the baby were checked out and declared healthy. She'd spent time checking all the fingers and toes, memorizing each nuance of her daughter's perfect face. She glanced to the side as Liam walked back into the room, pink balloons in one hand, pink roses in the other, and a bag dangling from his arm that she hoped contained a hamburger and french fries.

He walked straight to the bed, bent, and kissed her cheek, whispering, "Hey."

Smiling, she whispered in return. "Hey, back."

"How're my girls?"

My girls. She couldn't begin to process how his term of endearment moved through her, warming every cell of her body. It had been a long time since she'd been anybody's *girl,* and even though she was afraid to put any meaning into his words, it was hard not to think how easy it would be to get used to that. Seeing him still staring, she was startled. "Sorry. My mind is wandering. We're good… perfect, thanks to you."

He turned and set the flowers and balloons on a stand next to the bed, and from the delectable scents emanating from within, the bag that she was now sure contained a hamburger and french fries was placed on the bed tray. He sat on the edge of the bed and leaned with both hands on either side of her hips, bending further to stare at the tiny face. "I was terrified. If there are any thanks to give out, it's got to be to you who did what you needed to do and to Roberta, the 9-1-1 operator who talked me through it all."

"Don't diminish what you did, Liam. Just knowing you were there helped get me through. How's Rosie?"

"She's with my mom. They'll come by in just a little while." His finger traced gently over the baby's cheek. "What did you name her?"

The heat of a slight blush moved over her face. "Desiree. That was my other grandmother's name. So both girls are named after their grandmothers, Rose and Desiree. And her middle name is Leanne… after you."

She watched him startle, his eyes widening as they moved between her face and the baby and then back to her again. Feeling self-conscious, she rushed, "Please, don't think anything about it other than I just wanted her to be named for the person who delivered her, but it doesn't imply— "

Her words were stifled as he placed his finger over her lips. "Shh, Amy. You're ruining my moment."

"You're having a moment?" she mumbled underneath his finger.

"Oh, yeah. You named this beautiful miracle after me. You better believe I'm having a moment."

"I was afraid you would think I was pushing for… well, that I was—"

"Nope. I think it's perfect. Just as perfect as she is."

Peace descended, and they held each other's gazes until her stomach growled. Chuckling, he said, "I'll set your hamburger out." He organized the tray and rolled it closer, then stopped, an uncertain expression on his face.

"Here, you take her."

"What?"

She giggled at the squeak in his voice. "Liam, you held her when she came out. You can surely hold her now."

His large hand came forward, gently taking Desiree from her arms. He stepped to the side while she pulled the tray over and devoured her hamburger, fries, and soda. Just as she finished, a noise at the door caught her attention.

"Mommy…" Rosie's bright eyes told how hard it was for her to whisper, but she held onto Carolyn's hand as they came into the room.

She opened her arms and let Rosie climb up onto the bed, holding her close. "Oh, baby girl, I missed you."

"I was scared, but Miss Carolyn said I had a new sister." Rosie looked over at Liam. "Is that her?"

As Amy glanced up, she caught Carolyn staring at Liam holding Desiree, and the smile on his mother's face caused her breath to halt in her throat. The heartache that her mother would never see her grandchildren gripped her in a vise. But then, Carolyn's smile gave evidence that she loved seeing her son holding a baby. Refusing to consider whether Carolyn would feel the same if he was holding just any baby or perhaps just hers, she watched as Rosie slid down from the bed and made a beeline to him, cooing over Desiree as well.

Liam knelt so Rosie could kiss Desiree before he walked over and placed her back into Amy's arms. Then he lifted Rosie back onto the bed, making sure she was settled close to Amy and Desiree but giving them plenty of room. With both her girls in her arms, a tear slid down Amy's face, caught by him as he reached over and wiped her cheek.

"Don't cry, Amy," he whispered. "You've got the whole world in your arms right now."

Swallowing deeply, she nodded, then blew out a big breath trying to regain control of her emotions. "Don't say things like that if you don't want me to cry."

His reply was to simply grin. "Are you still being discharged tomorrow?"

Nerves slid over her as she wondered what she would do; no home, no nursery set up. Nodding, she said, "Yes. Tomorrow morning. Tori said she would check with me later today and I thought that—"

"Stop thinking."

Blinking, she jerked her chin back. "What?"

"Your job is to take care of Desiree right now. You'll come home tomorrow, and we have lots of time to figure things out."

"But—"

The look on his face quelled further discussion, and since she didn't want to upset Rosie, she just nodded.

"Good. Now, this girl and I have a date to get an I'm-a-big-sister milkshake."

Rosie looked up, her eyes bright. "Yeah, Mom, Mr. Liam says now that I'm a big sister, I should have a treat like a milkshake."

"Oh, he did, did he?" She leaned over and kissed her daughter—her *oldest* daughter—and grinned. "Desiree and I will leave the hospital tomorrow, but for the rest of the day and night, you need to be on your best behavior for Liam and Miss Carolyn, okay?"

Rosie rolled her eyes. "Mommy, I'm always the best."

"Hang on, we've got to get some pictures." Carolyn pulled out her phone and began snapping pictures. "Come on, Liam, get in there, too," she ordered.

He lifted Rosie and put her in his lap, sat down next to Amy, and the four cuddled close, huge smiles for the camera. Finally, he stood and set Rosie off the bed. Bending, he kissed Amy's cheek before barely touching his lips to Desiree's forehead, whispering, "I'll see you tomorrow." With Rosie's hand clutched in his, he started walking out the door.

Clutching Desiree tighter as uncertainty about the future moved over her, she watched Carolyn squeeze Liam's arm, saying, "You know, son, with you sitting on the bed with those three wonderful females, you had the whole world in your arms right then, too."

Before she had a chance to ponder those words, Desiree began scrunching her nose, her rosebud lips pouting. Smiling, she kissed her daughter before bringing her to her breast.

20

Liam couldn't remember the last time he'd had so many people in his house at one time. *Oh, yeah... never!*

His sisters, Ellen, Sue, and Marie, and his sisters-in-law, Gina and Vicki, were there with his brothers, Lenny and Corby, plus his brothers-in-law, Joe, Bill, and Saul. That alone would have made his house full to bursting. But with their combined seven kids running in and out of the yard, that made it even crazier. Thank God Carrie and Colt showed up with their pre-teen son who agreed to ride herd over the younger kids, managing to keep them outside most of the time.

Tori brought part of her girl-gang of Jillian, Belle, Maddie, Katelyn, Sophia, and Jade with her to make sure the kitchen was well stocked and there were plenty of diapers. In fact, he wasn't sure if Walmart had any more diapers left on their shelves because of the multitude of diaper boxes piled in his guestroom closet.

But that wasn't all. It seemed everyone he knew assumed he'd have no idea how to set up a nursery.

Mitch, Grant, Hunter, Hannah, and Dylan, plus more from the American Legion, showed up to put together a crib and a changing table and bring in a rocking chair with a leg-thingie that was supposed to be good for the mother while nursing. More items were brought in, put together, or stored.

Tori walked over and handed him a bag, pulling out what looked like a tiny, pink T-shirt covered in yellow ducks with snaps at the bottom. "Here are a bunch of onesies. More are coming."

Onesies... so that's what these look like. Christ, it's so little.

Finally, Aiden and Brogan MacFarlane, co-owners of the pub, showed up with coolers of beer, sodas, and water. Their wives, Lia and Ginny, provided the cups and ice. Food and drinks flowed for all the helpers.

By the time evening descended, everyone said their goodbyes, all stopping to talk to Liam and offer to bring more food anytime he needed it. His mother was staying the night to be with Rosie and had already gone upstairs to bathe the overexcited-but-tired little girl.

Mitch and Colt offered their hands. "You okay with everything?" Colt asked.

Overwhelmed, he had no idea what to say, so he simply nodded.

Colt grinned. "It hits when you least expect it. But life's coming at you fast, so hang on. But man, I gotta tell you, the ride is worth it." With that, he, Carrie, and their sons piled into their SUV and pulled down the driveway.

Tori stepped up, kissing Liam on the cheek. "Amy is

strong. She's been through a lot. But, as Colt said, life has come at her hard and fast. I'm glad you've got her back so she's not facing this alone."

He smiled at that. "I think she and I have each other's backs."

Mitch laughed. "Good, that's the way it should be." They left in their SUV after gathering their son.

Now, Wyatt was the only one left. He stood on the porch and held Liam's gaze. "Man, I can't say I have any words of wisdom. Part of me wants to ask if you have any clue what you're doing. The other part wants to ask if you're crazy."

He laughed, shaking his head. "Hell, I have no clue what I'm doing, and I'm probably crazy. But then, I've come to realize that not everything in life has to be planned or has to fit in a perfect box. Sometimes life just is."

"Well, when I see your face, I know whatever is going on with you and Amy, you seem okay with it all." He clapped him on the back and grinned. "Damn, I think I've just lost my wingman."

"Shit, like you ever needed anyone to help you out with women."

Chuckling, Wyatt started down the front steps. "Who knows? Maybe one day, someone will land in my tiny-ass town needing help and knock me on my ass, too."

With a wave, Liam turned and walked back into his house. Almost afraid to look, he should have known it was left perfect. The food had been put away, the nursery in the second guest bedroom had been set up, and his living room and the kitchen were clean. But with Rosie's toys in the corner and Amy's laptop still on the table, it looked more lived-in than when he had been by himself. *Was that only a week ago?*

His mom called him to come upstairs. Once there, he found a clean, smiling-but-yawning Rosie looking adorable in her nightgown covered in Disney Princesses.

"I want you to read," she announced, climbing into her side of the bed. Once under the covers, her face scrunched as she stared at the empty side where her mother would have slept. Looking up at Liam, she asked, "I can't sleep in this big bed by myself all night long. Will you sleep with me?"

He leaned back against the pillows, his legs stretched out on top of the covers. "I'm sorry, Rosie, but I can't do that."

"But why not?"

"Well, sweetheart, I'm just a friend. I'm not your daddy, so it wouldn't be right for me to sleep in here with you."

"But you could be my daddy." The words fell easily from Rosie's mouth, and she looked up at him through wide, blue eyes so similar to her mother's. Uncertain what to say to an almost-four-year-old that they'd understand, he was saved when his mom stepped into the room.

"I'm going to stay with you tonight, Rosie. It'll be like a sleepover."

Liam looked down, wondering how Rosie would take that compromise. Gratefully, she seemed to be excited about the prospect. With a big grin on her face, she snuggled down under the covers further. As tired as she was, he only made it through one book before she was fast asleep. Pulling the covers up tight around her ears, he bent and kissed her cheek lightly, the scent of her little girl shampoo already so familiar to him. Slipping from the bed, he turned out the light, leaving the nightlight on and the door open, and followed his mother downstairs.

He wasn't surprised when she made two cups of cocoa and they settled in the living room. Sipping the warm, comforting drink, his mind was filled with Amy. He missed that she wasn't sitting in the room with him.

"It's been quite a day," Carolyn said, interrupting his thoughts.

Snorting, he nodded. "I'd say that's an understatement, Mom."

"You were amazing, Liam. To deliver a baby with only an emergency operator to help you." She chuckled. "I certainly can't see your father doing anything like that."

The image of his dad having to assist with a birth struck him funny as well. As their mirth slowed, he said, "I couldn't believe what a trooper she was. I mean, I know she was probably scared out of her mind, but Amy was great."

"I'd say the two of you make a good team."

His chin jerked back, her words sounding right, and yet... *How can we be a team when we've known each other barely a week?*

Proving her mother's intuition about his tumultuous

feelings, she set her cup down and held his gaze. "Liam, after your father died, you took responsibility to a heightened level. I blame myself for that while thanking you all at the same time. But since then, you've always liked to put things in a neat mental box. Your family. Your time in the Army. Your career. And even your home and personal life. But, Liam, love is an emotion that defies logic. Love doesn't fit into a neat box. Sometimes it's messy, and crazy, and out of control."

"I understand that, Mom, but how can what I feel be love? I've known Amy for less than a week."

"How long do you have to know someone before you can tell you're in love? Is there a specific amount of time? I've known people who dated for years before they got married, some of them ending in divorce. And other people can know right away. Take your father and me, for example."

"You and dad?"

Laughing, she settled back against the sofa cushions. "I suppose I've told the girls, but you and your brothers never cared much about love stories. Your father was working over on the Barker farm when he graduated from high school, and after a few years, he moved up to be one of their supervisors in charge of getting some of the produce packed up for the local groceries. My family had just moved down from Maryland, and I got a job at the Food King store to earn a little money. I just happened to be taking my break and was in the back when a delivery truck pulled up. One of the men who climbed down from the truck looked over, and no lie, I was struck there on the spot. Tall, dark-haired, handsome. I think I stood there with my mouth hanging open like I'd been struck dumb. And then he smiled, and I was a goner. I barely remember anything after that, but your dad always said that I smiled back at him, and he felt like he'd been hit by lightning. That was it, Liam. People can say they don't believe in love at first sight, but just because they haven't experienced it doesn't mean it's not real for others." She leaned forward and picked up her mug from the coffee table, continuing to sip her cocoa. "Now I'm not saying that you and Amy are in love or soulmates. That's not for me to know or say. But I know you, son. And there is very definitely something between you and those two… well, now three beautiful females. I think you'd do anything to protect them if you thought Amy, Desiree, or sweet Rosie were in trouble, and that's not just your sense of responsibility."

Those words slammed into him; the idea of something threatening any of them made his chest depress as air rushed from his lungs. He knew in that instant that he'd fight to the death to protect them because of the feelings he had inside that had nothing to do with honor or duty or responsibility.

"What if she doesn't feel the same?" As the words left his mouth, his gut seized at the thought that she'd want to leave as soon as a rental house became available.

"You'll never know if you don't talk to her." Standing, his mom led the way into the kitchen where they stood next to each other, rinsing out the cups. Turning, she lifted her brow and pinned him with a hard stare. "But take my advice, Liam. When you talk to her, don't try to convince her that her staying here fits into anyone's idea of a neat box. Tell her what's in here." She lifted her hand and tapped his chest, directly over his heart.

"Now, I'll say good night because I've got a sweet little Rosie asleep upstairs, and I don't want her to be frightened if she wakes up alone."

Wrapping his arms around her, he pulled his mother in for a hug. Her strength and wisdom awed him, and another thought flashed through his mind as he kissed her cheek. *I hope I have the same strength and wisdom to pass on to Rosie and Desiree.*

21

Amy peered out the window as Liam turned onto his street. Desiree had slept in her car seat the whole twenty-minute drive from the hospital. Anxiety pierced her happiness. Anxious to see Rosie, who had stayed at Liam's home with Carolyn when Liam came to pick them up. Anxious about bringing a newborn to a place that wasn't ready for a newborn. Anxious that she didn't have permanent housing. Anxious—

"Stop worrying."

His words cut into her thoughts. Sucking in her lips, she glanced to the side at him. Liam had arrived early that morning to the hospital, his smile infectious as he tiptoed over to her, kissed her cheek, and then bent to touch his lips softly to Desiree's forehead. Amy had already showered while the hospital staff had Desiree, giving her a going-home checkup. She'd pulled her wet hair back into a braid and dressed in the only thing she had—stretchy maternity pants and a big, slouchy T-shirt. She had been so glad to see him, and her heart warmed at the way he reverently held Desiree in his arms as he stood rocking her gently, cooing to her while Amy had received her discharge paperwork.

Now, her anxiety had her wanting to scream that her life was spinning out of control and she had no idea how to make it slow down.

"Liam, I can't help but worry. I can't believe that she came early before I had a chance to get things taken care of."

"Don't worry about what might have happened or what happened that's already passed. Don't worry about what isn't under your control."

Snorting, she glanced back at Desiree to ensure she was still sleeping. "Since when did you turn into Sheriff Guru?"

He chuckled, and like her, glanced into the rearview mirror to ensure his noise didn't wake Desiree.

"Did you get the portable crib from the back of my trailer? And the sheets? And I think Tori said that—"

"Stop. I took care of everything." Pulling into his drive, he turned his head toward her and said, "Honestly, Amy. You and Desiree are safe and healthy. You've got a place to stay. It's going to be fine."

Before she had a chance to refute his definition of 'fine', Rosie bolted through the front door, jumping up and down on the porch with Carolyn right behind her, smiling widely. A whimper left her mouth as tears filled her eyes. "Oh, I missed her."

"Come on, sweetheart. Let's get you two inside."

As Liam walked around to open her door, she

shoved aside how nice it was to be called 'sweetheart.' *A common endearment, that's all. Just like what he would call Rosie or Desiree.*

He assisted her down, then turned to catch Rosie before she launched herself at her mom. "Easy, Rosie girl. Hug your mom gently, and I'll get your sister out."

Amy wrapped her arms around Rosie, welcoming the familiar feel of her daughter's body pressed against hers and the scent of her shampoo. Looking over Rosie's head, she smiled at Carolyn, hoping the older woman could feel her gratitude.

Liam stepped over to them, his arms full of the carrier, Desiree still sound asleep. "Let's get you ladies, inside."

Rosie was still jumping up and down but it was obvious she was trying to contain her excitement. "Mom," she whispered, "you're going to be so surprised!"

Amy wasn't sure she could take any more surprises but smiled and followed Rosie and Carolyn inside. Entering the house, she could see the living room looked the same, and yet, with Rosie's toys and coloring books on the coffee table, she felt the pang of self-consciousness that they were still encroaching on Liam's house. Then her gaze landed on the baby swing set up in the corner along with a small diaper changing station.

"See! You don't have to go upstairs to put a new diaper on Desiree!" Rosie practically crowed then softened her voice as Desiree stirred.

"Oh..." Words fled Amy at the nice gesture, but

before she could express her gratitude, Rosie pulled on her hand.

"You gotta come upstairs, Mommy!"

She felt sure that Liam had placed the portable crib in the bedroom that she was sharing with Rosie to keep them all together and to keep them from taking over too much of his house. He set the carrier on the sofa and Carolyn bent, immediately cooing.

Liam turned toward Amy, sweeping his hand out. "Lead the way, darlin's,"

She rolled her eyes at his increased endearments but followed Rosie up the stairs, aware that he was right behind her. At the top of the stairs, Rosie bypassed the room they were staying in and raced to the second guest bedroom. "Mommy, look!"

Brow furrowed, she glanced back at Liam to see him grinning as widely as Rosie, and yet, she could swear a nervous specter moved through his eyes. Stepping into the second guest room, her feet stumbled to a halt as her gaze swept over the refurbished room.

The top of the dresser had been repurposed into a beautiful changing table. Open shelves next to it housed diapers, a basket filled with various creams and lotions, and a baby wipe warmer sitting on top. The bed, which had extended out into the middle of the room, was now moved to the corner, allowing more floor space. A glider rocking chair and matching ottoman now sat in the other corner with a beautiful end table and lamp next to them. The bed was now covered with a multi-colored pastel bedspread with various pillows against the wall so that it could be used as a comfortable sofa as well as a bed. Topping it were several stuffed animals.

And opposite the bed was an oak crib, completely set up with soft yellow sheets covering the mattress.

Mouth open, Amy barely had time to take in everything before Rosie was pulling open the dresser drawers, squealing, "Look! Look! Desiree's got clothes!"

Her body began to shake as her fingers snapped up to press against her lips. Liam's hands landed on her shoulders as he pulled her back to his front, offering his steady body to help hold her upright. He bent, his breath warm against her ear. "I hope it's okay, Amy. Everybody came yesterday and helped. All my siblings and their spouses. Mitch and Tori. Colt and Carrie. All my friends and more from the American Legion."

"Mommy, the house was full! I had friends to play with."

The idea that Liam's quiet home had descended into chaos with so many people caused her chest to deflate. She turned, but his arms wrapped around her, holding her close as she faced him. "Liam, I don't know what to say. We've turned your life upside down and—"

"Yeah, you have," he chuckled.

She closed her eyes slowly, not wanting to see the frustration that must surely be on his face. His arms jiggled her slightly. "Amy," he whispered, his forehead almost touching hers.

Forcing her eyes open, she knew she had to face whatever he wanted to dish out.

"Do you not like it?"

She jerked slightly, her eyes widening. "What?"

"Do you not like it? I let Tori and the others decide how best to fix the room, but we can change it any way you want. Different colors, different furniture, different lights, different—"

Her hands landed on his shoulders, her fingers digging in slightly. "Oh, no, Liam, it's beautiful. It's perfect. I couldn't have even imagined a nursery this beautiful."

"Then what's wrong?"

"Rosie and I, and now Desiree, have barreled into your life and turned it upside down. And now you've changed part of your house to accommodate us. It's too much, and I don't want you to start resenting us or having regrets."

"It's true, my life has changed in the past week. Changes aren't always bad, Amy. Change can be necessary, and good, and right. That's how I feel about this. And that's how I feel about the three of you here. It's just right. At least, it feels that way to me, and I can only hope it feels that way to you, too."

She dragged her gaze away from his handsome face, once again taking in the room before looking down at Rosie's wide-eyed, expectant expression. Sucking in her lips to quell the giggle that threatened to erupt, she looked back at him. "Yes, this feels right. It feels amazing. And I promise, that as soon as we're able and something becomes available, we'll get moved into our own place."

His jaw tightened slightly as he said, "No rush." As

Rosie squeezed in between them, he bent and picked her up before snaking one arm around Amy and pulling them both in tight. Before she had time to revel in how nice that felt, she heard a cry from downstairs.

"I've got to feed Desiree," she said, pulling back.

As she walked downstairs with Rosie's hand in Liam's, she heard her daughter say, "I love this home!"

She winced, hating how Rosie was going to be so disappointed when they had to leave. *She won't be the only one!*

Two days.

Liam had taken two days off work just so he could be at home with them. As Amy stood at the living room window with Rosie, waving as he drove off, she still couldn't believe it. *That was more time than Marty had taken off when she'd had Rosie.* In the past two days, Liam had changed diapers and held Desiree after a feeding, slowly rubbing his hand over her back until she burped. He'd played with Rosie to keep her occupied so that Amy could take a nap when Desiree was sleeping. She knew he'd stepped out of his comfort zone, and yet, when she watched him performing these tasks, he seemed to do them with ease.

Desiree was sleeping after her morning feeding, and Amy spent some time curled up with Rosie as they read books and colored together. There had been no more discussion of her finding a place to live, and Liam had brushed aside any of her thanks for what he'd done for them.

"I'm glad we have a home with Mr. Liam."

Startled at how her mind had drifted, she glanced down to see Rosie staring up at her. "Oh, sweetie, I know you like it here, but this isn't our home. This is Mr. Liam's home, and we're staying here for a while until we can find our own place to live." Confusion passed over Rosie's face, and Amy hated that the situation was becoming muddled in her daughter's mind.

"But he loves us. He wants us to live here."

"I know he cares for us very much," she agreed. "And we'll still be very close when we find our place. I'm sure we can see him often."

"But I want him to be my daddy."

Closing her eyes, she dropped her chin for just a moment as Rosie's words speared her heart. She wanted to give her daughter everything but had no idea how to give her what had been taken away when Marty died. Once more, she felt inadequate and was so tired of that emotion. Sucking in a deep breath, she reached over and cupped Rosie's cheek. "I'm afraid it doesn't work that way, baby. But that's not something you need to worry about right now. You just need to be happy that you've got a mommy and a sister and friends who love you."

Later that afternoon, a knock on the door woke her from her nap. She swiped her hand over her hair and stood for a few seconds blinking as she pinched her cheeks to help wake up. Opening the door, she was surprised to see two older women standing on the porch, each holding what looked like a casserole dish.

"You must be Amy," one of them pronounced, her face not glaring but neither welcoming.

"Um… yes. Can I help you?"

"I'm Mrs. Traynor. I thought the Sheriff would be interested in my niece but it seems the rumors are correct, and he's off the market."

"Um… I'm not sure…"

"I'd thought my daughter had a chance but guess not. I'm Mrs. Mack, by the way. We wanted to stop by and see for ourselves if you really were staying here."

"Yes, but—"

"Of course," Mrs. Mack plowed on. "He's got a hero complex if you ask me. Always taking responsibility for others… feels an obligation."

"I agree," Mrs. Traynor joined in. "But then, she's got a baby with her. That's a lot for him to take in."

Wondering if she was going to be part of their conversation or was just the spectator in their dissection of her and Liam, their attention was diverted by three vehicles pulling into the drive and parking outside.

Carolyn climbed out, and with her were three women that, with their chestnut hair, green eyes, and ready smiles, could only be Liam's sisters. Their gazes quickly took in the scene, and without any hesitation, the quartet climbed the steps to the house, pushed past the two visitors, and entered, Carolyn stopping to kiss Amy's cheek as she passed her. One of Liam's sisters winked as she walked by, calling out, "Hey, Amy," as though they were long acquaintances.

"Humph," Mrs. Traynor grunted. "Well, the family's here, so I guess it's true. Sheriff Sullivan is off the market." She pressed her casserole dish into Amy's hand. "Welcome, dear. Hope you make it to the Methodist church on Sunday. We can't seem to get the Sheriff to come, but if he's going to be a family man now, he needs to get himself through the church doors." With a nod, she turned and walked down the front steps.

Mrs. Mack followed suit, but as she handed her casserole dish to Amy, she cocked her head toward Mrs. Traynor's retreating back. "She's right, but you really ought to find yourself at the Presbyterian Church. Good to have you here." Before Amy had a chance to say anything more than 'thank you', Mrs. Mack made it back to her car.

As she closed the door and turned, Carolyn and one of her daughters took the casseroles from Amy's hand. "I see we came at a good time. Those two old biddies are good people but they've been trying to marry off Liam for years." Laughing, she continued. "I wanted to bring Liam's sisters by to meet you. This is my oldest, Ellen. She and her husband live near me and they've got two kids. Sue is my middle girl. She's got one, and as you can see, she's got another one on the way. And then Marie's my youngest. She and her husband have only been married for a year."

She greeted them with enthusiasm, shaking her head

over the casserole brigade. "I had no idea what to say to them."

Sue piped up. "You won't have to worry about them anymore. Seeing us here has solidified that you are *with* Liam, not just staying here. They'll just be neighborly from now on."

"Maybe not Rachel," Ellen laughed. "That woman still hasn't landed husband number three. She won't be so friendly, but that's no loss!"

The others laughed, but it did little to ease Amy's concern. She sucked in her lips, her mind racing furiously.

Carolyn patted her arm. "I can see you are deep in worry."

"It's just that I don't want people to see me and my daughters as taking advantage of Liam."

Marie snorted. "Oh, Amy. Believe me, no one is going to take advantage of Liam."

She looked at the four women now sitting at the table sipping tea, all nodding and smiling. Rosie came down from her nap and was immediately beset upon by Liam's adoring family with promises to bring their children to play next time.

"In fact, we should take her to our houses to play," Ellen offered. "That would give you a break. My kids are six, four, and two. I'd love to keep Rosie sometimes, especially when you need to run errands, get some work done, or just rest."

Rosie's face shone with her glee, and Amy nodded. "That sounds really good. I know Rosie would love to have playmates. My job is from home, and I'm technically on maternity leave. But a little bit of time to work would be nice. Give us another couple of days, and I'll take you up on that."

Later, standing at the door, waving goodbye with Desiree in her arms and Rosie by her side, a sense of peace descended over her. As they walked back inside, her smile was easy for the first time in weeks.

22

DR. JAMES MALCOLM'S OFFICE

"Nathan, what do you have for me?" As soon as he'd seen who was on the phone, James jumped in, impatience lacing his words as he ignored social niceties.

"Not much," Nathan growled in return.

"You can't be serious!"

"I've searched what I can, and there are only two women with the name of Amy with their last initial as C. One of them is Amy Carson who happens to be eighty-two years old, and the other is Amy Canter who is ten years old."

"Damn, neither of those is right."

Nathan huffed over the airways. "You want to tell me what this is about?"

He stood and walked around his desk, shutting his door. Staring at it for a moment, he flipped the lock. His staff never just walked in unannounced, but he didn't want to take a chance. Moving back to his chair, he sat down heavily, the tension in his neck causing a headache to blossom. "Amy C. is the woman who has my account for transcribing medical notes. She works for the company I started using months ago when we increased our telemedicine business."

"Okay..." Nathan prodded, and Malcolm could tell his partner's patience was running out.

"I was transcribing and accidentally recorded part of a phone call to you where I was reminding you about changing birthdates and social security numbers for Medicare patients—"

"Are you fucking shitting me? Christ, what a moron! Do you have any idea—"

"Don't start with me!" Malcolm lost what little composure he had left.

"No? Well, it may very well end with you!"

The two men remained in a silent stand-off for a moment.

Finally, dragging in a shaky breath, Malcolm spoke. "The transcriptionist never sent anything back. As far as I know, she realized it wasn't connected to a record and therefore ignored it." He decided to leave out how he talked to the transcription company owner and discovered that the mysterious Amy C. had asked about him. Sighing, he said, "Look, she's said nothing. She obviously doesn't live on the Shore, so there's nothing we can do anyway. I thought that if she were local, your nephews could lean on her, but since she's not, then we just keep going."

"What a fucking mess," Nathan continued to growl.

Anxiety began to morph into anger in Malcolm's gut. "I admit it was a mishap, but damnit, Nathan, I've set this whole thing up from the ground floor. Got my two schoolmates involved. I'm the silent partner with the cash that set up your business here on the Shore. A business, I might add, that employs your wife and nephews. So don't get all high and mighty with me! This woman hasn't done anything with the message and her boss was wrong. She's not local, so she's out of our reach anyway. We just keep going and keep making money."

Not waiting for a reply, he disconnected, his heart pounding from frustration, anger, and a large dose of fear. Blowing out his breath, he startled when his intercom sounded.

"Dr. Malcolm, your three o'clock appointment is here."

Forcing a calm he didn't internalize, he replied, "Thank you. I'll be right there."

23

FOUR WEEKS LATER

Liam drove into Baytown for an American Legion meeting, his mind filled with the past month of having a baby and a pre-schooler in the house. *Four glorious, exhausting, amazing weeks since Desiree was born and five weeks since Amy and Rosie came into my life.*

If anyone had told him that he'd adapt to changing diapers, spit-up, toys on the carpet, late nights, and early mornings when Desiree fussed or Rosie had a rare tantrum, he'd have thought they were crazy. But after the past month, he'd grown to thrive on the chaos of life.

He'd hated leaving the girls tonight but had missed the last meeting and had words of appreciation to give out. As he drove, his mind settled easily over thoughts of what he had back home. He left work every day, anxious to pull into the garage, step into the house, and be greeted by Rosie's enthusiastic hug as she showed him the latest pictures she'd drawn or tell him about the fun she'd had with her new friends at Ellen's house. She had blossomed, no longer shy around him but offering hugs and smiles easily, each one melting his heart.

Then his eyes would search out Amy. Sometimes she'd be in the kitchen, heating one of the many dishes that had been brought to them while laughingly complaining that she'd soon forget how to cook. Other times she'd be in the living room, nursing Desiree or getting some work done while Desiree napped in her swing. Just having the three of them to come home to made him smile.

And then there was Desiree. While he'd certainly been around his nieces and nephews, the truth was he'd never paid close attention to how quickly they changed during the first month of life. But now, he could hardly wait to spend time with her each evening, noticing every nuance.

And his favorite times of all were when he and Amy had a little bit of time together alone. He could tell she was skittish, still afraid that his life had been turned upside down. But he loved it.

Looking back to his chaotic-but-fun childhood before his dad passed away, he remembered the baseball gloves in the dining room, shoes with cleats piled up in the laundry room, the scent of cookies filling the kitchen as he and his siblings bounced up and down waiting for them to cool, smudges on the window as they waited for their dad to get home in the evening, and lots of talking and laughter around the dinner table at night. He hadn't realized how much he'd missed that until his quiet home was now filled with the sounds of family.

They shared the chores, took turns with Desiree, and made sure Rosie felt secure. And last night, after the girls were sleeping, he and Amy had sat on the sofa, close together, his arm around her. His fingers trailed over her shoulders, and she relaxed against him. They'd been sharing a house for over a month and never kissed. He'd been terrified of taking advantage of her vulnerability. But as they'd grown closer, it was getting harder and harder to pretend that he didn't want her in every way.

Arriving at the building where the meeting would occur, Liam hustled inside. Stepping into the American Legion meeting room, his hand immediately extended to thank friends he saw who had come by to offer assistance, not only for Amy but for the two counties' storm clean-up needs. Many volunteers had helped the emergency response team's efforts to help their neighbors, making it easier on the law enforcement and community services.

After the meeting, he, Wyatt, and Colt chatted. Standing next to a group of elderly Legionnaires, he noted several had new walkers, leg braces, and a few wheelchairs. With a few of them hard of hearing and talking loudly, it wasn't hard to discern their conversation.

"I'm telling you, he's a miracle worker. My daughter spent over a year trying to get Medicare to pay for this walker, and Dr. Malcolm got it approved and paid for in less than a few weeks. And the Medical Supply of the Shore had it delivered straight to my house."

"Me, too," another said. "Got my brother a hospital

bed the same way. The only snafu was I got a call from Medicare about another patient with a similar name, but Mr. Caster at the supply store and Dr. Malcolm got that cleared up right quick."

"I have to wait on my niece to take me to the doctor," another man grumbled. "I don't know how long I'll have to wait to get in to see him."

"Don't gotta wait. He'll see you over the telephone."

"How the hell can he see me over the telephone?"

"You can do one of those face things, you know, where he talks to you over the computer or telephone. He did my sister that way, and she lives in North Carolina. I told her to skip finding someone down there. She talked to Dr. Malcolm, and the next thing she knew, Medicare was paying for her new walker, new wheelchair, and bed rails. Got them delivered from the supply store here on the Shore."

Colt waved a hand in front of Liam's face. "Hey, where'd you go? Too many late nights with the baby?" Wyatt, standing with them, laughed.

"Sorry, man." He moved slightly away from the group of older gentlemen talking. "Listen, have you heard anything about the orthopedic surgeon, Dr. James Malcolm? Or the Medical Supply of the Shore company?"

Colt's smile dropped as he immediately registered a serious look in his eyes as he glanced back at the men before holding Liam's gaze. "No, why?"

Liam looked at Wyatt and lifted his brow. "The medical supply store is in your little town. You heard anything suspicious?"

Wyatt, adopting Colt's immediate sharp-eyed gaze, shook his head slowly. "I know it's owned by Nathan Caster. He's got two nephews working there. They're kind of goonish if you ask me, but they work in the back and with deliveries. Nathan and his wife run the place. Never heard anything bad about them. What's up?"

"This came from Amy. She works for a medical transcribing company. From what I understand, when she was working full time, she'd receive files from her employer that came from hospitals, medical facilities, and individual doctors. She used to manage a medical facility so she knows the lingo and is a fast typist. After she had Rosie, becoming a medical transcriptionist was a way to have more control over her hours and be able to work from home. Dr. Malcolm not only has his orthopedic practice but he's the owner of a telemedical business where doctors can have clients from all over the country that they don't see in person but they can treat, diagnose, and prescribe over the Internet."

"No shit," Wyatt said. "I guess that makes sense for people who live in remote areas, but I just never thought about it."

"It sounds legitimate, but what's your concern?" Colt asked.

"She became suspicious that he was always prescribing medical supplies that appeared to be charged through Medicare, and yet, always came from the Medical Supply of the Shore, even if the patient was on the other side of the country. That didn't make sense to her, and it made her suspicious of fraud."

"Medical fraud?" Wyatt's hands landed on his hips, his brows lowering.

By now, Mitch, Hannah, and Dylan had joined them, and an impromptu Law Enforcement Leaders meeting occurred while standing to the side of the room, their voices low.

Shaking his head, Liam shrugged. "I don't know. To be honest, with everything that's gone on, it hasn't been first and foremost on my mind. But I was just listening to those gentlemen over there talk about how they've all gotten their equipment from Dr. Malcolm and haven't had to pay anything. And then they talked about knowing relatives and friends in other states that have gone through him as well. It may all be aboveboard, but I wanted to check to see if you had heard anything."

"Just because we haven't heard anything doesn't mean nothing's wrong. Manteague is in Acawmacke, but it's my little neck of the woods, too, so I'll work this with you," Wyatt said.

"I appreciate that. My sister is taking Rosie three mornings a week to her house so Amy can get some work done. Her boss is letting her work part-time. Dr. Malcolm's private telemedicine business transcriptions are the only one she now has. She still has concerns, but I simply hadn't thought much about it until hearing those men talk. It's worth checking if we suspect fraud." Glancing at his watch, he grinned. "I've got just enough time to get home and read a story to Rosie. I'll let you all know what I discover."

With smiles given along with the goodbyes, he headed out.

Thirty minutes later, he was sitting on the bed that Rosie still shared with Amy, reading Beauty and the Beast, her new favorite book. She seemed to make the rounds of all the Disney Princesses, each one, in turn, becoming her favorite.

Fresh from her bath, she smelled little-girl sweet and was dressed in her pink princess pajamas with her blonde hair curled around her shoulders. He reveled in their new nighttime routine. By the time the story had ended, she yawned widely, and he tucked her underneath the covers.

Amy walked in and passed Desiree off to him so that she could kiss Rosie goodnight. Then they walked into the nursery where, hopefully, the littlest one would go to sleep. Amy had circles underneath her eyes, and he knew Desiree's good sleeping schedule had recently changed. But the fates were with them tonight, and when he laid her in her crib, she stayed asleep. Backing out of the room, he left the door open and carried the monitor in one hand, taking Amy's hand in his other as they walked down the stairs.

Not wanting to let go, he led her into the kitchen, put the kettle on with one hand, and reached up to get the mugs.

She giggled. "Are you going to do everything one-handed?"

"Yes, if it means I get to keep holding your hand."

She blushed, her gaze dropping, but the smile staying on her lips. He gave a little tug, and she came to him willingly, lifting her chin so she could now stare at his eyes. They stood in the kitchen, desire and longing swirling around them like the steam from the teapot. His gaze dropped to her mouth, but not before noticing that hers did the same. He'd wanted to kiss her for weeks but kept looking for the right time. But with a pre-schooler and a baby, the right time had never presented itself. *Maybe we make our own right time, just like we've done everything—our own way.*

Not wanting to misread the signs, he swallowed deeply before saying, "I want to kiss you."

Her breathing pattern changed, her chest heaving as she nodded. "I want that, too."

Not moving closer, he confessed, "I've wanted to kiss you for a long time."

Her gaze never wavered from his but her lips quivered ever so slightly. "I've wanted that, too."

He didn't let go of her hand, but with his other cupped her cheek, drawing his thumb over the petal-soft skin. It was as though the blue of her eyes deepened in color and her skin warmed under his touch. Bending, he touched his mouth to the corner of her lips, hearing her tiny gasp. Lifting away, he moved to the other corner and touched her mouth there as well. This time, she sucked in her breath, and he could feel her anticipation meet his own.

He loosened her hand regretfully but wanted to hold her face in both palms when he finally gave in to the longing he'd carried inside for weeks. Lowering his face to hers, his mouth lightly touched hers before he angled his head and began moving his lips, drawing more gasps from her. Not wanting to rush a single second of the kiss, the need built inside, the anticipation overwhelming. Her full lips met his and the sensuous dance began.

Gliding over her mouth, he licked and nipped until finally giving in to his desires and sliding his tongue inside her open warmth. Exploring each crevice as her silky tongue moved over his, he felt the nerves tingle through his body in a straight line from his mouth to his cock. Each cell was vibrating with need. The need to feel her, taste her, kiss her. The need to know she was as affected by the kiss as he was.

Her hands were on his shoulders, but as she pressed closer to him, her fingers crept up, one hand clutching his neck and the other moving through his hair, her short nails dragging slightly over his scalp, creating more tingles. The result was his cock pressing against his zipper. He hoped she couldn't feel the arousal, not wanting her to overthink his desire.

As their tongues tangled, she moved her hips slightly, now straddling one of his jean-clad thighs, slowly rocking her core. Her actions gave him pause for only a few seconds. He hadn't planned on anything other than a kiss. He might be a novice when it came to new mothers, but he knew she had a few more weeks to be cleared for any sexual activity. But the more she continued to rub against his thigh, it flashed through his mind that she couldn't have intercourse… but there was nothing that said she couldn't have an orgasm.

Wanting to give her any pleasure he could, he slid one hand down to the small of her back, pressing her in tighter as he lifted his thigh slightly, giving her easier access. It was all he could do to not rub his leg against her core or glide his hand along her rib cage, moving it upward to her breasts. But he wanted whatever happened to be her choice, all about her.

So, he continued his assault on her mouth, her sweet taste driving him wild. Her hips moved at a frantic pace, little moans now slipping from between her lips, swallowed by him. Her fingers clutched tighter as she stiffened. The soft noises now became a deep groan pulled from her lungs as her body vibrated in his arms for a moment before her lips left his, and she slumped against him.

He held her weight easily, his hands gently stroking up and down her back, his lips now pressed against the top of her head. His cock pressed against her stomach but he knew he could take care of himself later. This had been about Amy and what he could offer her. *And it was hot as fuck.* Smiling, with his hands on her shoulders, he pushed her back gently so he could peer into her face, hoping to see the pleasure etched in her expression.

24

Amy stared up at Liam, her face burning with blush, horrified at her actions. It had started as a kiss, something he'd said he wanted, and God knows she wanted it, too. She should've known that a kiss with him would not be enough. Not considering she hadn't had sex since she'd gotten pregnant with Desiree.

His handsome looks and virility had captivated her from the first moment she'd met him, but living with Liam for the past month, she'd grown more aware every day of his kindness, endearing quirks and foibles, and the longing looks they'd shared.

And now, during their first kiss, a kiss he'd instigated but she had imagined and dreamed about, she'd dry-humped his thigh, her orgasm coming quickly while it had shaken her to her very core. *Oh, my God! What must he think of me?*

Desperate to say something, anything, her fingers clutched the material of his T-shirt. "Oh, Liam, I'm so sorry. I can't believe I did that. I can't believe… I… I'm so sorry!"

He jerked slightly, and she expected his hands to fall away from her, but instead, they held tight, pulling their hips together so that there was no doubt his erection was pressed against her. His glorious, long, hard erection.

"Amy, I have no idea what you're apologizing for. That was, beyond a shadow of a doubt, the hottest thing I've ever witnessed."

She blinked, opening her mouth, but he pressed his finger against her lips.

"No, I'm not going to let you spew any more apologies or fall into embarrassment. I've been attracted to you from the beginning. I know we started out as just me helping out someone in the storm, but you and I both know that changed a long time ago. But I needed to let you call the shots. I needed to make this about you. I needed you to take this where you felt comfortable going."

"I guess you got more than you bargained for, didn't you?" she mumbled, her face still hot.

With his knuckle under her chin, he lifted her head, keeping their eyes pinned on each other. "Oh, hell no. I got exactly what I was hoping for. But didn't know that I'd get pure, unadulterated *you,* so into our kiss that you wanted as much as you could get. Like I said, Amy, that was hot as fuck."

A giggle slipped out, but she pressed her lips together and shook her head. With her chin still lifted by his hand, she continued to hold his gaze. "Why did I need to call the shots?"

He sucked in a deep breath through his nose, letting it out slowly, still holding her close. "I don't see us as unequal, but I know you've struggled with the idea that you crashed into my life and interrupted everything. I know you've also struggled with the idea that I had a hero complex in rescuing you. I think you know me well enough now to know that if I didn't have a good feeling about you, I would've found other accommodations for you right away. And then, as soon as I got to know you and Rosie, I didn't want you to leave. I've wanted to kiss you for a long time. Hell, I wanted to do more than that but knew the time wasn't right. But there's no way I wanted to take advantage of your vulnerability or the situation. So, I was willing to let you know I wanted to kiss, but I needed to know you wanted it, too. And anything beyond that, I needed to know it was what *you* wanted."

His words moved through her, and she smiled, nodding. "I think it's pretty evident that it's what I wanted. But… um, even though I'd like more, I…"

"I know, sweetheart. I may be a bachelor, but I've had enough experience with friends and siblings who had had children, I know you haven't been cleared by your doctor. And that's perfectly fine. I want us to take things slow and make sure what we're doing is right. You were feeling it, and I was right there with you. You feeling the freedom to take what you needed, allowing me to be the one to give it to you… fuckin' amazing, baby."

She continued to nod in understanding, his motives soothing over her, lessening her embarrassment. He still held her close, his erection still pressing between them. She glanced down, before looking back up. "What about you? I definitely got what I needed, but let me take care of you—"

He shook his head, "No, not tonight. This isn't a tit-for-tat."

Another giggle erupted, and she shook her head, blush gracing her cheeks again. "Oh, my God, I resorted to sophomoric humor, giggling over the word 'tit.'"

Now it was his turn to laugh, and the tension eased as they both stood in the kitchen, arms now around each other. With her cheek pressed against his heart, she felt the steady beat and closed her eyes, reveling in the closeness. Now that she wasn't staring directly at him, she felt a little braver. "I don't want to make this awkward, but where does this leave us?"

"It's the start. Well, not technically *the* start since I believe that happened when you first moved in, and absolutely we were cemented when I delivered Desiree. And every moment since you've been here with me, we've been building toward where we are now, the next phase of *us*."

Sucking her lips in, her mind raced with the implications of what she was going to say but knew she had no choice but to press on. Needing to see his face now, she leaned her head back. "If I was younger and had no responsibilities, I could just float along, taking things as they came. And please, don't misinterpret this as me asking for a commitment or something stronger than either of us can give right now. I haven't had sex since I got pregnant with Desiree. I have responsibilities as a mom that are above and beyond anything else I might feel, including pure, physical desire. And I know how much Rosie cares for you, and part of me is afraid of doing anything that might interrupt or, God forbid, ruin that relationship."

His hands slid back up to her cheeks, holding her so that she had no choice but to keep staring into his handsome face. "Amy, there is nothing I would ever do or let happen to ruin the relationship I have with those two girls. And I refuse to think that either of us would do anything to bring us to that point. We're not just two people starting out. We've lived in the same house. We've shared our lives. We've experienced the miracle of birth, just you and me. Like you, I'd fight to the death to protect Rosie and Desiree, and that includes fighting for us."

Time ceased to matter as they held each other's gazes. She heard as well as felt her heart pounding in her chest, making it hard to breathe. Suddenly, she blurted, "I'm going to the doctor in two weeks."

His mouth curved upward in a slow, languorous grin. "I know. I'm counting."

Licking her now-dry lips, she swallowed down her nerves. "So, what do we do now?"

"This. Lots of this." His breath whispered over her lips just before his mouth sealed hers.

Amy had rushed around, trying to get organized so she could get out the door and to the doctor's appointment on time. She hated being late, but everything was conspiring against her. Rosie had woken up grumpy, and as though picking up on her big sister's mood, Desiree had fussed through her morning feeding, refused to take a nap, and had managed to blow through two fresh diapers and spit up on the first outfit Amy had put on.

Now, re-dressed, she kissed a pouting Rosie and a crying Desiree before grabbing her purse and sending a woeful expression toward Carolyn and Marie who were babysitting while she went to the doctor.

"I'm sorry—"

"Now hush," Carolyn said, shaking her head. "Nothing to be sorry for. You know as well as I do that motherhood isn't all sunshine and daisies. Your children are fine, so you go and take care of what you need. You'll feel better as soon as you leave. Do something besides just go to the doctor. Pamper yourself. And we'll be right here when you get back."

Finally, heading out the door, she made it to her car without crying. Carolyn was right, and by the time she walked into the doctor's office, she felt much lighter. No diaper bag, no huge purse, no carrier straining her arm, shoulder, and back. She felt guilty, but the little bit of freedom was amazing.

Less than an hour later, she walked out, feeling even lighter. Her weight was good, although the extra pounds she still carried seemed to be in her boobs and ass. All her female parts had been declared good as well, and she'd been given the go-ahead for sex. After two weeks of the most amazing kisses, her body was primed and ready. She loved the light kisses that were quickly stolen, loved the long, wet, and hot kisses after the kids went to sleep, and loved the ones that usually resulted in orgasms. She didn't tell the doctor that she had plans for her sex go-ahead, but she must have had a huge grin on her face since the doctor laughed, encouraging her to enjoy herself.

She sat in the car for a moment, trying to decide what to do with the hour she had allotted for her child-free excursion. She didn't get her nails done and didn't want to go to a coffee shop alone. There were no malls in the area, so that wasn't a possibility. Starting the car, she realized that she could have a leisurely stroll in a grocery store, buying what she needed without Rosie's desperate pleading for snacks or Desiree deciding to spit up in the middle of aisle three. In fact, there was a grocery store near the doctor's office that she had not visited.

Parking, her gaze drifted to the side, landing on a brick building with a large sign on the front. Medical Supply of the Shore. After nibbling on her bottom lip during a moment of indecision, she threw open the door and stalked toward the store. Entering, she wandered around, pretending to look at merchandise while an elderly couple was being assisted by the only clerk she could see.

Managing to weave her way toward the ongoing sales speech, she could easily overhear what was being said.

"You just have to have a prescription signed by a doctor, and then we can file Medicare for you. Once approved, we deliver the equipment to your home, help you set it up, and you don't have to pay for anything."

"Well, Dr. Malcolm said we should come here. I guess he was right."

"Oh, yes, indeed! Dr. Malcolm takes care of everything. And you're so lucky to have him here. Did you know that he sees patients all over the country?"

"We didn't actually go in to see him. Our daughter set up her computer, and we did it all over the internet. He looked at x-rays and told us what we needed. Best medicine around!"

The woman behind the counter looked over at Amy. "I'll be right with you, ma'am."

Smiling, she nodded and moved over a few aisles. She wandered through walkers, wheelchairs, travel chairs, lift chairs, canes, hospital beds, splints of all varieties, and just about everything else a patient could need. An idea formed as she continued to listen, and try as she might to ignore the desire to find the truth, it wouldn't be denied. Wiping her sweaty palms on her pants, she swallowed deeply as her mind raced to come up with a plausible reason for being in the store.

"Hello! Welcome to Medical Supply of the Shore, or MSS as we like to call it."

She turned and watched as the woman approached, having finished with the elderly couple. "Hello." She plastered what she hoped was a sincere smile on her face. "Um..." Deciding to go with her harebrained, not-well-thought-out scheme, she began again. "I hope you can help me. My father is coming to live with me, and from what he tells me, there are a lot of things he needs. A lift chair and a wheelchair are two things that I know of for sure."

"Can your father come in to choose the items himself?"

Smile drooping dramatically, she pressed on, making up her tale as she went. "Oh, no. He lives in West Virginia but can't live by himself anymore. So, he's got a friend who's going to drive him to my place here."

"And does he have a doctor who has diagnosed him?"

She pretended to think, then shook her head. "He's been to a regular doctor but not a specialist. He has arthritis and can't get up easily or walk well."

"Well, we have an excellent orthopedist locally that can see him once your father has arrived."

"That's wonderful, but he says he needs the wheelchair right away." She wrung her hands together. "I just don't know what to do. I surely can't haul him around, as big as he is."

Nodding, the woman agreed. "Oh, certainly not. Well, this orthopedist has a business where he can talk to the patient over the phone or by computer and can diagnose him that way. Does your father have Medicare?"

"Yes, he doesn't have any other insurance."

The woman smiled, still nodding. "That's wonderful, really it is. The orthopedist can write a prescription for him, and then we can order whatever your father needs."

"Can he do that without seeing him?"

"Certainly. It's done all the time. Modern medicine isn't like the old days, you know. Dr. Malcolm doesn't have to see your father to make sure he has what he needs. We'll just need your father's name and social security number or Medicare number. Once we have that, we can get the prescription and get Medicare to pay for everything."

"And if my father decides at the last minute to stay in West Virginia, can we use a supply store there?"

"Oh, no… I'm afraid that everything will still have to go through our store. But we can ship it anywhere."

Amy furrowed her brow with great dramatics. "But won't that cost more?"

"Not with Medicare paying for it all, sweetie." The woman smiled indulgently as though talking to a child.

Nodding, Amy exaggerated a huge sigh of relief. "I can't thank you enough. As soon as I get my father's information, I'll come back in."

Waving goodbye, she left with a smile, hurrying out to her car, ready to get out of there before the woman noticed her heart was pounding and her breathing ragged. Not wanting to draw attention to herself, she backed out of the parking space and pulled onto the road. All thoughts of grocery shopping or pampering flew out the window. Uncertainty flooded her. *Now I have more to fuel my suspicions of medical fraud, but what do I do with it?*

She changed lanes, a new destination in mind. Twenty minutes later, she was escorted into Liam's office. Thanking Margaret, she waited until the older woman left and closed the door. He stood, hurrying around his desk, a smile on his face but a curious look in his eyes. “Amy, is everything okay?”

“Yes,” she nodded emphatically. “Two things: first of all, I’ve just been to the Medical Supply of the Shore store, and I know what they’re doing must be Medicare fraud.”

He jolted, his head jerking slightly. “What?”

“And second, I’m cleared, so we can have sex anytime we want.”

25

Liam's mind had started to race when Amy mentioned the Medicare fraud suspicion but completely short-circuited when she mentioned sex. "What?" he repeated, this time his voice resembling more of an adolescent squeak than a sheriff hearing of a crime.

She laughed, her eyes bright. "Which part needed repeating?"

Swallowing, he shook his head, then lifted his arms toward her. "Um… honestly, my mind stopped at the word 'sex.'" He stepped forward at the same time she did and they collided in the middle of his office. Wrapping her close, her warm curves nestled against his hard body, he tried not to think just how *hard* he was. As luscious as she felt tucked into his arms, he sighed. "Okay, I guess the sex part of that good news will have to wait, or I'll be arrested for public indecency." She giggled again, and the gentle sound moved through him.

She leaned back, her head tilted so she could hold his gaze. "So, we need to focus on the crime part, right?"

"Yeah..." He let the word hang for a few seconds, then grinned. "For now. But later? We'll talk later."

"I hope that's not all we do."

Squeezing her waist, he slid his arms away. "Christ, Amy, don't say things like that. My dick is so hard for you, I can hardly think of anything else."

She stepped back, her gaze dropping to his crotch for just a second before lifting, her cheeks now pink with blush. Or desire. *God, I hope it's desire!* Clearing his throat, he got back to business. "Okay, tell me what you've got."

As she started to talk, he halted her and picked up his phone. "Wyatt? Are you able to come to my office? Now would be good. Yeah, I've got Amy here, and she has news on Medical Supply of the Shore. Good... see you in a few." He looked up and said, "The store is actually in Wyatt's town. Manteague is smaller than Baytown, but it has several businesses. Since the store is part of the county, it falls under my jurisdiction, too, but I want to involve him and there's no sense in you telling your story twice."

"He's the Chief of Police there?"

"Yeah. I've got Wyatt as the Manteague Town Chief. He's independent of me, but since his town is in Acawmacke County, we work together."

"What about the hospital? Is it just in the county?"

"It sits outside the town limits, so yeah, it's just in the county. But some of those doctor offices are actually inside the town limits." He picked up his phone again. "Mack? I've got Wyatt coming in. Can you meet me in the conference room in about ten minutes? I saw Agent Donaldson earlier in the building. See if he can come in with you." He looked back at Amy's confused face. "Mack is my Lieutenant of Investigations, and Donaldson is from the Chesapeake FBI office located in Virginia Beach."

"Oh," she replied, eyes wide. "That makes sense to call them all in."

He stepped closer. "You know what else makes sense?" When she shook her head, tilting it to the side in silent question, he grinned as his arms snaked around her again, lowering his mouth to hers. "Making use of the ten minutes we've got to ourselves."

Liam could not have been prouder of Amy. She sat at the large conference table, surrounded by law enforcement personnel which could have been intimidating to anyone, but she appeared nonplussed as she carefully and succinctly went over her involvement with Dr. Malcolm and Medical Supply of the Shore.

She explained her job as a medical transcriptionist and how Dr. Malcolm was using her company for his orthopedic telemedicine business. When Mack asked about telemedicine, she used Liam's computer to show them the websites available.

"Telemedicine has been growing over the past few years," she continued. "It allows doctors to reach people who live in remote areas where medical care is less prevalent. It also allows the elderly to have care when they are unable to get into a facility. When it works best is when a specialist can work in concert with the family doctor. But, yes, prescriptions can be given by a physician who hasn't *seen* a patient, at least not in their physical clinic. Therefore, it can open up concerns about a doctor diagnosing and treating a patient without all the information needed."

"Is it such a big industry?" Mack asked, his brow furrowed. "I guess I'm thinking about my elderly parents. They can only use their iPad to talk to the grandkids if someone is with them. Other than that, they have no idea how to use the computer to talk to a doctor."

She nodded. "It has limitations, no doubt about it. The large medical clinic I used to work for didn't use telemedicine. They tried it, but the doctors hated it and most of the patients did, too. They want to see a doctor. Or they were non-English speakers and needed a translator. Or they simply had no clue, as you indicated with your parents, how to use the internet to talk to a doctor without assistance." She shrugged, looking at the others around the table. "But it's still big business. Some doctors… well, let's say they don't abuse the system, but they interact with a *lot* of patients that way and get paid by insurance companies and Medicare regardless of whether it is in person or over the internet. And that's legitimate. There's nothing wrong with that, but they get paid for what might amount to a few minutes with a doctor."

"And your job?" Agent Donaldson prodded.

"Because I had worked for a large orthopedic medical facility, when I became a mother and needed to cut back on my hours, preferring something I could do from home, I joined a medical transcription company and they assigned many of the orthopedic physicians to me. When I decided to make a life change at the invitation of an old college friend to come to this area to live, my boss gave me Dr. Malcolm's telemedicine business to work on. Since I recently had another child, he was the only client I had."

"Can you review your transcriptions again, indicating the ones that involved possible Medicare fraud?" Agent Donaldson asked. "In the meantime, I'll get a subpoena to obtain a copy of those."

"Of course. As soon as you present me with the judge's orders, I can send them to you." She sucked in a deep breath and let it out slowly. "If I hadn't had a background in the business of a large clinic, I would have just transcribed and thought nothing of what I was working on. But, for me, alarm bells began to ring. He was prescribing things for the same patients but using different birth dates. He was always using MSS, no matter where the patient lived. Then, I found where he was double charging Medicare for the same session with patients."

Liam stepped in. "This is where I may have dropped the ball. Amy told me a few weeks ago that she had suspicions, but I didn't follow up. Well, I mentioned it to Wyatt and Colt, and then overheard some of the men at the American Legion talk about getting all kinds of equipment from MSS through Dr. Malcolm, even for their relatives that live elsewhere."

"It sounds so sloppy," Amy said. "It's hard to believe that he'd be so careless as to leave a trail of clues right there for someone to find."

"What about the other doctors in his telemedicine business?" Wyatt asked.

"Oh, that's right. I did a little searching, and it's amazing how easy it was to find out this information. The other two doctors that do telemedicine with him graduated from the same Caribbean medical school. In fact, they all graduated within a year of each other."

The men in the room nodded but shared a rueful smile. Agent Donaldson said, "Ms. Carruthers, that's how many criminals are discovered—by being just plain sloppy. And intelligent, educated white-collar criminals are not immune to becoming greedy and complacent."

She nodded, knowing the agent's words were true, just having a hard time wrapping her mind around the crime. "I suppose that considering most of the clients he uses telemedicine for are older or in remote areas, he feels somewhat safe that they won't compare notes and see anything wrong. Or, as Sheriff Sullivan indicated from the American Legion meeting, they're so grateful to be able to get what they need that they have no complaints."

"And if he's using double billing, or false birth dates, names, or Social Security numbers, then a certain amount is going to slide by Medicare," Mack interjected.

Now that Amy had given her information to them, Liam said, "If that's all, I know Amy wants to get back to the children." She sent a grateful nod his way, and he didn't doubt that she was desperate to nurse Desiree.

"Yes, yes," agent Donaldson said. "I'm going back to my office to check and see if there have been any reports or open investigations on this. Ms. Carruthers, if you'll get those transcriptions to Sheriff Sullivan as soon as I get the subpoena, I'll have him forward those to me."

She stood, accepted their thanks, and started to walk out the door. Liam took to his feet and said, "I'm walking Amy out. I'll be right back."

With his hand resting lightly on her back, they walked down several halls and out through a side door that led to the parking lot. Reaching her car, she turned but he was already in her space. "I know I've got to go into that building and deal with everything you just told us about Dr. Malcolm and MSS. You've got to go home and take care of the kids. But don't think for one second that I've forgotten the other piece of good news you gave me. Honest to God, Amy, it's all I can think about. You getting a clean bill of health and getting cleared for sex." Heedless of who might be around, he leaned down and kissed her. "Maybe, just maybe, if the kids go to sleep easily, you can sleep in my bed tonight."

Two hours later, Liam answered his phone. "Sheriff Sullivan."

"Liam? It's Donaldson. I checked FBI records on MSS and didn't find anything reported on them, but it seems that one of the doctors that is in the telemedicine group with Dr. Malcolm has a file open on him. Dr. Johnson from Mississippi. It was suspected Medicare fraud twelve years ago. The complaint was never fully investigated, and the case ended up like so many of the cases."

"Shoved into a file drawer, right?" Liam wasn't passing judgment. Too many crimes and not enough investigators. Sometimes, cases had to get prioritized and some were pushed to the back burner.

"You got that right. Anyway, it allowed me to get a judge to fast-track a subpoena. I'll get Ms. Carruthers's transcription notes and take a look at them." After a few seconds of silence, he added, "She's a smart woman."

Liam hesitated, uncertain what Donaldson's comment meant. "Yes, she is."

Donaldson chuckled. "She's beautiful and smart. She's in your house, and you delivered her baby. I'm not sure which of you is luckier that you picked her up in the middle of a hurricane."

Liam scoffed. "No doubt about it, I'm the lucky one!" Disconnecting, he looked at the time and grinned. The workday was over, but time with his family just getting started... and that included time alone with Amy.

The drive home couldn't go by fast enough. By the time he walked into the laundry room from the garage, he was greeted by Rosie slamming into him, talking a mile a minute about her day with Miss Carolyn and Aunt Marie. "We had a tea party with lemonade instead of tea. And we had cookies instead of sandwiches."

Bending so he could be on her level, he grinned at her enthusiasm. She threw her arms around his neck, and he stood, carrying her into the kitchen. "So, you had a lemonade and cookie party."

"No, no! It was a tea party!"

"Goodness, Rosie, keep your voice down," Amy admonished. "Desiree is sleeping." She approached Liam, her gaze darting from his eyes to the floor and back up again. He recognized the hesitation, and with Rosie still perched on his hip, he stepped close, wrapped his free arm around Amy, and leaned in, kissing her lightly. Moving back, a grin on his face at her wide-eyed shock, he set a giggling Rosie's feet onto the floor.

"Mommy and Mr. Liam kissed," Rosie sang out, her smile wide. She danced around the kitchen before heading into the living room to play.

"You… you… you kissed me. In front of Rosie," Amy sputtered.

He leaned in, stealing another kiss. "Yep, and if all goes well tonight, I'll kiss you and more, only not in front of Rosie."

Her lips pursed but she was only able to hold the expression for a few seconds before she grinned. "Dinner is almost ready. Rosie is wiped out from playing all day, and she didn't take much of an afternoon nap." Sighing, she threw her hands up to the side. "Desiree? Who knows, but if we get lucky, we can steal at least an hour while she sleeps between her fussy feedings."

"Sweetheart, I've been waiting for this for weeks. We'll do only whatever we feel like… no rushing, no pushing, no pressure. Just you and me and whatever time alone we can squeeze in." He bent to hold her gaze. "Deal?"

Grinning, she nodded. "Deal!"

26

Amy stood in the bathroom between the guest-room-now-a-nursery and the room she and Rosie had been sharing for almost two months. She'd managed a quick shower earlier and a hasty shaving and moisturizing with her coconut and shea butter lotion, glad to smell like something besides spit-up. She'd run a brush through her hair, honey blonde tresses shining in the light.

Now, swallowing deeply, she stared into the mirror. Her stomach was not toned, and faint white stretch marks streaked across the skin. At least her waistline had returned, but it would never look pre-baby, and her hips were generous. She almost snorted. She remembered reading that description in a romance novel about *generous curves.* Looking at her breasts spilling out of her bra, she nodded. *Yeah... I'd say more than generous describes this body.*

She pressed her lips together. The truth was that she was proud of her mommy body. She carried two beautiful children and accepted the bodily changes that went along with pregnancy and nursing. But wanting to feel sexy to a man as gorgeous as Liam created doubt. *But how can I teach my daughters to be proud of their bodies if I don't exude that same strength?*

She peeked in on Desiree, barely able to believe the baby had nursed easily and fallen straight asleep. Rosie was tucked into bed, fast asleep as well. She had no idea how long she and Liam might have before Desiree woke, but wasting time thinking of the nineteen-year-old body that she was never going to have again was foolish.

Sucking in a deep breath, she let it out slowly, pulled herself to her fullest height, and smiled. Then, as she lifted her hand to flip off the light switch, the gold on her finger caught her eye. She stared for a long time at the shiny band, twisting it around several times. Blowing out a long breath, she slid it off and dropped it into the small jewelry box on the counter. *I loved you, Marty. And you gave me two beautiful children. But it's time.*

Flipping the light switch, the bathroom was now bathed only in the glow of the nightlight. Slipping out of the room, she crossed the hall and into Liam's open bedroom, gently shutting the door behind her. She dropped the robe, now standing in just a bra and panties before she lost her nerve.

He stepped out of his bathroom, shirtless with his jeans hanging low on his hips, the top button unbuttoned. She licked her lips, the sight of his naked torso calling to her. She wasn't sure if she wanted her fingers to trail along the dips and curves of his washboard abs or if she'd rather explore the smooth skin taut over his muscles with her tongue. Just staring at him caused nerves to tingle throughout her body.

By the time she dragged her gaze up to his face, she realized his eyes were devouring her. Fighting the urge to suck in her stomach, she stood, allowing his slow, heated perusal to move from the top of her head to her toes and back again.

He stalked forward, not stopping until her back was against the door and his body was pressed against hers. He slid one hand behind her, and she heard the click of the lock, the small sound mingling with her heartbeat pounding in her chest.

"What I want to do to you, we need privacy." His voice was gravel, the words seeming to be pulled from deep in his chest.

She nodded, unable to think of a witty response. With his naked chest pressing against her body and his cock so prominent in his jeans, she was unable to think of *any* response. Finally, with absolutely no finesse, she blurted, "You're gorgeous."

Bending, his lips grazed her shoulder before gliding to the pulse point at the bottom of her neck, his teeth nipping slightly. "I think that's my line."

Her body broke out in a strange mixture of chills and heat. His mouth was barely on her, and yet, desire flooded her core. Her breath left her lungs in a rush as he leaned closer, her breasts now crushed against his chest. Her nipples beaded, an ache building, and she was glad she'd just fed Desiree.

Lifting his head, he stared into her eyes. "Confession time, Amy."

His serious words jerked her mind from her breasts to him. Blinking, she remained silent, having no idea what he was going to confess.

"I want to take my time. I want to explore every inch of your body. I want to make this good for you. I want to draw things out all night long until we're both sated and exhausted from lovemaking. But I know we're on borrowed time. I know Desiree or Rosie can wake at any moment. So I'm torn between a slow seduction or burning up the sheets."

With those words, she wheezed, "To be honest, Liam, both of those sound pretty amazing, so I think we're good either way."

He grinned and moved back in, kissing her ear, nipping the lobe, and trailing wet kisses down her neck to the plump mounds of her breasts. His hand left her waist and linked fingers with her, drawing her toward the bed.

Once there, he shifted their bodies so that her back was to the bed, and he unsnapped her bra, letting the satin and lace fall to the floor. Her breasts, without their support, hung slightly, the nipples large and rosy.

"Christ, you're beautiful." He palmed her breasts, and he bent, taking one nipple into his mouth. He sucked and licked gently, and her fingers dug into his shoulders.

Lifting his head, he said, "Don't be embarrassed. But tell me if I do anything you don't want me to do."

She cleared her throat as she shook her head slowly. "No, it's all good. Um… I'll leak some…"

"Babe, I know. And it's sexy as hell. Everything about you and your body is sexy as hell."

He sounded so sincere. But then, she knew that about Liam. True. Honest. Sincere. His words pushed away the last remnants of embarrassment over leaky breasts or poochy tummies, and she grinned just before he knelt and pulled her panties down her legs. Now, completely naked and exposed, she stood, allowing his gaze to freely roam. And if the flare of heated lust that moved through his eyes was any indication, he was not turned off by her *generous* curves.

A smile graced her lips as she sat down on the side of the bed, placed her hands next to her, and pushed backward, reclining with only her calves and feet hanging over the edge. Still on his knees, he pulled her legs over his shoulders, inhaling deeply. "God, you smell like heaven." Before she had a chance to speak, he dove in, and instantly, she was gone, her body and mind taking flight with the swirl of sensations that overwhelmed her. Her fingers grabbed the sheets, needing to hold on to something in case she truly did levitate.

His mouth licked her folds, his tongue working miracles as he thrust inside, and then, just when she thought her sensation overload could take no more, he blew his breath over her clit before sucking on the sensitive bead, and she cried out, slapping her hand over her mouth to stifle the noise as her body shook through her orgasm. Spots danced behind her eyelids, and the only sound heard was her ragged breathing and heart as it pounded out an ancient rhythm.

When she was finally able to catch her breath, she lifted on her elbows with her forearms planted on the mattress and watched his dark head lift from between her thighs as he licked his lips, peering at her with a huge smile on his face.

"Fucking fantastic, baby. Better than I could have imagined, and believe me, I've imagined a lot."

She fell back to the bed and laughed, no longer caring what body parts jiggled with her mirth. He stood, and as she heard his zipper, her head shot back up, eyes wide as she watched him shuck his jeans and boxers all in one swift movement. If she thought his upper body was gorgeous, his thick thighs, tight ass, and erect cock were downright heavenly. Suddenly, flooded with thoughts, she sucked in a quick breath. *Two babies, one only six weeks old. Things have got to be loose down there. What if it's not good for him? Or me?*

"Damn, babe, the look on your face is not good for my ego. You went from looking at me like I was the last popsicle in the freezer to discovering it was green apple and that's the only flavor you hate."

Shaking her head, another giggle slipped out. "Actually, I like the green apple ones."

Lifting a brow, he scowled. "Babe."

With that one word, she knew she needed to salvage what her worries were tearing down. She sighed heavily. "I'm sorry, Liam. It's kind of hard to just let go and feel when my mind keeps reminding me that my body is different. I'm afraid of disappointing you."

His face relaxed, and he crawled over her, settling his weight to the side, holding her close. "Amy, I met you on a stormy night when you were heavily pregnant, and I thought I was going to be delivering a baby in the car, so your body hasn't been a surprise to me since the minute I laid eyes on you. We've been together every day for almost two months. I delivered Desiree and have watched you nurse many times. I'm familiar with your body, and honey, I *love* your body."

"I'm not going to whine about my mommy body, but I'm getting used to the changes after baby number two. It's kind of new for me, as well."

He kissed her lightly before lifting away to hold her gaze. "If you've got other things on your mind besides what my body wants to do to you, then I'm not doing a good enough job. Let's see if I can rectify that."

He took the kiss deeper, his tongue gliding inside, tangling with hers as his hand kneaded her breasts and tweaked her nipples. Giving herself over to the sensations again, she cast everything else from her mind and allowed his talented hands and mouth to send her soaring. Just before she flew apart, he shifted, and she heard the crinkle of a wrapper, opening her eyes in time to see him roll on a condom over his impressive cock.

Lining up at her entrance, their eyes remained locked on each other as he glided the tip through her wet folds before easing into her sex. His eyes were hooded, his neck tight with restraint. Desperate for him, she moaned, "More. I won't break. Promise."

He still didn't plunge but continued his slow thrust until finally fully seated. She had no worries about being too loose. His long, thick cock filled her, their bodies perfectly aligned.

"Oh, God," he groaned. "You feel amazing. So fuckin' good. So fuckin' right."

He began to move, his thrusts alternating between slow and fast, shallow and deep. Kissing her, his tongue mimicked the movements of his cock. She lifted her legs, allowing deeper access, and wrapped her feet around his back, her heels digging into his ass, urging him on. With his upper body held up on his forearms planted next to her, their fingers laced, her breasts bounced with the movement, her nipples dancing against his chest.

He didn't need urging if his movements and the noises he made from deep within his chest were any indication. She kept her eyes open, not wanting to miss a moment. Every nerve tingled and even the air in the room felt electrified, sparks flying all around. The friction built as his cock dragged against her inner walls and she wanted to weep with how alive she felt. Clinging to his shoulders, she watched his handsome face, relief and excitement flooding her as ecstasy washed over his features. She felt heady with a feminine power that had nothing to do with being a mother. It was all about being a woman.

His hand slid between them, and as his fingers tweaked her clit, she cried out again, this time his shuddering matching hers. Stars hit the back of her eyes again, and when she finally opened them, his face was buried against her neck, his breath rasping warmly over her skin. She could have stayed entangled with him, not caring if they never moved.

Slowly, their bodies cooled, and her consciousness began to categorize each sensation. His heavy thigh pinning her to the mattress even as he lay to the side. His arm resting underneath her breasts, aware of a bit of leaking from her nipples. Her core ached deliciously. Turning her head toward him, she stared into his eyes. She tried to think of something appropriate. Something witty. Something loving. Something complimentary. But no words could possibly fit the moment, so instead, she kissed him lightly.

His smile let her know it was the best thing she could have done.

Liam sat with his back against the pillows piled on his bed, Amy sitting next to him in the crook of his arm. Desiree reclined on a long pillow in Amy's lap, her rosebud mouth latched onto Amy's nipple.

He reached out, his finger barely tracing over Desiree's cheek, grazing over Amy's breast. It was the most beautiful sight he'd ever witnessed. They had stayed entangled in bed until Desiree's cries sent Amy into the nursery. He followed, and when she was about to sit in the rocker, he asked her to come nurse Desiree in bed. She smiled and acquiesced. He'd seen her nursing many times before, but here in the bed where they'd just made love, with her naked, feeding her baby, he felt complete. He looked at her hand, the pale indentation at the base of her left-hand ring finger.

"You took off your ring." He barely whispered, not wanting to disturb Desiree but also in awe.

Her gaze lifted, her eyes shining with emotion. "It was time," she whispered in return. "Marty will always be their birth father, but he's no longer my husband. You said we're becoming *us.* So, it was time to take off the ring that represented my past." She kissed the top of Desiree's head and then turned her gaze back to him. "I put it in my jewelry box. I can have a jeweler make something pretty with it and give it to the girls when they're older."

His heart squeezed at her words. That was his Amy: honest, open, no games. "They'll love that."

She smiled and leaned forward, placing a kiss on his lips. Desiree fell asleep after burping, and since she'd already had a diaper change, they hoped she would keep sleeping. Slipping on shorts, he gently carried her into the nursery, laying her in the crib and patting her for a moment until he was sure she was still deep in slumber. Walking back into his bedroom, he spied Amy coming out of the bathroom, her naked body walking toward him. Her hips and breasts were lush, his absolute fantasy come true.

Kissing her deeply, he rubbed his thumbs over her cheeks. "Sleep with me."

She nibbled on her bottom lip. "What if Rosie wakes?"

"You've got the second monitor in here, so you'll know. We can set an alarm and wake before she does."

A smile curved her lips as her arms curled around his waist. "Okay," she whispered.

Brows lifted, he asked, "Okay?"

Nodding, she repeated firmly, "Okay."

Climbing back into bed, he tucked her into his arms, her head on his shoulder and her heartbeat close to his. As she fell asleep, he nuzzled her hair, thinking how lucky he was. She was the perfect woman, the perfect mom, and the perfect mate. Rosie and Desiree were his in everything but biology. And now, he needed to figure out how to make that permanent.

27

The LEL meeting's rotation had them at the Acawmacke Sheriff's conference room, but Liam couldn't concentrate. He'd spent time going over Amy's transcriptions with her, the same ones he'd sent to Agent Donaldson. In checking dates, names, birth dates, prescriptions, addresses, and Social Security numbers, he saw the pattern that Amy had become suspicious of. And while she had no special training in investigations and he had no special training in medical corruption investigations, patterns of fraud were evident. He'd explained to her that insurance fraud was a federal crime, and therefore, the FBI would handle an official investigation.

That hadn't made her happy, and she'd argued that that was how a lot of white-collar crime went uninvestigated and unpunished. He agreed, but all he could do was work with Agent Donaldson and hope the case would move to the next step.

"Liam? You with us?" Hannah asked.

He jolted slightly upon hearing his name, then shook his head and leaned back in his chair. "Sorry, sorry. Got a case on my mind. Or rather, an investigation that I'm turning over to our local agent."

"The Medicare fraud?" Wyatt asked. "Dr. Malcolm and Medical Supply of the Shore?"

"Damn!" Dylan swung his head around. "Dr. Malcolm was the orthopedist who saw me when I had shoulder trouble last year. I thought he was a good doctor, and he sure as hell knew his stuff."

"There's no question about him being a capable doctor. The question comes into whether he's stealing from insurance companies and Medicare, and initial evidence points to just that."

"Why do I get the feeling that Amy is the reason you're tied up in knots about this?" Mitch asked.

Scrubbing his hand over his face, Liam simply nodded. A knock sounded on the door and Agent Donaldson popped his head in. Liam offered a nod, inviting the agent into their meeting.

"Sorry to interrupt, Liam, but I just got the okay to move forward on the Dr. Malcolm and MSS investigation." Donaldson pulled up an empty chair, glanced around at the others, then settled his gaze on Liam. "I've gone through the transcriptions that Amy has done and sent them to one of our insurance fraud investigators. While Dr. Malcolm and MMS haven't been nearly as adept at covering their tracks as they think they might have, it's also not that uncommon."

"Well, Amy will be glad to know that somebody's going to be working on it. She hates the idea of them getting away with stealing on the backs of people who have need."

Dylan shook his head. "When you told us that those men were discussing how easy it was to obtain equipment from Dr. Malcolm and MSS, I can't believe someone didn't get suspicious and wonder if something was going on."

"Think about it, though. Those people were just happy that someone was paying attention to them, helping them get medical supplies they weren't having to pay for. To them, he and MSS are heroes. It never entered their minds that they were getting something for free that they shouldn't have."

Donaldson nodded. "Most people feel like insurance companies get rich on the backs of people anyway. So, as long as they're getting what they want and don't have to pay for it, they don't think twice about how it's happening. It's only when you have a whistleblower or someone stumbles across something like Amy did."

Liam nodded, proud of Amy and glad that the case would be handed off to the Feds and she could rest easy. Expecting Donaldson to leave, he looked across the table and noticed the agent shifting in his seat as his gaze dropped to the table, no longer looking at Liam. A sliver of unease moved through him, uncertain of its root. "Was there anything else?"

"We want to wire someone and send them in. Someone who can have a telemedicine videoconference with Doctor James. And then have that person go into MSS."

Liam nodded again. "Makes sense." Donaldson

remained quiet, and the sliver of unease grew until it rushed through Liam's body. "Why the fuck do I think you're going to tell me something I don't want to hear?"

"It was suggested that Amy go back into the store, only this time wired—"

"Abso-fucking-lutely not!"

"That's not really your call, is it Sheriff?" Donaldson bit out. "I'd say that's up to her."

Liam's hands were fists on top of the table, anger rolling through his body. His eyes bore straight into the agent, a man he'd respected up until two seconds ago. "You'd send in an untrained civilian instead of a trained FBI agent? When did the Agency start shirking their investigations?"

"Just because you've got a personal relationship with our informant doesn't mean you get to call the shots."

"Your *informant*? Amy is a medical transcriptionist who has a background in office management of a medical practice. She was never your *informant*. She discovered something and brought it to light as any good citizen should. That should be the end of her involvement."

"She's already involved. She's already gone into MSS and talked to them. She's already set up a scenario where her fake father needs medical equipment. They're already expecting her! Anyway, as I said, it's not your call. I've already talked to her, and she's agreed."

Feeling as though his head would explode, Liam leaned forward, ready to eviscerate Donaldson. A hand landed on his arm, and he swung his head around, staring at Hannah's calm expression. "I get it,

Liam, I do. But you blowing your stack isn't going to help."

He wanted to bite her head off but knew she was right. Sucking in a deep breath, he let it out slowly, willing the deep breathing to calm him but finding the maneuver did little to cool his temper. Turning back to Donaldson, he said, "Then I'll talk to Amy, and she'll un-agree."

"Why would you do that? Having a telemedicine appointment with Dr. Malcolm won't endanger her at all. She won't even be in the same room. And she's already gone into MSS. She goes in with her information from Malcolm, makes arrangements for equipment for her fake dad, and she walks out. It's easy. No risk. We'll have people close by. Hell, you can have someone close by."

Still angry, he grabbed his phone. "Amy? What the fuck did you agree to?"

"Whoa, bad move, man," Mitch grumbled under his breath.

Instantly, and a few seconds too late, Liam realized Mitch was right.

"Excuse me? What did you just ask?" Her voice was heard throughout the room.

Glancing around at the smiles and raised eyebrows of the others, he sighed, lifting a hand to squeeze the back of his neck. "Sorry, babe. It's just that Agent Donaldson informed me that you agreed to help in his investigation."

"I thought it was your investigation."

"It was, but remember, I told you that since insurance fraud is a federal crime, then they would be taking over."

"Yes, but he indicated that you'd be working with me, so I assumed you were in on all this."

He looked across the table, fire coming from the top of his head. "I'll call you right back, babe."

Disconnecting, he glared, for a moment not trusting that his actions wouldn't land him in his own jail. Finally, he breathed deeply and growled, "You told her that I was involved."

Donaldson had the grace to appear abashed. "That's not a lie. You are."

"She thought it was already approved by me."

"This doesn't have to be approved by you, Sheriff. I was giving you the courtesy of letting you know since you're shacking up with our informant—"

Liam shoved his chair back and was halfway around the table before Colt jumped to his feet and grabbed him, the others doing the same.

"Hold on, man. Don't do this. You gotta maintain your cool no matter how much this federal prick gets under your skin."

"That was fuckin' out of line," Wyatt growled toward Donaldson. His opinion was seconded by Dylan, with Hannah and Mitch chiming in.

Colt held Liam tightly, his words finally penetrating the red haze that surrounded him. As he nodded, Colt let him go, and he took his seat again.

Donaldson scrubbed his hand over his face. "Okay, look, you're right. That was totally out of line. I apologize. But if you'll chill, you'll see that she would never be in any danger. She sits in her home in front of a computer and has a remote *appointment* with Dr. Malcolm. She's already set up the scenario with MSS, so she knows what she said and how she presented it. If he takes the bait, then she gets wired and goes into MSS. We have someone in the store with her, agents around, and they will never know."

"Why can't you just go on what you have?" Wyatt asked.

"You know as well as I do that the wheels turn slow if we just take the transcriptions. If we get them caught in the act, then this can go to a grand jury much faster."

Liam's phone vibrated and he glanced at the screen. Sighing, he answered. "Yeah?"

"Honey, I have no idea what is going on, but I've already got a video appointment with Dr. Malcolm for tomorrow set up for my fictitious dad. I just thought you should know before you cancel everything. I don't mind doing this. Honest, honey. I want them stopped as much as you. It's people like them that drive up the costs of insurance for everyone else."

He said nothing for a moment, knowing she was right and her risk was almost nil. Finally, he sighed again. "Okay, babe. We'll talk it over here, and I'll let you know what's happening." It was on the tip of his tongue to sign off with *Love you,* but they hadn't gone there yet, and he wasn't about to have those words heard by her over the phone with an audience sitting in front of him.

Disconnecting, he set his phone down on the table. Pinning Donaldson with his hard stare, he nodded.

"She'll take the video appointment, but I'll be right next to her, out of sight, and I want no fuck-ups."

Donaldson grinned, rubbing his hands together. "You got it, Liam." With that, he stood and walked out of the room.

It didn't escape his notice that the agent used his first name when he got what he wanted. *Fucker.* For a moment, no one spoke.

"I know you're pissed, Liam." Mitch was the first of his friends to take a chance on incurring his wrath. "For what it's worth, I wouldn't want Tori to have anything to do with this, either."

"Hell, I was thinking of suggesting Katelyn Harrison since she and Gareth run a PI business together," Colt said.

"I was going to suggest doing it myself, but there'd be a chance they would know who I was." Hannah looked over at Liam, sympathy and her eyes.

"At least the videoconference can be with me right next to her, just out of camera range. But for MSS, that gives me a bad feeling."

"With her wired, you'll know exactly what's happening every second of the time. Then, between the Sheriff's Department, my Police Department, and the Agency, she'll be well protected," Wyatt spoke, but Liam noticed his friend's voice didn't match the certainty of his words.

28

"Have you changed your mind? You can, you know. It's not too late."

Amy looked at Liam, placing her hand on his arm. "Sweetie, you're going to make yourself crazy. All I'm doing is having a virtual doctor consultation concerning my fictional father's medical condition and needs. I've been briefed by Agent Donaldson and his partner, Agent Cox. This room is filled with people who are going to make me nervous, and I don't need you doing the same."

He leaned in, touched his lips to hers, and nodded, but she was sure he was anything but happy with what was getting ready to occur. It had been decided to have the laptop set up in the dining room, having taken down the artwork that was on the wall behind her. That assured that no one would identify where she was during the videoconference. She wore an unadorned light-blue T-shirt, something the agents suggested, plain clothes that gave no indication of wealth or lack of it. Her blonde hair was pulled back into a ponytail and her makeup was light.

She had gone over the story she gave to the salesperson at MSS numerous times, and with some coaching from the two FBI agents along with a few written notes, she was ready for the subterfuge.

Carolyn had come over and was upstairs with Rosie and Desiree, making sure to keep them out of the way. Amy had just nursed Desiree, so the situation had been set up as best as it could be.

Her instructions had been that five minutes before the video conference was scheduled, she was to get onto the site given to her by the doctor's office. Glancing at the clock, she nodded toward the others, her stomach now deciding to do flip-flops. Wiping her palms on her pants, she waited until Liam scooted to the other side of the table where the agents were sitting.

Since the doctor's office was in the town of Manteague, Wyatt had elected to be present as well since he was the Police Chief there. Plus, earlier, Wyatt had leaned over and told her that he'd make sure Liam didn't lose his shit. That caused her to laugh, and she appreciated his humor to ease her nerves.

The seconds ticked by slowly, then, finally, the screen came on and she stared into the face of a middle-aged, bespectacled man, his hair still dark with gray at his temples. Wearing the requisite white coat and white button-up shirt, she noticed his brightly colored tie.

He smiled warmly, then looked down at a file in front of him. "Ms. Carruthers, I believe?"

"Yes, and you must be Dr. Malcolm."

"That's me." He chuckled. "I used to say, 'It's me in the flesh,' but now, with the advent of telemedicine, I just have to say that it's me."

"This is so amazing," she gushed. "I've never had an appointment that was over the computer before."

"It's my understanding that your father is going to come live with you but he's not here yet. Is that right?"

She nodded with enthusiasm. "Yes, he's going to be moving in with me next month. But I know I need to have things ready for him, so I'm so pleased that you can have this appointment with me to go over his condition so that when he gets here, there won't be a delay. When I stopped by the Medical Supply of the Shore store, they told me that this was possible."

"Good people, there. They want to help others and are generous to point new patients my way. Now, before we get started, let's go over a few housekeeping items. You will notice that the link to get into this video appointment was in your father's name when you set up the account."

"Yes, that's what your office said for me to do."

"Right, good. That's because I need to have the appointment with the patient, but since he isn't with you I can just get the information from you, but the two hundred and fifty dollars new-patient fee can be charged to his insurance, which I understand is Medicare."

"Yes, oh, my, yes. Neither he nor I have that kind of money. So, we can do that even though you're consulting with me and not him?"

"Yes. Insurance companies can be such a problem, Ms. Carruthers. So, this way, we can get the help your father needs and just circumvent their silly rules that do nothing more than prove to be stumbling blocks."

Amy licked her lips, still smiling widely. "Thank you, Dr. Malcolm. This is wonderful."

"Now, I usually like to get medical records from a new patient's previous physician, but since I don't have anything on him, I'll get everything I need from you."

They began easily, reviewing the basic information she'd sent in when his office had called to set up the appointment. Father's age. Father's weight. Non-smoker. Nondrinker. Then, they moved to the information she'd set up when she'd talked to MSS.

"He has arthritis, and it's getting much harder for him to move around. He has a walker, but it's the kind that just scoots along, not the kind with wheels."

Dr. Malcolm listened and nodded. "Yes, you'll certainly want something easier for him to be able to maneuver. How is he getting in and out of bed?"

"He can get into bed okay but has difficulty getting out. When I was looking at MSS, they had rails that can fasten onto a bed that I thought might be good."

"We can do better than that. We can go ahead and prescribe a hospital bed with the recommended O-Rings that fasten on. They're more expensive than regular bed rails but are the ones that nursing homes are regulated to have to use."

Her brow furrowed and she sucked in her lips, adopting an expression of concern. "That's more than he needs right now."

"There's no reason to wait until the patient needs something before you go ahead and have it ready for them."

"But will Medicare pay for these things now?"

He smiled indulgently and nodded. "Ms. Carruthers, you don't worry about that. If I prescribe that he needs these things, then they will take care of it."

"I've seen some online providers of medical supplies that have cheaper costs than what the Medical Supply store here offers. Will I be able to order these things from the discount supply companies? They take Medicare, too."

His smile remained, but he shook his head. "No, no. You don't want to use a discount medical supply store. You have no idea what you might be getting. Now, I have a special arrangement with the Medical Supply of the Shore, and they'll make sure to get you the best of everything that I prescribe. You'll be able to have your house ready for your father as soon as he gets here. No waiting, no hidden fees, just everything you need, all paid for by Medicare."

She heaved a dramatic sigh of relief, placing her hand over her heart. "Dr. Malcolm, this is such good news. Thank you so much."

They spent the next five minutes going over more equipment that her fictional father could use, finally settling on a list that shocked Amy. She looked across the table at Liam's tight jaw, shifting her gaze instead to the two FBI agents. Donaldson rolled his hand, the signal that indicated she needed to get Dr. Malcolm to admit to a little bit more before the meeting was over.

"So, let me get this straight. Will you send me a list of the items that have been approved by insurance for my father and then I take it to the medical supply store in Manteague?"

"Since I work with them directly, I will send the list over as a prescription to them. In fact, I'll do that today. They will get Medicare approval and will call you to let you know when you can come in to make delivery arrangements."

"That's it? That's all I have to do? Doesn't my dad need to meet with you when he gets into town to make sure that everything you've prescribed is correct?"

"Your dad can certainly come in to see me for a regular appointment, or we can do another telemedicine appointment. But that won't be necessary for him to get the equipment that he needs."

"So when MSS gets Medicare approval, they'll call me, and I can make arrangements to have it all delivered."

"That's it, Ms. Carruthers. Your dad should be well taken care of. He's very lucky to have a daughter like you, and I'm sure he's very proud of you."

For the first time since starting the subterfuge, she allowed thoughts of her real father to hit her, hoping he would be proud of her for trying to do the right thing. Her smile was tremulous, but she thanked him again, disconnected, and sat for a moment, staring at the blank laptop screen, no one else in the room moving or saying a word. She finally let out a huge sigh of relief, closing her laptop with a click that sounded out in the silent room.

Suddenly, a whoop from Agent Donaldson and clapping from Agent Cox filled the air, and she slumped back in her seat, not realizing how tense she'd been. Liam was on his feet in an instant, circling the table and drawing her into his arms. She was embarrassed to realize she was shaking but rushed to assure him that she was okay. "I'm fine, I'm fine. It was all so surreal, but I hope I did everything the way we practiced."

"Babe, you were phenomenal. I know that was harder than it looked like it would be."

She swallowed deeply, allowing Liam's embrace to surround her with warmth. Looking over his shoulder, she spied Wyatt still leaning against the doorframe, offering her a smile and a wink. She grinned in return before pulling out of Liam's arms and looking at the two celebrating FBI agents.

"That was fantastic, Ms. Carruthers." Agent Donaldson inclined his head toward her laptop. "Everything was recorded, and we've got what we need on that. The next thing will be when you get the call from MSS that you need to go in and make the arrangements. That will give us the next piece of evidence where he's falsifying prescription records to defraud Medicare."

"I'm assuming you're not just going by this?" she asked.

"Absolutely not. We already have insurance fraud agents poring through past records of his and MSS. We're also looking at his two medical partners in his telemedicine business. If they're doing the same, then this could be breaking open a wider case than what's here on the Shore."

The two agents left, and Wyatt walked over and kissed the top of her head. "You did really good, Amy." Leaning closer, he whispered, "Glad you're here to take care of my boy." With that, he tossed his hand up in a wave and followed the agents out of the house.

Alone for a few minutes, Liam finally smiled, dipped, and took her lips. The kiss started light, but as with most of theirs, soon flamed into something much hotter. With bodies pressed together, they worked the adrenaline out of their systems with their tongues vying for dominance as they swirled around inside their mouths.

"Mommy! You and Liam are kissing!"

Amy startled, but Liam only lifted his head, not releasing her from his embrace. They turned and looked down at Rosie smiling up at them. Carolyn entered the room, Desiree in her arms starting to fuss. Glancing up at Liam, Amy laughed. "Duty calls. I guess my career as a super-secret agent has just been halted by the needs of my children."

Two days had gone by, and Amy had heard nothing from either Dr. Malcolm's office or MSS. She tried to put it out of her mind, but knowing she'd get the call when the fake prescriptions had been approved, it was hard to ignore the constant glancing at her phone.

She had continued her transcriptions that morning while Rosie was at Ellen's house, but now she'd picked her up and was going to attempt the grocery store on her own with both children. With Desiree safely snapped into her carrier and strapped into the grocery cart and Rosie right by her side, she was making quick work of the errand, sticking to her list after having bribed Rosie with her choice of a snack if she behaved in the store.

Several people had stopped to smile and chat and comment on the children. She tried to be polite but knew that every minute that went by was another minute closer to both kids losing their patience and having a mid-store meltdown.

Finally, they approached the cashier who, gratefully, was extremely efficient in gliding the items over the scanner and calling for an extra employee to bag them. Glancing to the side, she spied Rachel staring at her, the other woman's gaze malevolent as she glared at Desiree. Having no wish to have any contact with the other woman, Amy paid, thanked the cashier and bagger, and rolled her cart out to her vehicle. Her good luck gave out right as she finished loading the kids and the groceries into the car.

"You know," Rachel said, approaching, "I've known Liam since high school. He's such a good man, and it's so hard to watch others take advantage of him. You showed up, a poor, bedraggled woman caught in a storm, weaseled your way into his life and his house. And now, you simply won't leave, and you've saddled him with *your* brood. And he's too kindhearted to kick you out. I think it's horrible the way you are using him."

It was on the tip of her tongue to throw out one of several responses that slammed into her. *"He's too smart a man to let anyone use him." "He's the one that wanted us to stay."* And her particular favorite would've been, *"It's not me who's using him when he wants me in his bed."* Instead, she inhaled deeply, then smiled and turned, offering her cart to the employee who was collecting them. Without giving Rachel another look, she climbed inside her vehicle and backed out of the parking place, peripheral vision allowing her to see Rachel standing to the side with her hands on her hips, a fuming expression on her face. As hard as it was to have kept her mouth shut, she knew someone like Rachel liked to do as her grandmother used to say: *they like to stir the manure just to have it stink.*

That thought made her giggle out loud, pulling Rosie's attention from her snack. "Was that woman funny, Mommy?"

Sighing, Amy shook her head slightly. "Kind of funny, sweetheart." *But mostly mean.* She wished she could get Rachel's words out of her head, but dismissing a pesky problem was harder than being able to drive away from someone. And it didn't help when she received a phone message from Mr. Porter.

"Ms. Carruthers, I know you haven't heard from me in a long time, but I've been worried about you. I've got a friend who has a little house he wants to rent, and I thought of you. So, give me a call back, and we can go look at it. It's a nice little house in a nice little neighborhood for your nice little family."

Nice. With Desiree napping and Rosie playing in the

living room, Amy slumped into the dining room chair. Now the words she was so ready to refute came back. *"Take advantage of him... poor bedraggled woman... weaseled your way into his life and his house... you simply won't leave... you've saddled him with your brood... he's too kind-hearted to kick you out... horrible the way you are using him."*

29

Liam came home, anxious to see everyone, the stress of the day having taken its toll. He walked through the laundry room and into the kitchen, and just like he had grown to love, he was greeted by Rosie, today in a princess T-shirt with a hot pink tutu, purple socks on her feet. Her tiara had slid off the top of her head but caught and was dangling from one of her pigtails. Swooping her into his arms, he greeted her with the same enthusiasm that she offered him.

She told him all about the snack she was able to get from the grocery store. "Mommy was nervous, but me and Desiree were soooo good. I got a treat, but Desiree just got a clean diaper when we got home!"

Grinning, he turned his attention to Desiree reclining in her carrier seat, her chubby hands reaching for the soft toys that hung from the bar. Setting Rosie down, he knelt on the floor and tickled Desiree's tummy. Standing, he walked around the kitchen counter, his eyes pinned on Amy. Her back was to him as she stirred a pot on the stove, a stiffness to her that hadn't been evident when he'd left this morning. Quite the contrary, they'd both been sated and relaxed from their stolen moments of lovemaking.

Coming up behind her, he placed his hands on her shoulders and bent to kiss her neck. She twisted around and smiled. He was intimately acquainted with all of her smiles. The ones when Rosie was playing or learning something new. The ones when Desiree snuggled close. The ones when she heard a song that she liked. The ones when she managed to complete a transcription while Rosie was playing at Ellen's and Desiree slept. And the ones she gifted him when he surprised her, or cuddled with her, or after they'd made love. He knew all of her smiles, and the one on her face right now wasn't real.

"Something's wrong," he said softly, not wanting Rosie to hear.

She gave a quick shake of her head and lifted on her toes to kiss his cheek "Everything's fine, but we can talk later." He didn't believe for one second that everything was fine but respected her choice to choose when to talk to him about whatever was bothering her. Hating to put it off but understanding the reason, he nodded.

After dinner, he and Rosie played for a while working on puzzles, then he held Desiree while Amy gave Rosie her bath. All four of them piled into the bedroom while he read a story. Kissing Rosie's head, he turned out the light then followed Amy into the nursery. She sat in the rocking chair, nursing Desiree, and he sat on the bed, reclining against the pillows, watching mother and baby with the same awe and affection he felt every time he was with them.

Grateful both girls went down easily, he stood and linked fingers with Amy, stepping out into the hall. Turning to her, he whispered, "I know we need to talk. Is this a conversation that is better lying together in bed or downstairs where a glass of wine or a beer might make it better?"

She rolled her eyes, a true smile curving her lips. He bent and kissed her, loving the feel of her smiling lips underneath his. Without speaking, she led him downstairs, and he sighed. *Looks like I'll need a beer.*

Retrieving one, he fixed a cup of herbal tea for her and took them both into the living room. She settled onto the sofa, and he, not giving her any room, sat next to her, his long leg pressing against hers. Wrapping one arm around her, he twisted his head and said, "Okay, lay it on me, babe."

She chuckled and rolled her eyes. "Do you know how hard it is to have a serious conversation when you're sitting this close and your arm is around me?"

"I remember my parents having *serious conversations*, and I also remember my dad always keeping my mom close during those times. She'd complain that he wasn't giving her enough room to think, and he'd say that anything they needed to talk about as a couple could be done with their arms around each other."

She smiled and nodded. "Sounds like your dad was a very smart man."

"Damn straight. I'm just sorry he died before I was able to learn all of life's lessons from him."

"Sometimes I feel the same way. There's so much I'd like to still learn from my parents, and since they're gone, I can't. So, I stumble through life, hoping I'm not completely messing things up."

They sat quietly for a few moments, and while he wanted to prod, he knew she needed a chance to pull her thoughts together.

Finally, she said, "I ran into Rachel today at the grocery store."

Without giving Amy a chance to say anything else, he felt the heat rush through his body and bit out, "Don't listen to anything that fuckin' bitch has to say! If I need to tell her to stay the fuck away, I will!"

She placed her hand on his leg, barely calming his desire to grab his phone, call Rachel, and tell her to stay the hell away from his family.

"Honestly, Liam, I didn't let her get to me. Not right then. The girls had been so good in the store, and I'd just gotten them buckled into their car seats and given Rosie the treat she earned when Rachel came over. She was just blabbing how I was taking advantage of your kindhearted, good nature. How I was saddling you with my brood. And how horrible I was to have weaseled my way into your home—"

His feet went from the coffee table to the floor with a plop, and he stood, walking around the room, furiously wishing he had something he could punch. Turning toward her, he propped his fists on his hips. "Amy, babe, I'm not having her say those things to you. If you see her, you need to walk away. I don't want her around you, and I sure as fuck don't want her around the girls."

"Liam, listen to me. What she said is probably what other people in the county think. But I put that out of my mind until I got a phone call from Mr. Porter."

Blinking, it took Liam a few seconds to realize that Mr. Porter was originally going to be her landlord. Walking back around the coffee table, he sat close again, pulling her toward him. "Okay. What did he want?"

She held his gaze then looked away, licking her lips. "He said that he'd been concerned about me and had a friend that now had a house he wanted to rent out. Mr. Porter said it's a nice house in a nice neighborhood and he thought the girls and I would be very happy there."

Incredulity slammed into Liam. "I didn't know you were still looking for a place to live besides here." He heard the harshness in his voice.

"I haven't been. I've been perfectly happy here."

"Did you tell him that?"

"No," she huffed. "I wanted to talk to you about it. Coming right on the heels of what Rachel said, I thought it was worth us talking about."

He opened his mouth to refute the need to talk about anything but grimaced, shutting his mouth instead. Breathing deeply, he waited for a moment, then nodded. "Okay, sweetheart, I'm listening." He wanted to add that he didn't think he was going to like what came out of her mouth but kept that comment to himself.

She gave him a stink eye as though knowing what he was thinking, then sighed. "I'm not concerned about

Rachel's opinion of me. And while she's right, you are kind and goodhearted, I know that you're the kind of man who also wouldn't have the girls and me stay here if you didn't want us here. I'm not so insecure that I'm not sure of that. But the fact of the matter is that you brought Rosie and me here during the hurricane, then the house I was going to rent became *broken,* as Rosie likes to say. Before I had a chance to get anything else arranged, Desiree decided to come almost a month early. All of those things add up to me and the girls being here due to a series of extreme circumstances. The relationship you and I have built was born from those circumstances. And I never want you to look at us and wonder, *'What if.'* I don't generally waste time on the *what-ifs* in life, Liam. I learned a long time ago that you take what comes and keep moving forward. I can't change the fact that there was a hurricane, or you rescued us, or a tree fell on the house I was going to rent, or Desiree came early, and you had to deliver her. Those *what-ifs* I can't do anything about, so they don't take up any of my headspace. But having our own place and giving you a chance to discover if what you feel for us goes beyond just having us here all the time. That's a *what-if* that I'm now wondering about."

He blew out a breath, staring into her intense expression, the tension rolling off her. "There was a helluva lot in that speech, babe. But I listened, and I'm processing, but now I'll tell you how I feel. I like to think that I *am* a goodhearted person. That's who my parents taught me to be. But there's a difference between somebody who's goodhearted and somebody who lets others run over them. I didn't let my siblings run over me when I was helping to raise them. I don't let my deputies run over me in my job. And I sure as hell wouldn't let a stranger run over me. You came to this house, you stayed in this house, and you're still in this house because this is where I want you to be. Everything Rachel said is bullshit. She's been bull-shitting people since I knew her in high school and that's never changed. If she can't get her way, she will work to make other people feel bad enough that they'll let her get her way. So, everything she said, toss it into the garbage because that's where it belongs."

Amy shifted slightly so that she faced him. He wanted her close but didn't mind staring into her eyes as he continued. "Now, about the new rental house. If you, Rosie, or Desiree were unhappy here and didn't want to be here, then I'd be more than willing to help you find a new place. If we weren't coming together as a couple, building a family unit, then we would've already found someplace safe and good for you to live. But what we've got and what we're building is real and good, and you and those beautiful girls are exactly where I want you to be. If this isn't where you want to be, though, you need to let me know. Not because someone is throwing bullshit guilt at you but because you truly don't want to be here."

"Wow, talk about a lot being there," she said, her brows lifted. "Maybe we should have talked more and fooled around less, then we'd know where the other was at."

Grinning, he shook his head. "Nope, the fooling around part is exactly what we needed to be doing."

She laughed, playfully slapping his chest before resting her cheek against his shoulder, resting her fingers over his heartbeat. They sat quietly for a minute, then he continued. "People meet in all kinds of ways, Amy. Every couple who is a couple had to meet at some point when they were both strangers to each other. That doesn't make us any different than anyone else. What we feel is no less real because of the way we met. And you're right, things kept happening. That's called life. What we feel is no less real because of the life we've been living for the past couple of months."

He twisted around and placed his hands on her waist, lifting and shifting until she was straddling his lap. Moving his hands to cup her cheeks, he held her close. "I want you right here so that you cannot only hear the words I'm getting ready to say but feel them deep in your soul. I love you, Amy. I love you, Rosie, and Desiree."

He watched as moisture gathered in her eyes, and she blinked to keep the tears at bay but it was to no avail. One slid down her cheek and he leaned forward, capturing it with a kiss.

"Oh, Liam, I love you, too."

"My mom knew I was in love with you long before I did. And I'll never forget what she said to me. *'Love is an emotion that defies logic. Love doesn't fit into a neat box. Sometimes it's messy, and crazy, and out of control.'* That's what I've come to realize, sweetheart. I'm in love with you, and it doesn't matter how we met or what life threw at us. We are exactly where we were meant to be."

"So, I guess I'll call Mr. Porter tomorrow and tell him that we are not interested in the rental property."

Holding her so close that their lips were almost touching, he corrected, "Call him tomorrow and tell him that you're already home."

Their lips met, waves of emotions crashing over them. Heads moving to find the perfect angle, his tongue delved deep, raking over the warmth of her mouth, gliding over hers. Unable to get enough of each other, their noses bumped as they kissed wet and wild. His hands slipped underneath her shirt, dragging it over her breasts before tossing it to the floor. Unsnapping her bra, her breasts fell free into his hands where he palmed the mounds, tweaking her nipples before dipping his head and sucking one hard peak into his mouth.

Her hands clutched his head, and she grunted, "No. Not here. Rosie."

Lifting his head, he nodded. Standing with her still in his arms, she wrapped her legs around his waist and he stalked around the coffee table. Her hands still clasped his cheeks, pulling him in for another kiss. He was aware he was close to the bottom of the stairs but didn't want to take a chance on making noise as they tried to get to his bedroom. Changing his trajectory, he headed toward the kitchen, turning to enter his office. Whirling around with her still in his arms, he pressed her back against the door, then lifted a hand from her ass and clicked the lock.

His office was not large, consisting of a wooden desk, two chairs, and two bookcases that flanked the window. But, other than his laptop, his desktop was clean. He set her ass on the edge of his desk, shifting his body away from hers with difficulty. He grabbed his laptop and set it on one of the bookcases. Now, with his desk completely cleared for their pleasure, he grinned.

She sat topless, leaning back with her palms on his desktop, her full breasts with their dark-tipped nipples ripe for the plucking. Standing in front of her between her open legs, he reached behind and grabbed the back of his T-shirt, pulling it forward, exposing his naked torso. Pleased with her ravenous expression, he flexed his muscles just for show. She sat up quickly, her hands snapping out so that her fingers could trail over his pecs and flat nipples before trailing over the ridges of his abs.

A hiss left his lips as her fingers slid further and cupped his erection over his jeans. It didn't matter how many times they'd had each other, every time was like the first. The excitement. The anticipation. The knowledge that it was going to rock his world.

Not wanting to come too quickly, he gently wrapped his fingers around her wrist and shook his head. "Uh-uh, babe. It's my time to play." He slid her pants down her hips, and she rocked back and forth to assist in getting them over her ass. Pulling them slowly down her legs along with her panties, he dropped them to the side as they crossed her feet. Kneeling, he kissed her ankles before shouldering her legs apart and kissing his way up her calves, licking the sensitive skin behind her knees, and moving between her thighs, seeking the prize he so desperately wanted.

The scent of her arousal filled his nostrils, and he

dove in, licking her like a man starved for his last meal. The assault on her senses could not have been more than what he was feeling, and he was barely aware that she once again leaned back, her forearms planted on top of the wooden desk, her legs over his shoulders, and her moans meeting his.

She came hard, her body quivering underneath his. Tearing his mouth away, he knew if he didn't sink into her luscious body, he'd go mad with longing. He almost ripped his zipper as he jerked his pants down his legs, grabbing his boxers along the way. Circling his cock with his fist, he held her gaze, loving the smile that curved her lips.

He stopped, his hand leaving his erection, and bent over her as she lay on the desk. A question formed in the crinkle of her brow. His chest heaved with emotion, his hands slowly gliding up her thighs to her waist. Swallowing deeply, he said, "I love you. That's important... so important for you to know, Amy. I love you."

Tears formed in her eyes again as her face crumpled. A sob ripped from her chest as she nodded. "I love you, too."

With her legs wide apart, he glanced down to the most intimate place, marveling that she was giving her body and her trust, her life, her girls, and her love to him. Placing the tip of his cock at her entrance, he thrust ever so slowly, not wanting to rush the moment. With his hands planted on the desktop, he leaned over her body, slowly making love. Occasionally, he dipped his head to her breasts, suckling gently. He smoothed one hand over her stomach, breasts, and hips, his fingertips barely grazing the silky skin, loving the way she quivered underneath his touch.

Long, slow strokes of his cock dragging along her inner walls were met with her hips moving in rhythm with his. Watching the blush start at her breasts and move upward over her face, he grinned, knowing she was close. Which was good, because it was taking all his effort to not come too early. Gliding his hand down again, his thumb pressed against her swollen nub, and he watched as she fell apart once more, crying out his name.

That was all it took to send him over the edge, stars exploding behind his eyelids as the universe seemed to converge where their bodies connected. He pumped until drained, then gathered her in his arms and twisted, sitting on the desk with her straddling his lap, his cock still buried inside.

Arms banded about each other, their sweat-slicked bodies stayed plastered together. Breathing ragged, heartbeats erratic. Finally, his cock slid from her body, and he felt wetness on his thigh. Consciousness slowly allowed him to realize something was different. Jolting, he shifted her just enough that he could look into her face. "Oh, God, baby, I didn't use a condom."

She kissed him lightly, her expression warm. "I'm nursing, so I have a much less chance of getting pregnant now. It's not perfect, but we'll be more careful from now on."

He nodded, but then the idea took flight… Amy, pregnant with his child, giving them three. Swallowing deeply, the words slipped from his lips. "Would you want that? A child with me besides the two we already have?"

Tears welled in her eyes once more and she sucked in her lips, breathing through her nose, nodding rapidly. "I love hearing how Rosie and Desiree are yours. And I love thinking that we could have another one."

After tasting her lips once again, he stood and pulled on his boxers and jeans. Giving her his large shirt, they gathered the rest of their clothes and slipped upstairs to shower before climbing into bed together, at least until Desiree decided she wanted to be fed again.

30

The phone call came two days later.

"Ms. Carruthers? This is Nathan Caster of Medical Supply of the Shore."

She placed her finger over her lips as Rosie looked up at her. Rosie smiled and nodded before going back to play with her dolls.

"Yes, Mr. Caster, how nice of you to call. Ever since Dr. Malcolm told me what we could expect, I've been most anxious to see if everything was approved."

"Oh, we never have any problems. If you'll come in whenever it's convenient, then we can get you all taken care of."

"Do I need an appointment?"

"No, you just come in whenever you can. We're a family business, my wife and nephews are always here with me. If I'm not out on the floor, then you can just let them know I'm expecting you."

"Then I'll be in sometime tomorrow morning." Saying goodbye, she disconnected before calling Liam.

He groused as she knew he would but said he'd get everything set up.

That afternoon, he came home early, Agents Donaldson and Cox in tow along with Wyatt. They went over the plans, and Agent Cox explained how the wire would work. She laughed, saying, "I remember the days when a wire was actually a *wire* connected to a bulky recording device. God knows I had a few of those shoved in my bra before. You'll find that in the digital age, this will be much more comfortable." She showed Amy how the small transmitter would fit under her clothes and the camera was attached to the buckle on her shoulder bag strap. "Just remember, act very much like you did when you first went into the store and then again when you talked to Dr. Malcolm. Stay in character."

By the evening, after everyone had left, Liam was tense. Rosie was picking up on his mood, fractious also. By the time Desiree had fretted through her nighttime feeding and Rosie had cried because she couldn't find her favorite story to read, Amy was ready to scream. Digging deep to find her patience, she managed to get Desiree to sleep and Rosie to be satisfied with the story they'd chosen.

Downstairs, she found Liam sitting at the kitchen counter, a beer in his hand and a grumpy expression on his face. Sighing, she walked around to the other side of the counter, leaned forward with her forearms against the cool granite, and forced his eyes to lift to her. "It'll be over tomorrow. People go in and out of that store all day, every day. I'll be perfectly safe with you, Wyatt, and the agents just outside. I know what I'm going to say, and then it's done."

He held her gaze, the air leaving his lungs as though the weight of the world pressed against his chest. He pushed the beer bottle to the side and took her hands in his own, linking their fingers together. "I hate this shit, Amy. I can't stand the thought of anything happening to you."

"And what do you think I feel every day when you go to work?"

"That's different. I'm trained."

"You're trained to do the best job you can, but you know as well as I do that life can kick us in the ass. I'll go in tomorrow, and all I have to do is answer some questions and sign some papers for the delivery. Then I'm out of there. Easy breezy."

She leaned forward, and he met her halfway across the counter, their lips touching in a slow kiss. That night, as she lay in his arms after making love, she counted down the hours until it would all be over. She hated how becoming involved in the investigation had seemed to take over their life. And she was ready for their life to be just about them again.

Amy couldn't believe how easy it was. Nathan Caster was in the store when she arrived, so she didn't have to ask for him. He smiled and welcomed her, pulling out a file that he'd created on her fictional father, filled with papers from Dr. Malcolm and what looked like

Medicare letters of approval. There was very little she had to do, and with the surveillance camera and recording on the buckle of her purse that was wrapped around her shoulder, she felt they were getting the information they needed.

"So, everything that Dr. Malcolm thought Dad would need, we can get? The lift chair, the walker, the hospital bed… "

"Everything, Ms. Carruthers. He also prescribed several other things that he thinks your father will need, and we've gotten approval for all of it."

"And there will be nothing that I or my dad have to pay?"

He placed his hand over his heart and smiled. "Absolutely nothing."

She heaved a sigh of relief and shook her head. "Isn't it amazing how in modern times the doctor can deal with the patient without actually having to see them? This is all so wonderful."

Nathan chuckled, nodding. "Dr. Malcolm and we here at Medical Supply feel that everyone deserves to have what they need. Now, I just need you to sign these forms, and since we don't have your dad's identification, I just need to see your ID. Then, I'll take a look at our books, and let you know when my nephews can deliver everything."

He filled out a few more papers, had her sign, and then handed her ID back to her. "Give me a day or so to check when these items can come in and we can get you on the delivery schedule. I'll give you a call, Ms. Carruthers. It's been delightful to do business with you."

She smiled, then turned and walked out of the store. She climbed into her car and pulled onto the street, giving no evidence that there was anyone else around interested in what she'd just done. Within ten minutes, she pulled into the Sheriff's Department parking lot. Climbing from her vehicle, she turned to see three more vehicles pull in close to her. The two FBI agents leaped from their vehicles, high-fiving each other. Liam climbed down from his truck, hustling straight toward her where he wrapped her into his arms and twirled her around. Wyatt came over and clapped Liam on the back, kissing her head as soon as Liam set her down.

"We did it!" she cried out.

"Thank fuck that's over!" Liam said.

As much as she wanted to celebrate with them, she knew she needed to get back to the kids. Waving toward the others, she turned to Liam and kissed him quickly. "Okay, sweetheart, my undercover days are over. Anyway, I promised Rosie that she and I could make sticky buns this afternoon, so I've got to go." She kissed him again, only this time he didn't let go for a long moment, and she forgot they were standing in the middle of the parking lot in full view of anyone coming and going into the Sheriff's office. It wasn't until the whoops and catcalls from a few of the deputies as they walked by that she separated, blushing. Leaning in, she whispered, "Tonight, we can celebrate in private." Catching his wide-eyed grin, she climbed inside her car and drove home.

Dr. Malcolm's Office

His staff had gone home for the day, but as always, James Malcolm had more work to do. Looking up from his desk, he was surprised at the visitor who walked in. "Nathan? What brings you here?"

Nathan Caster walked in briskly and took a seat. "Thought you might be interested in the client I had come in today."

James laid his pen down, not in the mood for Nathan's games. "Why don't you just spit it out? I've got things to do."

"Yeah, well one of those things might be trying to figure out how to stay out of jail."

Blinking, he leaned back in his chair, his elbows resting on the chair arms, his fingers templed together.

"The young woman you sent to me. Ms. Carruthers."

"Yes? She's the one whose father is coming to live with her. I thought you said Medicare approved everything."

"I needed to see her ID, and guess what her first name is? Something you never bothered to find out?"

Malcolm's brow lowered but he remained silent.

"Amy Carruthers. Amy C."

His breath rushed from his lungs as his heart jolted. Not for the first time, he wondered if he was having heart palpitations. Or worse. "Fuck…"

"Yep, my sentiments exactly, partner. But that's not all."

Afraid to ask, Malcolm swallowed deeply, managing a curt nod for Nathan to continue.

"After she left, I realized the address she gave me didn't match the one on her new Virginia driver's license. So, I did a quick search on the internet for her name. Guess what hit I came up with?"

Mouth dry, Malcolm continued his silence.

"I found her father's obituary. He's been deceased for years."

At that, James sat up straighter, his brows lifted.

Nathan gave a rueful snort. "The little bitch is trying to scam us."

"Shit!" James bit out. "Why?"

"I don't know what her game is, but I'd say she's trying to get free medical equipment, possibly to turn around and sell."

"Do you think she's working for investigators?" Malcolm asked.

"Nah… too amateurish. But she has no paperwork from me, and I've destroyed whatever she signed today. And I'm not waiting around to see what she's playing at. I'm having my nephews pay her a little visit tomorrow just to make sure she knows that *her* health will stay good if she forgets whatever she thinks she knows. And your silent partner days in the medical supply business can stay just as it is."

"Tell your nephews to make the threats stick. I won't have some scammer try to ruin what we've built."

Nathan stood, a smirk crossing his face. "Don't worry. They'll have no problem making sure she knows exactly what will happen if she thinks about crossing us." His face hardened as he stood and walked toward the door. "But no more fuckups. We lay low for a bit. Keep everything legit just to make sure."

Malcolm nodded, his head jerking as Nathan walked out. The money they'd made had built his nest egg tremendously and he wasn't about to jeopardize it. Not for some little bitch that had decided to play detective.

31

Amy and Rosie had spent the early morning making cinnamon rolls, pecan sticky buns, and caramel rolls. They'd wrapped them up and after feeding Desiree drove into Baytown where they took them to Jillian's Coffee Shop and Galleria. Jillian greeted her with a wide smile and hug, kissing Rosie and cooing over Desiree.

"Everything you've managed to bring me has sold out in no time," Jillian said. "When Tori told me you could bake, she wasn't kidding! I just wish I could get more from you."

Amy smiled and said, "Well, I'm not sure how things will go, but I'd love to be able to make a career change."

Eyes wide, Jillian smiled. "Please, I'm praying to the gods of bakeries that you'll start baking more, and I promise I'll sell it for you."

"Oh, Mommy! Are we going to be bakers?" Rosie asked, clapping gleefully.

"I have no idea, baby." Looking back at Jillian, she

crinkled her nose. "Things are a little up in the air right now with me. I'm only working part-time as a medical transcriptionist, but I'm thinking about making a career change if the time is right and the money is right. But please, don't say anything yet. I haven't had a chance to talk to Liam, and I need his input."

Jillian reached out and squeezed her hand. "I won't say anything, I promise. But I really hope we can go into business together. But until then, I will certainly sell these delectable treats you brought in!"

Driving home, she could barely keep the smile off her face. So much had been happening with the investigation that she hadn't talked to Liam about the many ideas running through her head. What had started as a love of baking had grown into the possibility of a small business. She had no desire to run a bakery, but with Jillian's Coffee Shop and others in the area willing to sell her baked goods, she decided a small bakery from home just might be what she wanted to do.

Pulling into the garage, she lowered the door and unbuckled Rosie, who raced into the house. Making a silly face toward Desiree and kissing her tummy, loving the giggles she elicited, she lifted her from the car seat and followed Rosie inside. Moving into the living room, she looked around. Liam's perfect house was now home, one he told her often how much he loved.

She walked upstairs and fed Desiree, changed her diaper, and put her into her crib. The outing had obviously tired Desiree and she fell quickly to sleep, much to Amy's happiness. Walking back downstairs, she looked out the kitchen window and noticed Rosie had gathered her dolls around the back deck, getting them ready for a pretend tea party.

Glad to have a few minutes to herself, she fixed a cup of tea. A knock on the front door surprised her, not expecting visitors. She peeked outside and saw two men with MSS on their shirts, the delivery truck parked out front. She hadn't received a call letting her know that the equipment was going to be delivered, and this wasn't the address she'd given to Mr. Caster, having used the address the agents had told her to use. Uncertain what to do, she grabbed her cell phone and called Liam.

As soon as he answered, she rushed, "The delivery men from MSS are here! They didn't call, and I wasn't expecting that! I don't know why they're here at this address! What should I do?"

"Don't answer the door. I'm already out on the road, and I'll be there in about five minutes."

"But Liam, they have no idea that this address belongs to the Sheriff!"

"Then I guess they'll get a surprise, won't they? Don't worry about it, babe. I'll be right there but I don't want you to open the door to them. Stay on the line with me."

She continued to peek out the security peephole, watching as the two men shifted their stances, looking first at each other, then at the door, then back at each other. Neither looked very friendly, scowls on their faces instead of smiles. About the same height, they both had dark brown hair, although one looked younger than the other. The one appearing older knocked again, and she hoped they would either leave or Liam would get there soon. Putting the phone back to her ear, she whispered, "They're still here."

Suddenly, the two men turned and looked toward the side of the house, a smirk appearing on the face of the one that she could see more clearly. "Hey, little girl."

"Shit, Rosie's out there!" Without giving Liam a chance to say anything, she shoved her phone into her pocket and threw open the door. She pushed open the screen, causing one of the men to step back. "Oh, I'm sorry, I didn't hear anyone ring the doorbell." She tried to smile but knew it was as hard as she felt inside. Looking to the side, she called out, "Sweetie, go into the backyard to play." Praying that Rosie would obey without question, she tried to keep her breathing steady. Rosie held her gaze for a few seconds, then pouted but turned and obediently ran toward the backyard.

Now that she was out on the porch, she could hardly ignore the men. She took a step back, noticing they both stepped forward. "May I help you?"

"We're looking for Amy Carruthers."

"I'm Amy. I see you're from MSS, but I was supposed to receive a phone call letting me know when the delivery would be made. I'm afraid this isn't a good time. If you'll excuse me, I'll go inside and call Mr. Caster to set up a more appropriate time."

She turned and managed to get the storm door opened. Before she had a chance to move through it, it was jerked away from her as a beefy hand landed on it and slammed it shut. Whirling around, her heart pounded as she realized how close the two men had crowded toward her.

"Mr. Caster knows all about you."

Blinking, she couldn't imagine how they had discovered anything. "I don't know what you're talking about but please, step back."

The younger one leaned closer and grinned. "We're here to give you a message. Mr. Caster knows you're trying to scam the system by getting equipment free and then turning around and selling it yourself." He lifted a finger and dragged along her cheek. She jerked back but he just laughed. "You're not getting shit from us. And if you try this again, the next thing I slide over your cheek will be a knife."

Afraid her legs were going to give out from her, she prayed Liam was close. Refusing to say anything, she simply nodded.

The two men looked at each other, sly grins on their faces before turning back to her. This time, the other one said, "Just to make sure you get the message, maybe we'll go around and visit your little girl in the backyard."

Those words sent a chill running through her that only lasted a few seconds before her vision flamed into blistering red. Screaming at the top of her lungs, she rushed forward, her hands landing on the man who dared to threaten her child, catching him by surprise and shoving him so hard he toppled backward, rolling down the front steps. The younger man jolted in surprise, his head jerking toward his brother now groaning at the bottom of the steps. A broom rested near the front door, and without thinking, she grabbed it and swung wildly. It caught the other man on the back of the head, and he roared as he turned, his fist flying out. She managed to duck and swung again, hitting him once more. Unable to stop, she continued to swing, whacking him over and over as he cursed, unable to duck before getting hit in the head again.

He raced down the steps to get away from the broom before turning toward her, his eyes glittering, his jaw set in anger. He started toward her again, his boots stomping on the steps, but the sound of sirens filled the air, and both men halted, turning to look down the driveway at the same time.

Seeing Liam's SUV skidding to a halt followed closely by several more vehicles with lights flashing and sirens blaring, she raced into the house and slammed the door, locking it. Desperate for Rosie to be in her arms, she ran through the house and out the back door, seeing Rosie sitting on the steps of the deck, her elbows on her knees and her head propped on her hands. Rushing to her, she grabbed her up, eliciting a cry of alarm from Rosie. Not explaining, she ran into the house from the deck, slamming the back door, locking it as well.

Moving into the hall, she leaned her back against the wall, and with Rosie and her arms, she began to sob, her whole body shaking.

"Mommy! What's wrong?" Rosie cried.

Unable to speak and having no idea what to tell her daughter, she managed to make it to the front window with Rosie still in her arms. Deputies had the two men in handcuffs, and Wyatt was holding Liam back, his face filled with fury. He strained against Wyatt, his voice like thunder. "No one threatens my family!"

Her legs gave out, and she slumped to the floor, keeping Rosie wrapped tightly to her. She barely heard the front door unlock but looked up just in time to see Liam rush forward, dropping to his knees and wrapping them both in his arms.

"Baby, are you all right? Are you all right? Christ Almighty, are you all right?"

She nodded, wiping her face, hating that she'd scared Rosie. "I didn't know what to do when they'd seen Rosie—"

"Shhh, it's okay. I heard everything. I'd already called for backup and had several deputies close by. Wyatt happened to be nearby as well."

With his strong arms around them, she knew they were safe but could hear the shaking in his voice. She looked up and cupped his cheek with her hand. "We're good, it's all good." She looked down at Rosie and kissed her daughter. "Oh, Rosie girl, you were wonderful. You did exactly what Mommy asked you to do."

"Were they bad men?" Rosie's eyes were wide.

Not wanting to frighten her daughter, uncertain what to say, she looked to Liam.

He leaned over and kissed Rosie's forehead as well. "They were men who were wanted by the police for having done some bad things. And you were perfect when your mommy asked you to go into the backyard and you did. I'm so proud of you. I'm proud of both of you."

Just then, the baby monitor sounded as Desiree cried, waking up. He smiled, kissing Amy lightly. "Let's go get all my girls together."

All my girls. She loved the sound of that.

Liam looked across the table as Agent Donaldson talked about wrapping up the case against Doctor Malcolm and MSS. The LEL meeting was in Easton, hosted by Hannah, but with the federal news dominating their discussion, the FBI agent dropped by.

"So, it turns out that the other two doctors in Malcolm's telemedicine business were also involved in the fraud. They were using MSS that was under the contract they had with him, gaining a kickback from it. And it turns out that Malcolm was a silent partner in MSS, so the web of his fraud case gets wider. He's being charged along with Nathan for fraud, and the two nephews were in on it, too. So, we've shut them all down."

"How big was the case?" Mitch asked.

Grinning, Donaldson preened, giving evidence that the bigger the case, the bigger the glory for him. "It was a multi-million-dollar Medicare fraud. It'll hit national news when the story goes live."

Liam fought the urge to roll his eyes. Donaldson stood and leaned over the table, his hand extended. "Sheriff Sullivan, I'm sorry things got tense between us. You're a good officer, and I wish there had been a way for us to do things as quickly as we did without using Ms. Carruthers."

Liam paused, his jaw tight at the danger Amy had been in… his whole family had been in. But, digging deep, he stood and shook Donaldson's hand, offering no more than a chin lift in response as the other man left the room.

Wyatt had been quiet, but it was obvious he wasn't happy. Looking toward him, Liam asked, "What are you thinking?"

Wyatt sighed. "Manteague is a tiny-ass town with not much going on. And not a lot of businesses like Baytown. MSS was a big player in the town. Brought in people who would stay and eat at one of the restaurants or shop at another store. Their tax dollars helped the economy. Now, with them shut down… I don't know. It just worries me that Manteague will struggle."

"It was a good business," Colt interjected. "Not the way they ran it, of course, but it was the only medical supply store in either county. Someone could come in and take over. Make it completely legitimate."

Nodding, Wyatt agreed. "I hope so. Otherwise, my little town might just dry up if some excitement doesn't roll in soon."

As the meeting concluded, the group of friends walked out of the building together, climbing into their separate vehicles. Looking at the time, he grinned. Deciding to stop at his house before heading back to his office, he drove quickly, his heart light as he pulled up to the front.

Stepping inside, he walked around the toys in the

middle of the living room floor, ignoring the crayons on the coffee table and the blocks on the carpet. He smiled at the dolls lined up in front of an easel, knowing Rosie had been playing school with them.

Hearing singing coming from the kitchen, he walked down the hall, stopping at the doorway, taking in the scene.

Rosie sat on her knees on top of a stool, stirring something gooey in a bowl. Globs of batter sat on the counter, and she wiped her sticky hands on the green skirt she wore over yellow and black striped leggings. Broken eggshells sat next to her, a bit of the raw egg oozing over the counter. Desiree was sitting in her highchair, a big toothless grin on her face as she slapped her hands onto the tray, her little fingers moving in goop which might have been pudding in front of her. And behind the counter, singing while shaking her lovely hips, was Amy, rolling out dough. Flour and sugar were scattered about the counter as well as the front of her shirt and a swipe across her cheek.

His house might be a mess but his home was filled with love.

All at the same time, the three women in his life looked over, saw him, and squealed with delight. *Best sound ever.*

He kissed Desiree and Rosie, then walked to the other side of the counter to wrap his arms around Amy. Kissing her soundly, his heart filled to overflowing. Unable to stop… or wait for a more romantic time… or when he was alone with Amy… or any of the other things he thought he would need, he blurted, "Let's get married."

Her body jerked, and she blinked her large blue eyes at him. "What?"

Now that the words were out there, he glanced over at Rosie, seeing her wide blue eyes staring back at him as well.

"Let's get married. I love you. I love Rosie. I love Desiree. I want this family that we've built to be permanent."

"Seriously?" she asked, her lips curving, her flour-covered hands clutching his shirt, leaving streaks of white over the tan, formerly-pressed uniform.

Nuzzling her nose, he grinned. "Yeah," he whispered. "If you'll have me."

A tear slid down her cheek as she nodded. "I love you, too. There's nothing I'd love more than to marry you."

He kissed her soundly, the feel of her lips sending tingles straight through his heart. Lifting his head, he turned her so that she was tucked close and looked over at Rosie. "How about it Rosie? You want to make it official? Be a family with me?"

He expected the little girl to shout with excitement, but she continued to kneel on the stool, her body strangely quiet. Finally, she whispered, "Will that make you my daddy?"

A little gasp flew from Amy's lips as she lifted her hand to press her fingers against her mouth. He tightened his grip, and after sucking in a deep breath, nodded. "If you want me to be, then there's nothing I'd love more than to be your daddy."

Faster than he could imagine an almost-four-year-old to move, she flew from the stool, around the counter, and straight toward him. He barely had time to let go of Amy to grab Rosie, picking her up, holding her close.

She grinned and grabbed his cheeks with her sticky hands. "I've wanted you to be my daddy for a long time!"

Amy walked over and picked Desiree up from her highchair, making her way back to him in the middle of the kitchen. Together, they hugged, kissed, and danced. His mom's words came back to him. *Love doesn't fit into a neat box. Sometimes it's messy, and crazy, and out of control.* With his girls in his arms, he threw his head back and laughed, his heart full of love.

Five years later

Liam sat on his sofa, hoping the photographer knew how to wrangle a lively family. Desiree and Rosie, preening in their new clothes, sat on one side of him, their bodies close. Balanced on his knee was his son, four-year-old Robert. Amy, looking as beautiful as ever, was on the other side of Desiree, their one-year-old daughter, Carol, squirming in her arms.

It was impossible to get everyone to look at the photographer and smile at the same time, but he didn't care. His family was healthy, happy, and his home was full of love. What more could a man want?

"Look over here and say 'cheese'," the photographer called out.

Weeks later, as Liam double-checked the doors on the house before going upstairs for bed, he stopped at the fireplace and looked at the large photograph on the mantle. It was a miracle, but for that one second, everyone looked forward, big smiles on their faces. He wouldn't have cared what the photograph looked like, but had to admit it was a stunning picture. And on either side of the framed picture were jars of brightly colored sea glass, reminding him that what had been broken was now beautiful.

Walking upstairs, he checked on the kids, finding them all fast asleep. Entering the main bedroom, he smiled as Amy stepped out of the bathroom. Her smile met his and he stalked straight toward her, wrapping her in his embrace. Holding her tight, he whispered, "Did you hear the weather news on TV tonight?"

She leaned back, her brows lowered as she shook her head. "No. What's happening?"

He grinned and nuzzled her neck. "A hurricane is coming. A possible direct hit for the Shore."

She held him close. "Well, then we'll have to go look for sea glass when it's passed."

"Best decision I ever made was bringing you and Rosie here during that storm. You smoothed my rough edges."

"Back at you, Liam. You smoothed the rough edges of our lives."

They climbed into their bed and made love, and when their bodies were sated and Amy finally fell asleep in his arms, he decided this was the best way to spend a dark and stormy night.

For the next Baytown Boys, Wyatt's story, click here!
Protecting Her Heart

ALSO BY MARYANN JORDAN

Don't miss other Maryann Jordan books!

Lots more Baytown stories to enjoy and more to come!

Baytown Boys (small town, military romantic suspense)

Coming Home

Just One More Chance

Clues of the Heart

Finding Peace

Picking Up the Pieces

Sunset Flames

Waiting for Sunrise

Hear My Heart

Guarding Your Heart

Sweet Rose

Our Time

Count On Me

Shielding You

To Love Someone

Sea Glass Hearts

Protecting Her Heart

For all of Miss Ethel's boys:

Heroes at Heart (Military Romance)

Zander

Rafe

Cael

Jaxon

Jayden

Asher

Zeke

Cas

Lighthouse Security Investigations

Mace

Rank

Walker

Drew

Blake

Tate

Levi

Clay

Cobb

Bray

Hope City (romantic suspense series co-developed with Kris Michaels

Brock book 1

Sean book 2

Carter book 3

Brody book 4

Kyle book 5

Ryker book 6

Rory book 7

Killian book 8

Torin book 9

Blayze book 10

Griffin book 11

Saints Protection & Investigations

(an elite group, assigned to the cases no one else wants…or can solve)

Serial Love

Healing Love

Revealing Love

Seeing Love

Honor Love

Sacrifice Love

Protecting Love

Remember Love

Discover Love

Surviving Love

Celebrating Love

Searching Love

Follow the exciting spin-off series:

Alvarez Security (military romantic suspense)

Gabe

Tony

Vinny

Jobe

SEALs

Thin Ice (Sleeper SEAL)

SEAL Together (Silver SEAL)

Undercover Groom (Hot SEAL)

Also for a Hope City Crossover Novel / Hot SEAL…

A Forever Dad

Long Road Home

Military Romantic Suspense

Home to Stay (a Lighthouse Security Investigation crossover novel)

Letters From Home (military romance)

Class of Love

Freedom of Love

Bond of Love

The Love's Series (detectives)

Love's Taming

Love's Tempting

Love's Trusting

The Fairfield Series (small town detectives)

Emma's Home

Laurie's Time

Carol's Image

Fireworks Over Fairfield

Please take the time to leave a review of this book. Feel free to contact me, especially if you enjoyed my book. I love to hear from readers!

Facebook

Email

Website

ABOUT THE AUTHOR

I am an avid reader of romance novels, often joking that I cut my teeth on the historical romances. I have been reading and reviewing for years. In 2013, I finally gave into the characters in my head, screaming for their story to be told. From these musings, my first novel, Emma's Home, The Fairfield Series was born.

I was a high school counselor having worked in education for thirty years. I live in Virginia, having also lived in four states and two foreign countries. I have been married to a wonderfully patient man for forty years. When writing, my dog or one of my four cats can generally be found in the same room if not on my lap.

Please take the time to leave a review of this book. Feel free to contact me, especially if you enjoyed my book. I love to hear from readers!

Facebook

Email

Website

Made in the USA
Middletown, DE
03 August 2022